"As a critic of the macabre, in closeness Lane is unsurpassed. As a fiction writer h prose is spare and sharp, his vision is br treasures of our field."

> – Ramsey Campbell, author of *The Overnight*, and
> *The Darkest Part of the Woods*

"Over the past twenty years Joel Lane has quietly and prolifically built up a body of work that has brilliantly chronicled lives led in the wastelands of the UK, as well as charting some of the awful territories that exist within all of us. His prose is honest, unflinching and horribly gorgeous. In my opinion, he is a writer without equal."

> – Conrad Williams, author of *London Revenant*,
> and *Use Once, Then Destroy*

"Joel Lane is a master at creating moods of disturbing and disorientating strangeness set against backgrounds of urban decay."

> – Karl Edward Wagner, editor of *The Years Best Horror* series

"Joel Lane's writing has the quality of dark glass shattered and reconstituted."

> – Joseph O'Neill, author of *Breezes*, and *Blood-Dark Track*

"Joel Lane draws us into an alarming world where the simple realities of his characters' lives are liable to give way, at the turn of a page, to strange miracles and surreal horrors described in a language of almost visionary intensity."

> – Jonathan Coe, author of *The ClosedR Circle*, and *The Rotters' Club*

"…sex, alcohol, desperation and suicidal despair – without ever resorting to cliché or stereotype"

> – *Gay Times*

"Lane has blended the dark, decaying industrial Birmingham… to paint… an intriguing, if not a little foreboding, place. Dark stuff indeed"

> – *The Barcelona Review*

THE LOST DISTRICT

Other books by Joel Lane include:

From Blue to Black
The Blue Mask
The Earth Wire and Other Stories

THE LOST DISTRICT
AND OTHER STORIES

Joel Lane

NIGHT SHADE BOOKS
San Francisco & Portland

First Edition

ISBN-10   1-59780-039-2
ISBN-13   978-1-59780-039-6

Night Shade Books
Please visit us on the web at
http://www.nightshadebooks.com

For John Howard
in memory of restored texts,
conjectural editions
and horrible imaginings

Acknowledgements

Thanks are due to the editors of the magazines and anthologies in which most of these stories first appeared: Andy Cox, Ellen Datlow, Stephen Jones, David Sutton, Ramsey Campbell, Jack Dann, Dennis Etchison, Chris Kenworthy, Richard Chizmar, Robert Morrish, Mark McLaughlin, Steve Lines, Trevor Denyer, Christopher Roden, Barbara Roden, Andrew Haigh, D.F. Lewis and Michael Kelly.

Thanks are also due to the following for their support, advice and encouragement over the past ten years: Nicholas Royle, John Howard, Christina Morris, Simon Bestwick, Mick Scully, Chris Morgan, Kate Pearce, Mum, Steve and Ann Green, Mat Joiner, Emma Hargrave, Gul Davis, Deborah Fields, Graham Joyce, M. John Harrison, Ramsey Campbell, Michael Marshall Smith, Conrad Williams, Chris Kenworthy, Mark Morris, Gary Fry, Dad, Jonathan Oliver, Elly Tams, Peter Crowther, David Sutton, Peter Coleborn, Jan Edwards, Mike Chinn, Stan Nicholls, Anne Gay, Stephen Jones, Rog Peyton, Pauline Dungate, Lynn Edwards, Tindal Street Fiction Group, Anne Faundez, Chaz Brenchley, Dave Mathew, Chris Monk, Simon Avery and Mark Samuels.

CONTENTS

THE LOST DISTRICT

These lost streets are decaying only very slowly. The impacted lives of their inhabitants, the meaninglessness of news, the dead black of the chimney breasts, the conviction that the wind itself comes only from the next street, all wedge together to keep destruction out; to deflect the eye of the developer.   —Roy Fisher

Quite recently, I heard some kid on the TV saying "Nothing ever changes." It made me think about Nicola. Are we really blind to what happened before our own lives? This was just after the General Election, the first change of government in eighteen years. There'd been this joke going round that all the parties had trouble canvassing in the Black Country, because none of the local people would go outside the street they lived in. Which again reminded me of her, and made me want to go back to Clayheath and see what, if anything, had changed.

Back in 1979, I was in the fifth year at secondary school. It was an odd time for me. People think "teenage culture" is just one thing that everybody gets into. But it wasn't that simple. In our school there were punks, second-generation Mods, long-haired heavy metal kids and fledgling Rastas. Each crowd had its own language, politics and drugs. The rebels had gone by then, disappeared into casual work or streetlife or youth custody. Those who remained were only playing with fire, not living in it. Like the girl who was sent home for wearing a slashed blazer. We were too obsessed with our needs and resentments to communicate. None of us knew what to say, what to feel, what to believe in. It didn't matter: nothing was going to change.

After school, at a loose end, I often walked or ran through the long strip of parkland along the Hagley Road. The first half was neatly laid out, with flowerbeds and bowling greens. The second half was nearer woodland, an overgrown and sometimes marshy surface flowing around huge trees. Now that I no longer had to do Games, I missed the exhausting cross-country runs that had made me feel connected to places like this. It had been my only chance to look good in front of the heavy lads who could fillet me on the rugby pitch. Out here, I could leave them panting and clumping while I raced against the heartbeat of an invisible partner, on into a mist of adrenaline and sweat. But at sixteen, I was too lazy and self-conscious to race against anyone.

One chilly, bright day in April, I was strolling along the boundary between

1

the halves of the park: a ragged line of birches, their silvery trunks slashed with rust. Phrases from my German homework were flickering through my head, alongside The Jam's "Going Underground." A pale-faced girl was sitting on a bench in front of a cedar tree, not far away. I walked past her, noting her short, dark hair, white blouse and black skirt. In the thin afternoon light it was like a scene from an old film. Her eyes followed me impassively.

Driven by a sudden impulse to try and impress her, I ran up to the cedar tree. It was as wide as it was tall. I clasped my hands around the lowest branch and pulled myself up, kicking to gain height. A momentary shiver of sexual excitement passed through me. Using the rough trunk for leverage, I climbed another three or four branches. I felt a cold breeze shake the leaves around me, and didn't dare climb any higher. Below me, the girl was standing. I could see her upturned face, almost featureless at this height. A sudden vertigo snapped my eyes out of focus and I could see two of her, no less alone for it.

When I'd succeeded in climbing down, we stood awkwardly for a while. "Which way are you going?" I said.

"Don't mind." She smiled; her teeth were strong and very white. "You just come from school?" I nodded. "I'm from Clayheath. Y'know, out past Quinton. Came here on the bus." Her accent was Black Country with a touch of something else, perhaps Irish. It was an old person's voice. We walked along towards the road, where the traffic was beginning to thicken.

"Why are you here?" I asked.

"I have to get out sometimes. Just anywhere. It's bad at home." I knew what she meant. I was in no hurry to get back to our narrow house in Smethwick: my tired parents bickering and shouting, my brother turning up the sport on TV to drown out everything, chores undone, dinner a communal stare. "You don't know where Clayheath is, do you?"

I'd never heard of it. "Never been there. Is it far?"

"Not really. It's just nobody goes there. Or leaves." Along the Hagley Road, the lamp-posts were hung with election placards: mostly blue, a few red. Traffic punctuated our conversation. Her name was Nicola; she worked part-time in a garage. I guessed she was the same age as me. She looked unhappy even when she smiled; it was something in her eyes, always trying to run away. Her skin was stretched tight over her cheekbones, as pale as a Chinese paper lantern. I wanted to make her blush.

When we reached her bus stop, Nicola said "What are you doing on Sunday?" I shrugged. "D'you want to come to Clayheath?" She gave me directions that involved catching a local train to Netherton, then taking the number 147 bus as far as the swimming baths. She'd wait for me there. "Promise you won't let me down." I promised. We stared at each other nervously until the Quinton bus arrived. Then Nicola leaned forward and kissed me, her eyes shut. Her lips were so soft I could hardly feel them, just her teeth and a whisper of breath. When the bus drove away, I turned round and walked back into Bearwood. After a while, I realised I'd passed my stop and was in a street I didn't recognise. All the shops had closed.

The train to Netherton stopped at Sandwell, Blackheath, Cradley Heath and some other towns or districts I'd never heard of. The gaps between towns were a mixture of rural and industrial features: forests, wasteground, factories, scrap yards, canals. Parts of the line ran close to the back yards of terraced houses, where clothes jittered on washing lines and blurred figures moved behind windows. I pictured Nicola in such a room, brushing her hair. The only other people in the train carriage were three teenagers, not much older than me, who'd got on at Blackheath. The two girls sat behind me, whispering to each other. The boy sat in front of me, on the other side. He was wearing a brown jacket which he'd pulled up so it covered his head. After a few minutes of sitting like this, leaning sharply forwards, he twisted his face around and snarled, "A wooden vote for th'Layba." The girls didn't respond. His pale, staring face rose above the seat like a mask. "Ah said, a wooden vote for th'Layba BARSTAD." Then he relapsed into his leaning posture, forehead pressed against the back of his seat, jacket pulled over his ears.

The bus stop was in a narrow, old-fashioned high street with half-timbered buildings and wooden pub signs. The approaching streets were the usual Black Country mixture of small factories, houses and less easily identified buildings. Nothing was derelict, but everything had been patched up and reallocated many times over. Most of the buildings had the soft, grimy look of long-ingrained pollution. A faint sunlight filtered through the streets without catching any surface. Opposite a grey churchyard, there was a tall Victorian building with stone steps: the swimming baths. As I got off the bus, I saw Nicola step out from the shadow of the wall. She was wearing a pale grey jacket and black jeans. I walked towards her, wondering if I should kiss her or wait for a better opportunity. Her pale hand gripped my arm; her lips brushed my cheek. "Glad you made it here," she said.

We walked together through the centre of Clayheath, if a place so marginal could be said to have a centre. All around us were raw traces of industry a hundred years old: canals just below road level, a brickworks wearing a loose scarf of smoke, black cast-iron railings and crudely worked flowers, walls studded with blue-green pieces of clinker from glass manufacture. By contrast, the houses themselves were coldly uniform: narrow grey terraces arranged in regular grids like the lines on a chessboard. The district seemed overcast, though the sky was dead white.

Nobody much was around. I remember a white dog pissing on a lamp post; a young woman pushing a pram; a few nondescript grocery and hardware shops with figures moving behind the window displays. "It's dead here," Nicola said quietly. "Nobody comes here, nobody goes away. It's always the same. Nothing ever changes." She was shivering; I put my arm cautiously round her shoulders. A faint smile ghosted her mouth, nervousness mixed with resignation. She took my hand and curled it into a fist.

"Where do you live?" I asked.

"We've just passed it," she said. I remembered a street of narrow terraces, unlit basement windows behind iron railings like display cases in a museum. "Don't matter. We can't go there." The houses at the end of the street were derelict: windows smashed, doors clumsily boarded over. Ahead, a new expressway crossed a stretch of canal where rotting barges clung to the towpath. Drivers raced over Clayheath without seeing it. I wanted to be with them. I wanted Nicola, but not this featureless place where she seemed little more at home than I was. Light flickered between strips of pale cloud. The road dipped under a railway bridge, part of a viaduct made from tiny bricks and blackened by industry. Frozen worms of lime poked through the brickwork overhead. In the shadow of the bridge, Nicola stopped and kissed me. For the first time, I was really aware of her vitality: a fierce, bitter energy, like the charge you felt if you put a battery to your tongue. My hand moved from her shoulder to her breast, from the shape of bone to the shape of flesh. "Come on," she said. "I know somewhere to go."

Beyond the railway, a footpath led behind a row of allotments. They didn't seem to have yielded any crop except leaf-mould and scabs of black ash. A few small lumps of greenish clinker studded the earth, like jewellery on a drowned body. As we walked, I told Nicola about my school, my parents, my hopes of being a journalist if the O-levels worked out. "I never took any exams," she said. "I was ill, and then it was too late. Makes no difference around here." Her voice seemed more accented than it had been in Bearwood: the vowels flattened, worn out. In front of us, the outlines of buildings repeated themselves as if the sun were a cheap Xerox machine. "I like it here. Away from the houses. It's here too, but you have room to be yourself." I didn't know what she meant.

Ahead of us now, I could see the sun setting through trees: warm petals of orange and pink that belied the growing chill. A park. We stumbled through some undergrowth, skirting a pond that was crusted with grey flakes. The trees around it were short and wide, their branches tangled together. There was a smell of decaying wood and fungus. Nicola tripped and fell; I knelt to help her up. "Are you ok?" She stared into my eyes. I put my arms around her. After a while, we spread our coats beneath us on the mossy ground.

It was too cold to undress, but we displaced our clothes to allow our bodies as much contact as possible. I remember the slow warmth of her, the sudden incredible heat. Then it was over. As I wiped her thighs with a tissue, I thought of all the times I'd wiped my residues from the centrefold of a magazine. She showed me how to give her pleasure with my fingers, and I felt less guilty. As we covered ourselves, Nicola laughing softly, I had an unmistakable sense of being watched.

Going from the wasteground to the park was like stepping back into the town. The edge was marked by a straight line of poplar trees, their shadows like the bars of a giant cage. We held hands as we shuffled through the grass; Nicola was still laughing, and I realised that something like love was keeping pace with us. Then she stopped, the smile dissolving from her face like smoke. "All laughing," she said. "All laughing, all dust, all nothing." I kissed her. As if sex were a bandage for all kinds of unease and despair. You can be a lot older than sixteen and still do that.

Dusk was beginning to isolate the town, reducing it to a cluster of lights surrounded by industrial wasteland. Perhaps it wasn't a town after all. I was still wondering what was the matter with Nicola as we returned from the uncomfortably tidy park to the grey streets. A cat waddled past us like a drunk. "Can't you feel it?" she said. "They're used to it round here. But you'm not." I frowned at her, then shook my head. Nicola shrugged with a quiet irony I already recognised as characteristic of her. "I've got to go to work now."

The garage was a small plastic-roofed box, between the expressway and a short block of flats with iron railings in floral patterns. It had a long car park that smelt of petrol and old newspaper. There were two or three cars that looked abandoned, well away from the pumps. As we stood in the light of the garage window, the red above the houses fading to the blue of night, two figures emerged from the shadows. Boys, a year or two older than me. I registered the similarity of their denim jackets and blow-waved hairstyles before I realised they were twins. Nicola smiled at them. "Hello."

"Who's this one?" Nicola introduced me. I don't remember their names. They both seemed to have the same crooked half-smile; their eyes were hollows of darkness. "What are you doing here?"

"He's doing her," the other said. Like an echo.

The first one looked at Nicola and said, "Why do you bother?" She pulled at my sleeve nervously.

"This isn't your place," one of them said to me. Maybe it was the failing light, but I couldn't see their teeth when they spoke. They were both shivering, but making no effort to get warmer.

"Whose place is it?" I said, inwardly preparing myself for trouble. I'd been through some fights in school and knew where to hit. But I had no illusions about violence being romantic.

"You'll learn." Another blank stare, a half-choked snigger. "Time's running out." A car drove past, white eyes turning a dull red. Nicola tugged at my sleeve again, holding it. "Let's go inside," she said.

The twins watched us through the window, as faint as reflections in water, before moving on. Nicola lifted a wooden flap and stepped behind the counter, then fiddled with a display of cigarette cartons. A middle-aged man with greying stubble around pink cheeks nodded at her sardonically and went back to writing figures in his accounts book. I fidgeted, bought a chocolate bar, touched Nicola's fingers when I gave her the coins. "You'd better go home," she whispered; not coldly. I nodded and turned away, then felt in my coat pocket for my diary and stub of pencil. I wrote down my name and my parents' phone number, tore out the page and gave it to her. She brushed it across her lips before folding it and slipping it into the pocket of her white blouse.

Outside, the cold went through me like a voice. I ran towards the lights at the higher end of the road, blinking, seeing double. I found the high street by chance and worked back to the swimming baths. The train rattled through a landscape of night shifts and distant fires. I stared out of the window and thought of home: my father asking "Where the hell have you been?", my mother somehow knowing.

Ten days passed before she rang. In that time, spring hardened into early summer. Light poured through trees, slipped on wet pavements. The rain tasted of smoke. Every morning, I got up half an hour early to deliver papers. They were full of the election, every tabloid but the *Mirror* hailing Thatcher as the saviour of England. I remember the election itself. Her clotted, suburban voice quoting St Francis of Assisi: *Where there is conflict, let us bring peace.* The newsagent whose papers I delivered was quietly jubilant. "Now we'll get things back the way they were. The way they should have stayed." Years later, I heard he'd been jailed for seducing a fourteen-year-old girl who was helping in his shop. He took her to bed, then gave her ten quid, a packet of cigarettes and a hot meal. The local paper said he'd been a pilot in the Second World War.

My paper round covered a strip of roads in between our house and the local primary school: the territory of my childhood. There was the fire station that sometimes jerked awake in the night, sending out wailing engines. The railway bridge where local bullies waited in shadow for younger boys to spit on or throw eggs at. The little car park with its row of disused garages where, when I was eleven, the twin girls who lived up the road led me through a broken wall into a sealed-off alley where they showed me their vaginas. There wasn't much to see, of course: just two scraggy folds of pale skin that reminded me of bacon left too long in the fridge. I had to expose myself too; it was probably the first time I had an erection, which I took to be somehow an effect of the cold.

Nicola phoned me late one evening; my father frowned at me as he passed me the receiver. She didn't say much. When I asked her what she'd been doing, she said "Nothing." Then she asked if I wanted to see her on Sunday. Same place, slightly earlier time. I agreed. It suited me to be away from home when I saw her. There was some interference on the line, making us echo each other's goodbyes—a verbal entanglement that felt somehow intimate. I put the phone down and slowly opened my eyes to see my father staring at me from his armchair. I said nothing.

Sunday was lukewarm and overcast. The train crawled through unconvincing stage sets of old factories and new housing, or vice versa. Rain chipped at the windows. I chewed a bag of aniseed sweets I'd bought in the chemist's shop that morning, having gone in to buy a packet of Durex and been inhibited by the young female assistant. In retrospect, I'm amazed at how little Nicola and I knew about each other's lives. I don't think that ever changes, but it's more obvious at a distance.

When I got to the swimming baths at Clayheath, Nicola wasn't there. I waited while a succession of ageing swimmers emerged slick-haired and red-eyed from the baths. Clayheath appeared to be dissolving into the rain. Blinking away ghosts of narrow buildings and metallic trees, I didn't see Nicola until she was close enough to touch. Her black umbrella covered us both as we embraced. "Come with me," she said. "There's a place I want you to see. And we'll need somewhere to shelter from this." As we walked along the high street, the umbrella a patch of darkness just above our line of sight, I slipped an arm around her pale jacket. She was tense, braced against the cold. Around us, the wind tore up scraps of light.

Nowhere seemed to be open. The narrow streets looked more compact than ever, as if the spaces between buildings had closed up, the district shrinking into itself. We walked past the edge of the park, the line of poplar trees like huge railings. There were no leaves on their symmetrical branches. I hadn't noticed that before.

Outside a scrap yard where rusting car parts were stacked up in mounds, two men were arguing. Something about a failed engine, where to find a replacement. I couldn't understand most of what they were saying, though it wasn't really dialect. It was like ordinary words in mouths that weren't quite alive. A dog started barking from behind the wire fence as Nicola and I passed. The sound echoed along the street. The sky felt as close as an iron lid.

"They've shut down the junior school," Nicola said quietly. "Not enough children to go there. It's been closed for years." She pronounced *closed* with a break in the first vowel, almost making two syllables. "But some of us who were there, y'know... we miss it. So we go back." She laughed silently. I didn't see the joke. I somehow never did with her. We kept walking as the trees disappeared and more of the buildings began to seem derelict, their windows smashed or boarded. The canal network was visible every few blocks, crossed by narrow bridges, underlying the street plan like a mapmaker's grid.

The premature darkness of the rain clouds had begun to clear when we reached the school. It was like a smaller version of the swimming baths: a thin, Victorian red-brick structure with an elaborate carved lintel above the door. The green chain-link fence on either side of the rusty gates was twisted and torn in several places, as if small animals had broken in. A thin strip of concrete playground ran across the front of the school and down the left-hand side. The windows were unbroken, but furred with whitewash on the inside. Some of them were covered by rusty wire grids.

"This way." Nicola tugged my hand and led me along the side of the building, which was protected by spiked railings. At the back, two large dustbins were lying side by side. One railing was missing; Nicola squeezed through and I followed. To one side of the boarded-up door, an iron grille covered the basement window. The bars had been forced apart, the glass dismantled. Nicola smiled at me. Cautiously, but with a skill that suggested experience, she lowered herself feet-first into the gap. It swallowed her eagerly. Her knuckles were white above the bars as her feet kicked in empty air. Then she fell, landing with a soft thud that I hoped was cushioned by more than dust. She climbed to her feet, breathless, and took something off a shelf. An electric torch, the batteries weak but not dead.

As I worked my way through the bars to join her, I had a sudden conviction that we were being watched. Not by human eyes, perhaps: a hidden camera, an electronic security system, or a guard dog that had been trained not to bark before it attacked. Then I was falling, too abruptly for vertigo, flailing in a sheet of damp air before landing on several thicknesses of rough sacking stitched with dust.

Nicola's torch cast a circle of pale light, wide but fading steeply from the centre. I could see a boiler and a series of pipes, lagged with dusty whitewashed bandages. Some used condoms littered the floor. It was very quiet. Nicola shone the torch in my face, dazzling me. When my vision cleared, the torch was off. By the grey light of the basement window, I could see Nicola removing her blouse. We stripped naked, then wrapped ourselves in our coats. The near-darkness helped me to relax, slow down. It was just the way a wet dream is. I mean all the different things superimposed, as if an hour were folded over or spliced into each minute, or as if we both had many bodies to make love with. Time and again.

A pigeon moaned outside as we finally separated and fumbled for our clothes. Dressed, Nicola was different: at once more confident and less self-possessed. "I want to show you something," she said. Holding the torch in front of her, she led me up the stone steps and through the open door to the hallway. The green-painted walls were livid with damp and mould. Strips of paint curled from the ceiling. Behind one of the side doors, something ran across the room to scratch the wall. Nicola glanced back, but didn't flinch. "That was my classroom," she said. The failing torch beam jittered in a huge cobweb, making it seem alive with darkness. Nicola tore it in half and stepped through. "This is the hall where we sat for assembly. We did the Nativity play here. I was Mary. The baby was a doll from Woolworths." She stopped, her torch beam lost in the cobwebbed vaults above the dead mercury strip lights. I kissed her and realised, with a shock, that she was crying. "Come on," I said.

The first door in the next corridor had been locked, but the lock was smashed. "The staff room," she said. It was empty like all the others, smelling faintly of disinfectant. A side door, with no glass in it, was open by a crack. Nicola pushed it with her shoulder. The hinges snarled. Inside, shelves and crates were blurred with dust. "This is the store room." I stood beside her, my eyes following the weak torch beam as she moved it from side to side. First trying to make out what was there, then trying to make sense of it.

One set of metal shelves was filled with oblong wooden boxes, a foot or so long. They might have been games equipment, or costume items for a school play. Their lids had been crudely nailed in place. Another set of shelves, on the other side of the narrow room, was filled with murky-looking glass jars about a foot high. We stood there for minutes, Nicola banging the torch with her palm to make the battery keep working. The jars stank of formaldehyde.

It was a collection of preserved babies—or rather fetuses. I'm not sure they were entirely human. Were they deformed, or somehow a kind of hybrid? They floated, blind and colourless, shivering in the unstable light. Whatever their source, they'd been born without life. Perhaps others had survived, and these were the failures. Some had umbilical cords, I noticed; others were too distorted for anyone to tell where a cord might begin. A few looked like pairs of Siamese twins, so poorly separated that, in a photograph, you'd take them for a double exposure.

I stepped away from Nicola, walking until the darkness wrapped itself around me and I had to stop. For a moment, when she touched me, I wanted to push her away. Then I let her guide me back towards the steps and the basement, where the red sun glowed through the opening. We helped each other to climb out, then walked to the road in silence. Nicola glanced at her watch. "I'd better go home," she said. "My shift's in half an hour."

"Leave here," I said. "Come to Birmingham. Stay with me."

We embraced briefly. "There's no point," she said. "It's always the same. Nothing ever changes." We might as well have been talking to ourselves. I remember thinking that everything changed, but that somehow you never noticed.

From the train, I watched the last residue of daylight spill like oil onto wet rooftops and roads. I got home late in the evening and showered, then went straight to bed. More than Nicola's body, I remembered kissing her. How soft her lips were, like shreds of tissue paper over her perfect teeth.

It was nearly a month before she rang again, late at night. My parents were out. I was listening to The Specials' "Do Nothing" and trying to revise *Hamlet*. Her voice sounded faint and echoey; I could hear traffic going past. She must have been in a call box. "Simon? Simon?"

"Nicola? Is that you?" The darkness of the living room tensed around me. "Are you ok, love?"

She was crying. "Simon, I'm frightened. Please listen." Her breath caught in her throat, and I thought she was going to choke. Then, suddenly, she was calm. "I'm pregnant."

"Oh, no." I felt cold with guilt. As if I'd thrown up on the table and the whole family was watching me. "I'm sorry, Nicola. It's all my fault." She made an odd, throaty sound. "What do you want to do?"

The same sound again. I realised she was laughing. "Oh, Simon. You'm such a div sometimes." There was a pause. "It's not you. I mean, it wasn't you. It's not yours." In the silence that followed, I heard a car drive past; then another. I couldn't do anything but put the phone down. She didn't call back.

That weekend, I went to Clayheath. After a day spent with my revision notes, endlessly rereading the same text, I caught the train in mid-evening. I thought I'd try the garage, maybe leave a message for her there. By the time I reached the swimming baths, it was already dark. Sodium light painted the roadway. The garage was on the far side of the park. Or was it the near side? I tried to super-impose a memory of the district on the blank grid ahead of me, but all I could imagine was Nicola's face. And her body. Abruptly, I turned a corner and saw a featureless office building I didn't recognise. Two roads diverged from a traffic island with a tilted bollard. They were both lined with unvarying grey terraces, no lights visible behind the drawn curtains.

As I struggled to hold onto a sense of direction, a van swung around the corner from behind me. At the same time, a small dark shape loped awkwardly across the road towards me. The two collided with a scream of brakes and pain. The van slowed, then sped away. Its tires left a thin, red wound in the tarmac.

A cat. Probably the same cat I'd seen here a few weeks earlier. From where I stood, I could see that it was beyond help. I could also see what had made it so clumsy. Spilling from its torn gut was a litter of bald, helpless kittens. They must have been kittens. But in the flickering light of the streetlamp, they reminded me of what I'd seen in the glass jars. Their enlarged heads, blind, swollen eyes, tiny clutching hands with pale fingers. There were seven or eight of them, all exactly the same. Unable to live or die. Unable to change.

Swallowing a mouthful of acid saliva, I turned and walked slowly back to the swimming baths. Caught the bus. My head was a whorl of milky light, a finger-print on an icy road. On the train going back to Birmingham, I began to feel steadier. What made me vomit, weeping tears of pain and relief, was going to the urinals in New Street Station and seeing a coin-operated Durex machine.

There isn't much more to tell. I stayed in Birmingham, took my O-Levels and passed most of them, applied myself to the task of growing up in Thatcher's new Britain. Instead of becoming a journalist, I became an accountant. Somehow, my curiosity about the world had gone. In 1990, I moved to Guildford and became a financial consultant. I put on some weight, bought a maisonette, had a succession of girlfriends. Somehow I could never resist a new face, or experience affection without desire.

One weekend in the spring of 1997, I was up in the Midlands on business. Election fever was at its height, reminding me of 1979. I drove through South Birmingham, playing The Jam on my car stereo: "The Butterfly Collector," "Going Underground," "The Dreams of Children." That night, I decided to go back to Clayheath.

But it wasn't there. When I looked for it in my new A-Z, the district no longer existed. I wasn't even sure which districts it had been absorbed into. I decided to let the train and bus route take me to it; but the branch line had been discontinued. Finally I checked the Yellow Pages for swimming baths within a few miles of Netherton. There was only one.

It took me a long time to find it, driving through the narrow Black Country streets on a quiet Sunday morning. The sky was tinged with pink, like marble. Perhaps I was distracted by images of streets that no longer existed; or perhaps I didn't want to find real evidence of a place I'd long ago bulldozed and redeveloped in my mind. But at last I drove up a long straight road, behind a bus that stopped outside a tall Victorian building with a carved lintel and several deep steps. My neck stiffened, as if I had a chill. I parked the Audi and got out.

Apart from that building, nothing was the way I remembered it. In place of the crowded terraces, a jumble of housing blocks and prefabricated industrial units sprawled between the pitted roads. I couldn't see the park, nor any trees at all. A new expressway cut across the end of the high street before circling around a giant plastic-fronted garden centre, like a rubber ring around a baby floating in a pool of whitish concrete. I turned back towards the swimming baths. It wasn't only the image of Nicola that made me start to cry at that moment. It was the knowledge of how I'd been, then and ever since. Eighteen years of selfishness and waste. I blinked, rubbed my eyes and stared at my hands. Then I started running towards the car.

Ten minutes later I was speeding along the Halesowen Road into an acid sunlight, telling myself that what I'd seen had meant nothing. For those few moments, as I'd walked past the steps outside the old baths, I'd seen my hands somehow turn into hands that weren't left and right, that weren't mirror images of each other. They were the same hand twice: both palms up, both thumbs pointing to the right.

Nothing ever changes. We just tell ourselves it does.

THE PAIN BARRIER

After midnight, the city centre was an island of light and activity amidst the blank vacancy of the industrial and commercial districts. The ring road that surrounded the centre was flanked by building sites and wire fences. Aston, on the north side of town, was a mist-clogged blur of walls and road signs; Lee still had trouble finding his way around. He was drinking in a nightclub when he saw the face. At once, it took him back. He remembered sitting in a little private cinema, or alone in a dark room with a video. It was the same face, but no longer in pain. Except, in a way, it was. He was standing against the mirrored wall at the back of the dance floor. As the overhead lighting shifted, red and white lamps blinking off and on, his face disappeared and then came back. Lee finished his drink quickly, trying to remember the name; but he had never known it.

The lounge was a quieter, less crowded room to one side of the dance floor. When the youth moved through there to the bar, Lee followed him; they exchanged glances. He was less sure now, seeing a real face (and an uneasy one) rather than an image. The actor, if it was him, bought a measure of something and drank it almost at once. He appeared to be on his own. Lee hung back, where a red curtain covered the fire exit in the side wall, and looked around. A few small groups were clustered around the tables, talking; solitary figures passed between the doors and sometimes back again. Five couples were sitting on the imitation-leather sofas lining the far wall. Lee counted them, and saw how the shadows welded each couple together. An old torch song was playing from the speaker on the near wall; beneath it, he could hear and feel the thudding beat from the disco. His blood felt thin again. Was that just the effect of fear? The friction in his muscles was like particles of ash. When he looked back at the bar, the youth was watching him. Lee crossed the room and asked if he wanted a drink.

They were both drinking gin and lemon. Tony was his name. He looked about twenty, three or four years younger than Lee. "I haven't been here in a while," Tony said. "Nobody I know is here tonight. I don't think people like to go out now. Unless they're too lonely to stay in." He smiled; Lee didn't recognise the smile. It

13

was something else he hadn't seen. Tony said he worked for a glass manufacturer, packing and delivering windows in reinforced glass for new government buildings, prisons and the like. Lee had done jobs like that in the past, chiefly undeclared. The black economy had been steadily growing for years, as more services were deregulated and real jobs evaporated like so many verbal contracts. You learned how to improvise. Perhaps it was surprising that Tony wasn't working in films anymore. But perhaps it wasn't. Lee didn't say anything. They danced together in the circular pit of the disco, where the figures jerked like anxious puppets in the strobe light. The music, heard like this from the inside, was hard and metallic; it gave nothing away. A cold smell of amyl cut through the dense air.

Afterwards, they sat in the front bar and had another drink. Lee could feel cramps building up in his thigh and calf muscles. He felt undermined by his own body. More exercise might improve the circulation. He held his glass in both hands to keep it steady. "You recognised me, didn't you?" Tony said. Lee nodded, with some reluctance. "That was why I looked back at you. But from?"

"*Mercury. Scar Tissue. Never Cry.*" They were the names of films: short films without dialogue, or at least without words. Films that located pleasure in suffering. Or the other way round. All made by Carl Austin, and circulated privately and illegally. "I've seen others… of his, but those are the only ones I remember you from."

"Surprised you want to remember them. To most people, they're just bad pornography. Or did they turn you on?"

It was an unexpectedly direct question. Lee didn't know how to answer it. He looked away. "They bothered me. I don't know… something I couldn't understand. They're not sex films. They hurt."

Tony laughed slightly. "Tell me about it." The nightclub would close in half an hour, but people were still coming in. "So what's your interest? Carl?"

God, he was sharp. Lee shook his head. "Not even the films. Just you." He hoped that was the right answer. It probably wasn't the truth.

Tony looked at him, then seemed to reach an inner decision. "Where shall we go?" They couldn't go back to Lee's room: the hostel staff wouldn't let Tony in. Lee explained that his freedom was limited. He was on parole now. Tony didn't ask from what, though the answer would hardly have shocked him—possession of drugs and illegal films. "I'm homeless," Tony said in reply. "But I've found a house to stay in. We can walk, it's not far."

Outside the club, the first thing they saw was a fight. Five or six men had stopped a car in the road and one was trying to pull the driver out from behind the wheel. There were two men in the car; the passenger had blood on his face, so the attack must have started on the pavement. One of the attackers was holding an empty bottle. Lee and Tony walked away quickly. As they turned the corner, Lee heard glass break; he couldn't tell if it was the bottle or the car window.

They walked on in silence for some time, unable to look at each other. Lee thought of a joke he'd heard in school, eight years before: the city council was building a special graveyard for witnesses. It hadn't been funny then. They passed the barracks on what used to be the university site, and crossed the canal bridge at a strange junction of new roadways and old buildings; the streets had names like Lister Street and Oxygen Street. Further out of town, the lights thinned out and fibres of mist clung to the upper walls. Three cooling towers stood like chess pieces above a factory complex, walled in on all sides. The narrow streets were lined with parked vans and lorries; a continuous stream of traffic passed down the expressway, supported on concrete pillars above ground level.

A lot of these factories and offices had closed down. Every viable property was surrounded by a wire fence: warehouses, scrap yards, car parks. And building sites, which were everywhere in the inner city. Not because much was being rebuilt; the best way for government to save face, where a district had been mutilated by successive riots and continuing neglect, was to fence off the damaged areas and place an array of signs in front of the view. Here and there the rubble had been levelled, and the ground marked out with trenches and wooden posts.

Nobody stayed here except vagrants. Lee felt as though the wire fences were built to shut in the streets. He thought of the hostel at Five Ways, where he'd been transferred a couple of months before: the naked rooms, dim corridors, policemen waiting in the reception hall. There seemed to be no nameplates here to identify the roads; only signs to direct traffic. "You sure you know where we're going?" Lee said.

"Don't worry, I was brought up round here. I'm a walking map." Tony caught hold of Lee's arm and squeezed it for a moment. "We're nearly there." In the next road, a café was open; a few people, either vagrants or patrollers, sat inside. You couldn't tell the street gangs from the militia a lot of the time. That was the point: authority was everywhere. A few drinkers were sitting or kneeling on the pavement outside the café, like performers on stage just before the lights came on. One was singing to himself, a love song. The February night made everything chilly and stark. There was a crisp moon that shivered as clouds blew across it.

Further on, the buildings were largely ruined, though that didn't mean they were unoccupied. New doors and padlocks showed where ground floors were being used for trading or storage. They were somewhere between the industrial estate and the jewellery quarter. Tony stopped outside a three-storey house on a street corner. It could be a workshop or a patrol HQ or a tenement building. You never knew around here. Windows were either boarded up or protected by wire grids. "Here we are," Tony said. Lee stared at the front door; two planks of wood were nailed across the doorframe. "This way." Tony stepped into a narrow side passage between one house and the next; Lee followed him. It was utterly dark, smelling of damp and split stone. At the far end, Tony fumbled with a latch and stepped through into a back yard. There was gravel and mud underfoot. A light shone in the distance; Lee focused on it by reflex. He could see a railway line on the other side of a wire fence. "Are you all right?" Tony said.

"Sure." Their hands joined for a moment. Tony pointed to the fire escape at the back of the house. It was quite easy to climb, though the black-painted steps were hard to see in the moonlight. Flakes of paint came off on Lee's hands and elbows. On the second floor, two windows were close together; the left-hand one was boarded. Tony removed the board from the frame, like someone taking a patch off an eye. There was no glass behind it.

Inside were two chairs, a small table, a mattress. You could see all there was to see by moonlight and the distant railway lamp. Lee felt an uneasy sense of recognition. The iron-framed mirror above the table showed him only a negative image, like a shadow, of his own body. This was where they had made at least one of Austin's short films. "*Never Cry*?" he said.

Tony nodded. "And *The Pain Threshold*. They used the fire escape, too. Remember?" There was an awkward silence. Lee rubbed his hands on his coat, trying to wipe off the fragments of black paint. Surely there couldn't still be blood, after all this time. Fake blood, he reminded himself angrily. It all seemed more disturbing than at the club. A film was a film, wherever it was shot. But how had it really been? He remembered seeing a youth (Tony) chained to the fire escape, against the background of the city at night: streetlamps, tower blocks, distant fires, stars overhead. Austin's technique of cross-cutting had made this landscape appear to be projected onto the wall of a prison cell. The youth was being beaten by two faceless attackers. Burned with strips of magnesium. In isolated frames, semen drying on his neck. It had excited Lee, but he didn't know why. He didn't know what it meant. But then, Tony was exactly his type: short, black hair, pale skin, dark eyes, the narrow features of someone starved of comfort.

Lee sat down at the table, staring past Tony at the empty window-frame. Tony moved towards him, stopped. His eyes were black pits, devoid of expression, in the weak light. He gripped Lee's hand, leant across the table and spoke. Lee saw his mouth form the words before he registered their sound. "When you see a film, you don't ask yourself what's real and what's acted. Let alone what's been created by editing and dubbing in. It's all just there. Even the effects of how the film's been copied and botched up—illegal films go through nine or ten generations on video. Chinese whispers. Even the place you see it in, and what's in your mind at the time. You get me?" Lee nodded. "For actors, it's just the same." Tony sat down, his hand on Lee's arm.

"I worked with Carl for three years. Even when I knew how little he cared about what we were doing. He never actually had me, you know. Or if he did it was by proxy. What is he to you? A sexual rebel? A subversive artist? To me, he wasn't anything *in particular*. He was everything we had. Whatever he did, whatever we did for him. A complete world. Do you understand?" Lee said nothing. He tried to form an image of Carl Austin from the photographs, articles and fragmentary interviews he'd come across over the last few years. Blond hair, a determined face, a constant half-smile. He was an underground figure, a man perpetually on the run; but, Lee thought suddenly, one who had never been jailed. Nobody was sure what (if anything) he stood for. Lee had learned a lot about the porn trade during his six months in prison. It was like the drug trade: the police used it as a network, a chain of connections that they could tap into at various points. By applying pressure in one place they could affect things from a distance, assert control, gain information. It was one of their maps.

Lee thought of a remark Austin had made in a magazine interview: "Pain is a universal drug. My films show you how it feels to cross the pain threshold. They take you to the edge of identity—the point beyond which death comes to life, darkness becomes light, pain becomes the most intense pleasure." At the time, Lee had thought he understood what Austin was saying; but now, the words seemed empty of meaning. *I don't know about reaching nirvana through pain,* he thought. *But I know about punishment. And I know about police surveillance. Is Carl the same? Or is he a visionary? I'm not. I'm just a voyeur.*

When he spoke, it was to ask something he could never have imagined asking. "Was it real? The torture?"

"Yes," Tony said. "And no. There was more to it, there always is…" He leaned over and kissed the side of Lee's neck. "The pain was real. Even if the rest was fake. That's why I went on with it." He put his hand on Lee's shoulder, pushing himself back. "Have you wondered why I'm here? I'm trying to break away from the group. Carl's people. I want to go where nobody knows me. Even in this city, shithole that it is, I've got too many connections now. But I'm an exile, you understand? If I register for work or accommodation, they'll trace my records. I'll go to prison. Because I used to work for Carl. And I don't have any protection now, because I've gone." Lee stared at him, feeling cold. His hands were numb. "I want to live for myself. When I got to Birmingham I couldn't find anywhere to sleep. I knew about this place, so I came here. Not much good at escaping, am I? You can never escape. Do you know who Walter Benjamin was?"

"Sorry?" Lee was totally confused. "Who? Did he work with Carl?"

Tony shook his head. "He was a writer in the last century. A Jewish socialist who was captured by the Nazis and committed suicide. I read somewhere something he said about the Holocaust. He said, *The real death is the death of the witness.*"

The moon had crossed the window, and it was near to complete darkness. There was no light bulb, and probably no electricity supply; Tony lit a candle and stood it in a mug on the table. He lit a cigarette from it; the smoke was metallic, a mixture of tobacco and some narcotic, probably manufactured. In between drags, he took pills from his shirt pocket and chewed them. He crossed to the window and fitted the board back in the right-hand frame. There was an ancient oil heater in the corner of the room; Tony, with some difficulty, got it to light. A blue and orange flame jittered in the heater's oval mouth.

Lee felt the cramps returning to his legs and making his fists close up. A brief sense of helplessness passed through him. He took three capsules of plasma from his coat, along with the pen-sized injector. The only clear light was at the table, so he rolled back his sleeve and injected there. It made him angry—having to depend on drugs from other people's bodies. The anger was an image on the screen of fear.

Slowly, his muscles returned to their normal tension. His vision cleared slightly, the focus moving outward. He got up to go the toilet. The bathroom, at the end of the hallway, seemed too bright; the light made a silver web in the frosted glass. Then he realised the moon was still visible from this side of the house. There were crystals of ice on the walls, glinting; when he touched the plaster surface, they crumbled. The powder stuck to his fingers. It was cold enough to hurt. He rubbed his hand on some tissue paper, staring at the wall as though it held a secret pattern that would reveal itself, given time.

When he walked back into the room where Tony was still smoking, Lee could see the tiny ice fibres encrusted on the ceiling and upper walls. They made vague geometrical patterns in the candlelight. Perhaps he was hallucinating. It was like one of Austin's visual effects. Or like the effect of repeated copying. Tony looked at him. "You're thin-blooded," he said. Lee nodded. He supposed it was widespread now; people were less afraid of it than when he had developed the condition. The first cases were less than a decade ago. It was known to be an effect of contamination, though whether the cause was radiation or some chemical agent was still not clear.

"How long have you been like that?"

"Three years." It limited his power to live alone.

"You're lucky. It killed my mother. Five years ago, before they could treat it. Her muscles just seized up. She became like wood. My father panicked and left. He was afraid it might infect him. I watched her die. It should have been my father. He used to hit her. I remember. He called her a lunatic. When he beat me, he'd shout, *You're like her, you're wrong in the head, you'll be put away.* I was fourteen when my mother died. A couple of years later I started working with Carl. I was doing porn films already. Made some contacts, got in touch."

"The death of the witness, you see. I thought being a victim would save me. And more… it was something to belong to. An extended family. People who'd look after me." He laughed. "That was my trouble. I didn't just want a lover. I wanted a community. Outside all this shit. But they… well, they were either in it for Carl or for themselves. They think they own me. Now I want nothing. Except this." He stubbed out the cigarette on the table, went across to Lee and embraced him. Lee felt at a loss. He wanted to talk, but the script was missing. It had been years since he'd seen any film that didn't separate people into attackers and victims. He took it for granted, even when he wasn't sure which he was himself. Tony stepped back and took off his coat. They'd be cold, despite the flickering heater.

There were blankets on the mattress. Lee had been in worse places; he sat down to unlace his shoes. He felt more sure of himself watching Tony undress than he had holding him. There was too much about this situation that felt unreal, as though these were parts that Carl Austin had written for both of them. In the light from the table, Tony's shadow was a blurred giant. Lee could just make out the narrow white scars running down and across his back. It was like a chessboard. When Tony turned round, Lee saw the same crisscross pattern on his chest and stomach. Somehow, the cuts seemed too deep and regular to be the work of human hands. They had the look of something industrial.

Tony's fingers moved over Lee's body, slowly, finding its shape. They knelt on the bed, facing each other. Lee tried not to look at the scars. There it was again: the starved look on Tony's face. Like someone who needed to be whole, but couldn't be. Tony gripped Lee's shoulders and pulled him close. Their mouths clasped together like open hands. He seemed so hungry; they both did. And then they were lying side by side, kissing each other's bodies, biting, hardly able to breathe. There were no roles. Lee felt terrified at being close to this man he had wanted so badly; though he still didn't know *what* he wanted. Was this really the same one? He was shaking with tension. However tightly they held each other, it seemed there was no security, no peace.

They came into each other's mouths, almost at the same moment. Lee swallowed the chalky fluid with a compulsion he'd never felt before. Then he sat up and looked at Tony's face. Very briefly, the other man smiled. Leaning over him, Lee kissed the sweat from the rough hollow of his cheek. Pain echoed in his head, harsh as a guitar note. Not a pain that could be filmed. He was trapped in himself again. They hadn't spoken.

Minutes later they were curled together on the bed, trying to sleep. They both faced the window, Tony in front; Lee's right arm was folded across Tony's chest. For a few moments, his left hand traced the lines in Tony's back. He closed his eyes and tried to imagine meeting Tony a long time before, perhaps in early summer; a close friendship that had flowered into romance. That eased the stress in his head. His own body felt still and unfamiliar. The scars kept him at a distance; a fence that wouldn't let him through. They seemed to link the sleeping body to the city outside. *An extended family. Too many connections. A walking map.* The cold in the walls and the outside world wrapped itself around their little shell of warmth.

Not long before daybreak, Lee dreamed of a wire fence, too high to climb and sharp enough to cut your hands if you tried. The fence stood between him and a mass of people who were trying to reach him. It was night; there was mud and gravel underfoot. Distant trees were narrow cuts in the view. What he had at first taken for the moon was some kind of white lamp positioned high overhead. By its light, he could see some of the people moving behind the wire. They looked thin and distorted, as though they were suffering from malnutrition. Though they pressed their faces and hands against the wire mesh, they didn't seem to be aware of him in particular. Their faces were like pictures from newspapers, the features stubbled in with carbon. The eyes were gaps; the mouths were scars, healed shut.

Lee turned and began to pace along the wire, wondering what was on the far side of the enclosure. He turned a corner and found the desperate figures still just beyond the mesh. It caught the light here, made a grid of silver lines that mapped out all of the panic and loss filling his view. He was unable to turn his back to the wire. But he walked on until he had made a complete circuit, several times over; without once finding a way out. And without meeting anyone else on the inside.

When Lee woke up, it was daylight. Tony was still asleep beside him, half-curled and facing the window. Lee couldn't move his own arms or legs; at first, he thought the cramp had come back. Then he realised that his limbs were joined to the other man's. Their bodies were half-merged, around the edges of the barrier. There were faint traces of blood on Tony's back now, darker at the nodes where the scars crossed. Lee stared for a long time. Then he started to pull himself free. It felt strange, as though he were becoming divided. But it didn't hurt at all. He raised his arms, crouched and then stood up, leaving the shapes of his night tangled inside the still figure on the bed. He needed to inject some plasma; he'd have to go back to the hostel for that. He dressed, as so many times before, and left by the fire escape.

It took him an hour to reach his hostel on the other side of town. The sky was white; rays of sunlight glinted through the torn clouds like crystals, reflecting from steel crash barriers and broken glass. Such a waste of light, he thought, when there was so little to be revealed. But perhaps what you saw wasn't as important as how you saw it. Traffic shot past him on the expressway, feeding substance to the patches of faintly glowing mist that hung over the office buildings. Lee wished he had a cigarette; it would make his breath more solid.

When he got back to his room, he would close the curtains and listen to some tapes and find something to eat. Beyond the city centre, a few naked trees lined the roadway. Three tower blocks stood on a hilltop, their upper windows glittering in sunlight, as though nothing lay behind them but the sky. The building where he lived was one of them.

THE BOOTLEG HEART

My first love was a girl I never actually met. In the autumn of 1984, I came to Birmingham to study psychology at the university. It was the first time I'd lived away from home. My parents were as concerned about my choice of subject as they were about my falling into bad company. They made me promise to attend the university chapel regularly, and to continue my Bible studies as an antidote to Freud's denial of original sin. My first accommodation was a bedsit in a converted house on Gillott Road, close to the city reservoir.

After the uniform greyness and silence of Walsall, living in Edgbaston was something of a revelation. There were half-dressed prostitutes shivering in the streets after midnight, and ugly kerb-crawlers in still uglier cars. Lanky Rastas marched to the slow beat of their ghetto blasters. The same beat was louder in the crowded pubs where packets of weed changed hands for crumpled tenners, beyond what I could afford. Gaunt-looking hotels lurked on street corners, like spivs in old suits. There were teenagers everywhere: boys in tracksuits, their hair cut in wedges or spikes; girls in budgie jackets and white skirts, their hair knotted in or braided out. Bitter kids with nowhere to go, trying out models of adult life.

University was another world again: towering red-brick buildings, crowded lecture theatres, a storm of voices. The girls wore jeans or striped leggings, and cheap ethnic jewellery. I was slow to make friends, especially with the opposite sex. The habits of obsessive studying and solitude hung on even when I'd consciously rejected them. I spent the first term arguing furiously with my lecturers—but only in my head. The psychology course was obsessed with behaviourism and psychometrics. In retrospect, I suppose that was the mood of the time. The liberal humanism my parents had felt so threatened by didn't get a look-in here. They force-fed me Skinner and Eysenck, while asserting that R. D. Laing was "discredited." And if I wanted to hear about Freud, I had to go to the English Department.

One Friday night just before half-term, I was lying in bed listening to the traffic

21

in the street outside. My room was on the second floor. The water pipes groaned softly through the walls. Then I heard something else. A different groaning, quick and breathless. Was someone in pain? Then I heard the creak of bedsprings, a rhythm that kept pace with the cries. At once, I felt a tension building in my prick. I'd never heard these sounds in real life before. If my parents made love, they did it in silence. I suspected they didn't do it at all.

Of course, I'd heard sounds like this in films. But this wasn't acting. They weren't performing for a camera. They were alone together, and they had no idea that I was listening just a few feet below them. I hardly dared to breathe. The cries became sharper, more frequent. Her voice rose to a taut, helpless scream, then died away again, then built up a second time. Finally, she gave a low laugh of relief and happiness. The darkness around me prickled with stars. I rubbed the semen into my belly.

The next morning, I lay in bed for hours and listened. Eventually, I heard the door to the attic room close and feet rattle on the stairs. That night, I went to bed early, hoping to catch them at it. But I didn't hear them again, until the next weekend. In between, I saw the new tenant of the attic room: a dark-haired lad I recognised from university. He was probably a year or two older than me. But I didn't see her. In my mind she was short, with dark hair and a feminine build. She had a dazzling smile, but her eyes were serious. Whenever I saw a girl in lectures or the library who resembled my mental picture in any way, I couldn't help asking myself: *Is that her?*

It happened twice the next weekend. The sounds on Saturday morning, just before dawn, were almost violent: deep, choked cries, driven out of her in a steady rhythm. It was an old house with high ceilings; I was surprised that I could hear so much. There was no traffic outside. The cries echoed around me all day, on the bus, in the library. Late on Sunday night, they had a protracted session. She came four times. I came twice, staining a crumpled handkerchief. Rather oddly, I couldn't hear them talking at any time. I was sure that the different patterns of cries meant different positions, or even different acts.

My other great obsession at that time was music. The small cassette player and box of tapes I'd brought from home seemed hopelessly dull and provincial now. Other students had turned me on to a world of dark passions and unknown pleasures: Lou Reed, Joy Division, Nick Cave. And Bob Dylan in his drug phase. My friend Alan, an English student, had taped *Blonde on Blonde* for me; I played it endlessly, listening for clues to the link between sex and religious enlightenment. One song in particular, "Visions of Johanna," seemed to explain and justify my obsession with the girl upstairs. I saw something Jungian in the contrast between the real girl in Dylan's arms and the mysterious one in his visions.

Despite the vast amount of time I was spending in my gloomy bedsit, it took me weeks to realise that damp was spreading through from above. One morning, quite by chance, I looked up to see where a spider on the wall had come from and saw a ring of yellow mushrooms around the hall light. More fungus, pale and wrinkled, was growing in a corner of the ceiling. I knocked it all down with a broom. By the time the landlord came for the rent, it had grown back. He was a middle-aged Brummie with wary eyes. When he saw the fungus, he gave a dry chuckle. "That Trevor's got a cracked pipe under his sink," he said. "I've had it fixed, except apparently not. I'll go up and have a look a bit later." In my next essay, I wrote: *Cyril Burt's influence on Eysenck reflects the latter's reliance on scientific method, except apparently not.* My supervisor commented: *What this subject requires is hard facts, not sarcasm.*

One night, I dreamt that trapped cries of ecstasy were turning to water between the floors, staining my ceiling with the shape of a naked woman. I woke and turned on the light, but couldn't make out anything from the scattered bruises of damp and the cracks in the wood-chip wallpaper. As I was about to drift back into sleep, I heard a faint stirring and a dull moan, then a long shuddering wail. I curled into a fetal position as my crotch spasmed uncontrollably, impregnating the dark shape of my dream. In the morning, my supervision partner asked me: "Are you ok, Matthew? The bags under your eyes, they wouldn't let you through customs." I said I had a lot of emotional baggage.

Although the tenement houses around Edgbaston Reservoir were packed with students, they tended not to use the local pubs. The student union had a subsidised bar and a less threatening vibe. Or a group might stock up on cheap sherry and extra-strength white cider at one of the local off-licences before going back to somebody's room. With our heavy coats and bottles of cheap booze, we looked more like sad old men than the hard-faced, over-dressed youngsters who crowded the pubs.

One Friday in early December, I completed an essay on "How Reliable Is Eyewitness Testimony?" just in time to hand it in to my supervisor before he left his office. I'd been up most of the night before, writing it. I went home, ate a bag of grease-sodden chips and fell asleep. When I woke up, it was nine o'clock. I'd made no plans to see anyone. Feeling disorientated, I pulled on a clean shirt and went out. Highlights of rain glittered in the bare trees. The rusting gates of Edgbaston Reservoir were a cage around darkness. At the foot of the cross made by Gillott Road and Rotton Park Road, there was a low-key pub called The Duck where I occasionally saw people I knew. The rain broke in waves against the curtained windows as I stepped inside, blinking at the smoke.

Two men were playing pool with a studied intensity that broadcast their lack of skill. A middle-aged couple was snogging in a corner, under a blackboard with no message. There was no one here under forty. Still, I bought a pint of Tennant's Bitter and shook the rain off my coat. Then I saw a face at the back, almost in shadow, that looked familiar. I leant over: it was Trevor, my neighbour. He was blasted. There were two empty bottles of Diamond White on his small table. *Maybe I'll get to see her.* My mouth went dry at the thought. But nobody joined him. His face was blank, hanging over the bottles like a mask on a stick. He didn't see me, though his eyes were open. He was drinking alone.

I went over to his table. "Hi. I'm Matthew. I'm in the room under yours." His dull eyes searched for my face. "Mind if I join you?" He shrugged. "D'you want another drink?" He pointed to the empty bottle and said, *Cheers.* I bought two more bottles of Diamond White, one each. The combination, together with my lack of sleep, made me dizzy. We talked about work. He was a medical student, hoping to become a pathologist. I told him I'd decided to go into human resources. Psychology was doing my head in.

Trevor woke up a little as he gulped the white cider, wincing at its antiseptic taste. His eyes refocused every few seconds. His voice seemed to come from a kind of disembodied cavity, somewhere behind him. *Dissecting rooms... drugs... pointless... no soul to it.* I remember he gripped my hand at one point and slurred: *When you've cut out the heart and injected it with adrenaline, what happens to love?* I had no answer to that. I wanted to ask him about his girlfriend, but was afraid of betraying my obsession. No matter how drunk he was, I couldn't have asked him what I wanted to know.

At last orders, he got a round in. There seemed no hurry about drinking up. The games of pool continued. The pub was full now: women with perms set like dog turds, men whose beer-slicked mouths shone as they talked. The Gents' stank of chlorine. When I came back, my neighbour was slumped against the long seat. He looked like an empty coat. I shook him awake; he seized his bottle and drained it. As we were leaving the pub, he stumbled and fell over a bar stool. Luckily, he didn't hit anyone. The barman snapped: "Get the fuck out of here." I helped Trevor to his feet and guided him hastily to the door.

Outside, it was still raining. A streetlamp flickered, projecting shapeless faces onto the wall of a closed-down cinema. Young women stalked up and down Gillott Road in shiny black coats, tracked by car headlights. Stains of blood and vomit dissolved slowly in the rain, like a modernist kind of pavement art. Trevor groaned as I helped him along the road, weaving and staggering dangerously close to the kerb—not that many of the cars were moving fast enough to do any damage. He held out a shaking hand, watched it fill with rain, then clapped it to his mouth.

When we got inside the house, Trevor collapsed in the hallway. His dark hair was clotted together, shapeless. I saw bubbles in the corner of his mouth, and was terrified that he'd throw up before we reached his room. He muttered something, and I leant over to catch the words. *Love is the only thing that... matters... don't understand... the only real thing.* Sure. Right. I wanted to know all about love. I didn't want to be manhandling another male up the stairs to his bed. However drunk I was, boys weren't part of the plan. But I didn't mind holding him. We climbed slowly to the third floor. The dusty 40-watt bulbs stayed lit for half a minute, then died. I had to press every timeswitch we passed. I guided Trevor into the bathroom and looked away while he vomited heavily into the ancient ceramic bath. It sounded like breaking glass.

I had to drag him to his room and find the key in his trouser pocket. The light bulb flickered, then popped. "Got a torch?" I said. He shook his head. *Matches... on the fire.* The hall light went out. Stumbling in the dark, I opened a curtain. The yellow streetlight showed me a large, single room with a bed, a Baby Belling cooker and a table. I glimpsed faces watching me from the walls. The gas fire was framed by a real fireplace; the mantelpiece was piled high with cassettes. I found a box of matches and struck one.

Trevor had slumped on the bed, his face like a wet paper lantern. Books, papers and cassettes were scattered over the floor. A dark stereo was surrounded by piles of LPs: Roberta Flack, Dusty Springfield, Janis Joplin. The faces in the walls were floating, about to speak. Before I could focus on them, the match went out. I lit another one. Trevor groaned; but it wasn't his groans I could hear. The walls of his room were covered with black-and-white photographs of women. Or rather, a woman. She was young, with long fairish hair, a sad mouth, eyes full of light. Most of the shots were face or head and shoulders, but at least one showed her naked above the waist. The match stung my fingers, and I had to drop it.

The stark light from outside cast my shadow over the bed. I stood there look-ing down at Trevor's still figure, no more than a sketch. Then I said, very quietly: "When she moans like that, what's happening? Are you under her? Behind her? Is your tongue in there? Can you feel it when she comes, or do you only know from the sounds?" He showed no sign of having heard me. I shook the box of matches: one left. I'd better find him a bowl, in case he threw up again. There was nothing in the sink, but a small cupboard was underneath it. I knelt and lit the match.

The first object I touched inside the cupboard was a tall glass jar. It was filled with something like spider's web: long pale threads, looped and tangled. I could see a reddish tinge in the coils, a ghost of flame. Next to the jar was a locked wooden box I couldn't lift. There was nothing on top or behind. I put the jar back and closed the doors. They didn't fit very well. The match burnt down to my fingertips; I blew it out. As I stood up, dazed, the streetlight glinted from one of the photographs, and I realised what I'd seen in the jar.

It was hair. I stepped carefully round the bed to the doorway. Something plastic cracked under my foot. I closed the door behind me. My room smelt of damp, worse than before. Clearly it was getting in from outside.

Shortly before Christmas, a friend of mine threw a party in Smethwick. It was a shared house, more comfortable than the one I lived in. The front room and living room were decorated with paper streamers and foil stars. The people were mostly English or music students, dressed in black with spiky hair and black eyeliner. The boys too. The music seemed more appropriate to a funeral than a party—I think one of the songs was called "The Funeral Party," which summed up the mood—but everyone seemed to be having a good time. Cheap wine, cider and lager were ranked in the narrow kitchen. All the coats were in a mound on a bed in the spare room, where couples periodically sneaked off to be alone.

If Trevor was here, I hadn't seen him. Or his girlfriend, whose image hung like a photographic negative behind my eyes. I drank some strong cider, then some wine, then a mixture of the two. A tall girl dressed as Catwoman, with a black cape and whiskers drawn in eyebrow pencil, smiled at me and asked me to fill her glass. Her name was Susan; she was studying architecture. I made some feeble remark about climbing up tall buildings; she just smiled. We drifted into the front room, where a ring of Goths were sharing a joint and talking about Madonna. *She empowers women by deconstructing the feminine,* one of them said. *By hiding behind a succession of identities, she proves that identity itself is a mask.* Susan and I sat down together, giggling. I stroked the tight black fabric over her arm. Soon our mouths locked together.

An hour or so later, after several drinks and a furtive grope in the upstairs hallway, I asked her if she'd like to come home with me. *Okay,* she whispered. "It's a couple of miles," I said. "Are you happy to walk?" She nodded. Outside, frost glittered in the black roadway. There was a cemetery on the corner: grey headstones like books without covers. A dog barked at us from behind railings, but I couldn't see it. Lights shone in the basements of factories where night shifts were starting. It was cold; Susan and I held hands, pretending to be a couple rather than two strangers who'd drunk too much. The city was like a black-and-white film set. I kept seeing faces from the party, melting into shadows or each other. At the bottom of Gillott Road, a truck was being loaded from a curtained building. The wooden crates reminded me of the box in Trevor's room. I could smell the sea.

Back in my room, I apologised for the chaos of books and clothes. "It's fine," Susan said. "But it's cold in here." I lit the gas fire and turned off the electric light. We undressed each other slowly and stretched out on the bed. Then I heard the floor creak overhead. At once, I froze. I couldn't help myself. But there was nothing. Susan ran her fingers through my hair. "Are you okay?" she said. I closed my eyes and thought of the bed upstairs, the couple tangled together. As I penetrated her, Susan breathed softly against my face. I thought of the glass-covered photographs. The first time she moved against me, I came hard. Lying beside her, I kissed and rubbed her until she whispered, *Yes, yes,* and my fingers were wet.

Then I curled up with my head on the pillow, listening. I could hear her slow breathing. I could smell perfume and sweat on her neck. Eventually, I knew she was asleep. I strained to hear, but there was still nothing. So this was what it was all about, except apparently not.

At the start of the next term, Trevor and the unknown girl seemed to be making a go of it. I heard them almost every night, and the loss of sleep was more than compensated by the relief. But somehow, I knew this level of intensity was bound to lead to a break-up. It did, but not in the way I was expecting.

My brother's wedding was the start of it. I had to go home for the weekend, only a fortnight into the term. Throughout the ceremony and the long, drunken reception, I kept replaying the cries I'd heard in the early hours of the previous day. *Trevor! Oh—oh, God! Trevor!* It was the first time I'd heard her call his name. Guilt about remembering that in church brought me down all through the evening and the dark, rainy morning that followed. The bus journey back to North Birmingham took a long time, and her voice became clearer with every mile. When I got back to Gillott Road, I sat in the dark and listened to a bootleg tape of Dylan's "Albert Hall" Concert from 1966: the slow, haunting journey through "Visions of Johanna" leaving the audience baffled; the sneering venom of "Ballad of a Thin Man" provoking audience fury and a cry of *Judas!* Then Dylan's enraged *I don't believe you! You're a liar!* and the raging, desperate finale of "Like a Rolling Stone."

At last I slept, dreaming something about Mary Magdalene washing Christ's feet with her hair. The dream ended with a creak of bedsprings from overhead. With the first muffled gasp, I was wide awake. Her cries marked the accelerating rhythm of their bodies. She came fast, then began to approach a second climax. It sounded almost the same as on Thursday morning. *Trevor! Oh—oh, God! Trevor!*

No, not almost the same. It was exactly the same. Note for note, it was a perfect copy.

Thursday, Sunday. Was there a pattern I didn't normally get? Because I'd missed two nights, I'd heard the same tape twice running. Otherwise, I might never have noticed. But even now, with the truth in my veins like ice, my hand was still pumping hard. Semen dripped onto my belly, and the voice upstairs laughed. I knew I couldn't go back to his room.

You probably know the rest, if you saw the papers that Easter. The police interviewed all the tenants of the house. I didn't have much to tell them. Before it came out in the press, my landlord told me what the police had found. Apparently they'd been trying to trace the girl since November. They'd interviewed Trevor at the Medical Centre; he'd claimed not to recognise her bus-pass photo. Some other bit of evidence—maybe someone who'd seen them together—had made them visit him in the house, where they'd seen the photographs.

Then they'd found the jar. And the wooden box. I can still remember my landlord's expression, as if he'd felt a sardine come to life in his mouth. A mixture of disgust and awe. "The police say they found a locked wooden box full of bones. Including a skull. And all the teeth. Can you believe it? Taken apart, like bits of a jigsaw puzzle." Exactly like bits of a jigsaw puzzle.

The main thing the newspapers picked up on was that he refused to confess or to defend himself. At his trial, they could hardly get a word out of him. I think he ended up in a prison psychiatric unit. What became of his collection of tapes, I have no idea. Maybe I'll visit him one day and ask. What's kept me away is a mixture of fear and jealousy.

I never saw her. Maybe I never truly heard her voice. I hold her in my sleep, feeling her silent terror shake into the core of my hollow flesh. Joanna, her name was. Joanna. And I'm jealous that he had her first. But even more, I'm afraid that if I reach out to him, he'll take her away.

SCRATCH

Do you know, I can't remember the name my mum gave her? All I can remember is my secret name for her, Sara. Without an "h". It was my sister's name. Don't get me wrong, I wasn't trying to pretend she *was* my sister. Unless what you call things changes them. But I don't even believe that. I just think there are patterns. Like music or revenge or love.

I never knew my father. Or if I did, I didn't know it was him. My mum only knew him for a few hours. He never left his phone number, and she couldn't contact him when she found out she was pregnant. The only thing she ever said to me about him was that men who didn't have the sense to use condoms weren't fit to be parents. Which made me laugh. Sara's dad hung around a bit longer, a few months I think. So she was my half-sister really. But she always called me her brother. She was about eighteen months older than me.

We lived on a council estate in Oldbury. Oldbury's a nice town but the estates aren't part of it: they're stuck out among the factories and power generators, where there's non-stop traffic but no shops or houses. There were two main housing estates. One was a street lined with three or four layers of identical cubes, like something in a nursery school. Now they're all smashed up or burned out, and hardly anyone lives there. The other one was a group of tower blocks clustered together on some sloping wasteground. That was where we were. On the ninth floor. All the windows had wire grids to protect the glass. Any time of year, the building was cold.

After I was born, my mum got depressed and had to be treated. The neighbours helped look after us for a while. After that, she had an operation to stop her conceiving again. One of the ways people are different from cats is they go on fucking whether they can make babies or not. Lots of different men stayed in the flat when me and Sara were little. Sometimes just for the night, sometimes for weeks. There was one who came on and off for about a year. I know he was married, because he and my mum used to row about what he was going to do: leave his wife or not. He didn't.

29

Some of the men brought things for my mum. But she was never on the game. Some of them took things, I mean apart from what they all took. All I can say for our many daddies is they didn't usually outstay their welcome. But one did. It happened when Sara was eight. She was off school with the flu. I was just starting at the local primary, the same one she went to. When I came home, there were police in the flat. Mum was very pale. She was trying to drink a cup of tea, but her hands were shaking too much. When she spoke her voice sounded torn, as if she'd been screaming for hours. I don't remember what she said. When I tried to go through into the next room, where Sara and I had our beds, a policeman stopped me.

They never caught him. Mum never forgave herself for trusting him to look after Sara when she was at work. I'd liked him: he'd been nice to me and Sara. I suppose he would be. When I went back to school after the funeral, they all seemed to know more about it than I did. I learned two new words: *raped* and *strangled*. But nobody talked to me much. Kids who'd picked on me were afraid of looking bad, and kids who'd been friendly were afraid of saying the wrong thing. Or they thought I was bad luck. Mum didn't say much to me either. All she talked about was the chance of finding him, and what she'd do. She started to collect things like knives, razor blades and pieces of broken glass. Sometimes she'd spread them out on the table and look at them, test how sharp they were by scratching her arm. All I could think of was Sara. Every day, wherever I was, I could see her smiling, hear her voice when she told a joke, feel her hands when she shook me awake in the morning. It was all too bright, like the things you see when you've got a temperature.

There were no more men for a long time. A social worker came round every Tuesday and talked to my mum. A few times, she talked to me on my own. Asked me if I'd be happier somewhere else. I didn't know. Mum had told me if I was taken into care I'd probably get beaten and used. I went on a fostering list for a while, but no one wanted me. Later I realised if you've been through shit, people don't like you because you're not innocent. Most people want innocence because they like ignorance. Some people want innocence so they can abuse it. I wasn't either ignorant or innocent. I was just kind of shut off. Looking back on it, I realise I hardly spoke to anyone for three years.

Except Sara. The cat, that is. My mum bought her for company in the flat. The council was going to rehouse us, but there was nowhere to go that wasn't worse. If we'd moved outside the area, it would've been harder for my mum to keep her job and look after me. It was only packaging on an assembly line, but unemployment was getting really bad in the Black Country.

The cat was a smallish female. She was mostly black, with a few patches of white: upper face, front paws and tail. And those narrow grey-green eyes that never stopped watching you. My mum put a gravel tray out for her on the landing. A tower block's a fuck-awful place to keep pets, but she managed to find her way around. In spite of the security system that kept strangers out of the building. She wandered round the estate a lot, sometimes bringing back dead sparrows or mice until my mum discouraged her. In the flat, she just sat a few feet away from the electric fire and did nothing at all. Neutered cats are generally like that. I don't think she ever forgave the human race for taking her identity away.

People say there's no such thing as a domestic cat, and it's true. Females in particular. Whatever you feed them, they still hunt. When they bring you something they've killed, it's not a gift. It's a lesson. They're trying to train you, like you're a kitten. And when they rub against you, it's not love: they're leaving their scent to mark you as part of their territory. A cat's world is full of territories, friends and enemies, safe roads and dangerous roads. Patterns.

I don't know why I started calling her Sara. Or why she took to me so well. Sometimes she'd follow me round the flat and come with me if I went out for a walk or to buy something. At night, she'd often curl up at the end of my bed. I got used to her almost-silence, and the careful way she moved. Without her I felt—not alone, because I always felt alone, but like I wasn't all there. My mum was quite happy to let me feed Sara. She had other problems to worry about. Boyfriends came and went like before, but now there were often screaming matches in the middle of the night and the sound of things being thrown or smashed. Sometimes there was blood in the hallway, where a man had left injured. Some of them hit back—she was hospitalised twice. I used to cover my head with the pillow and lie there, with Sara curled up on the other side of the duvet like a kind of guardian angel. My mum must have got a reputation for being crazy, because the men became less and less frequent.

Years went by and nothing much changed. Just being able to carry on seemed enough, to both of us. But it wasn't. Sometimes it's easier to be a victim than a witness.

After I started at the secondary school in Warley, I was out of the flat a lot more. I used to go into Birmingham and just wander around, window-shopping or drifting through music and video shops with enough money to buy a can of Coke. Evenings were better, I could take Sara with me—except on the bus—and visit friends or hang around the town centre, watching people. It was a bit like cable TV: as many different faces and voices as you wanted. Making friends outside school was hard. My age scared some people off and attracted some others I didn't like. But I was quick on my feet, and good at hiding. I didn't know what I was looking for. There was some image in my head of an extended family, people who belonged with each other but nowhere else.

My mum got used to me staying out at weekends. Sometimes I'd sleep on friends' floors or in spare beds. Girls my own age liked me because I was quiet and seemed grown up. I didn't have sex much. A bit. At thirteen it seems strange, like a dance to music you've never heard before. I liked being in groups, where you all sat together and went to sleep in one room, and I could feel myself slipping from one mind to the next. School was a waste of time. My teacher called me the Invisible Man because he never saw me. I wasn't being a rebel, I just didn't care. But after they sent the truant officer round a couple of times and my mum hit the roof, I had to try and keep them happy. Not that they ever expected anything of me. It was a circus: sawdust on the classroom floor.

What I really liked was walking in the town at night. Or between towns—industrial estates and bypass roads and canal routes. With Sara. She made me see things I couldn't see on my own. Telegraph wires like webs stretched out between buildings. Splinters of glass across empty windows. Pieces of electricity generators left out to blacken. Things moving on the ground until the rain nailed them. The silver. The red. I used to stop in doorways, fall asleep, wake up with an erection and a mouthful of dust. Once, crying, I found a pack of cigarettes and smoked them all for warmth. Those nights seemed to go on forever, and I hated them but didn't want them to end.

One night on Snow Hill, I was standing outside Hamley's, the big children's toy store that closed down a few years ago. The building's gone now. But then there was still a big window display of toys and posters and things. The street was quiet, only a few dazed-looking kids waiting for the night bus and a vagrant hunting through the litter bins. Then I saw the mice inside the window, walking in a line. A mother and about six children. There was a strange high-pitched sound, like someone screaming a long way off. The mice disappeared into the wall. A few moments later, the mother crawled out through a ventilator near street level. Her children followed her.

The crying sound was coming from behind me. It was Sara. She was perched on a low wall, beyond the grass verge at the opening to the subway. Her mouth was wide open, and her shoulders were quivering with tension. Her eyes followed the mice as they came towards her slowly, one after another. As if they were walking into a blizzard. Sara jumped down onto the grass, where a drainage ditch ran close to the wall. The mother stepped awkwardly past the edge of the ditch and fell. Sara struck once. One by one, the others followed. It occurred to me that I'd never seen her kill before. It was only when a whole dead family of mice lay there that she started to eat. And the high thin voice became silent.

She kept one baby for me. No, I didn't eat it. When I told Mikki about this, she said Sara was the Pied Piper of Hamley's. But that was much later. When I was trying to go back to the things I'd escaped from.

A few days after the Hamley's incident, I spent a night with a stranger in Birmingham. My mum and me were getting on really badly, and I didn't want to go home. But I had no money and hadn't eaten since the night before. It was getting late in the evening. I was sitting on the wall of a car park, watching Sara try to catch a starling. As the bird finally took off for the roof of a Chinese restaurant, I noticed this guy looking at me. He was about to get into his car—a white Metro. Feeling really embarrassed, I asked him if he could spare a quid. He came closer, looking nervous. In fact scared, but not of me. He was about forty, cropped dark hair, glasses.

"Are you hungry?" He said. Pause. "Would you like to go for a pizza, maybe?" I left Sara to fend for herself. He didn't ask my age, and I didn't want to scare him off by telling him. At that time I was fourteen, but looked older because I spent so much time on the streets. I murdered the pizza (ham, pepperoni and black olives) and he asked me if I wanted to come back for a drink. In the car, I told him I needed somewhere to stay the night. His face lit up with relief.

It was different from when I'd gone to bed with girls. Not really because he was a man, more because this wasn't about what we could share—it was about his power over me and my power over him. In that way, I had an instinct for it. In the final moments I seemed to be watching myself through a mirror: crouched over him, my fingernails dug into his sides, my head down like a cat lapping up milk. When I woke up, he was fast asleep in the bed beside me. It wasn't yet dawn, but I could see ok. My clothes were wrapped up in a bundle on the floor. Next to them, his jeans were lying half under the bed. I checked the pockets: twenty-five quid plus some change. I took a tenner, thinking he might not realise he'd been robbed. And if he did he'd see it was need, not greed. When I looked up I could see him watching me. I pocketed the money and left the flat. Somehow I already knew the way back into town. Sara found me within an hour. All that day, no matter what I ate or drank, I couldn't get rid of the taste. After that I always asked for money.

It was me that found her. One cold, still day in March. I'd come home just before dawn and gone straight to bed. When I got up around three, the flat was silent. I sat watching TV with the fire on, wondering where my mum had got to. It was Sunday, so she'd normally be there. Lately she'd been threatening to get rid of me, have me classified as *estranged*. The flat was a mess. I thought if I went round with the vacuum cleaner, it might put her in a better mood. The last room I did was my mum's bedroom. She was lying there on the bed, unconscious. No breath. No heartbeat. I gave up trying to revive her when I realised how cold she was.

They told me she'd died of a morphine overdose. Asked me if she was an addict. I said no, but I didn't really know. The police contacted her sister in Bromsgrove, who I'd never seen before. She was like an older, heavier version of my mum. Lived with her husband in a little terraced house, no kids. They looked after me and Sara for a while. I didn't cry at the funeral, not until a few days afterwards when I went back to the graveyard on my own. Suddenly I began to remember what it had been like at first, before my sister was killed. Her grave was there too. When I found it I started crying, then screaming. A kind of white numbness grew in my head like scars. I fell onto my hands and knees. Then I punched myself in the face until the gravestone blurred. I begged my mum to forgive me for not helping her. The only answer was the scream in my head. It was a quiet morning, bright, really cold.

A week later, I got moved to a private hostel in north Birmingham. It was like a place for teenagers with "problems." All the rooms were painted a kind of frog green, with spots of damp like warts. The windows were tiny. There was always rubbish on the stairs that nobody bothered to shift. The kitchens and bathrooms were all smashed up, nothing worked properly. It was run by three fat men who sat around all day in an office behind a heavily barred glass screen, talking about their legendary fighting and fucking exploits.

At least I kept my room clean. Had some old photographs and some pictures I'd done in school. I used to light cheap candles and imagine I was in a cellar under a bombed city. Because I was still fifteen, a social worker came round to see me every week and check I was going to school. She hated the building too. Most of the other kids were older than me and like complete deadheads. Slow, I mean. Or they'd got that way from boredom or solvents. Or they were too scared to face the world. A few were dangerous. One threatened me with a knife to get a blow job. Whenever I went with anyone in that place I seemed to end up with crabs or scabies or some not quite accidental injury. I collected apologies the way some people collect empty bottles. Going out onto the canal towpath at night was better. There was a huge stone bridge with alcoves half-full of rubble. The police never went down there. Some of the men were drunk and clumsy, others were almost romantic. I used to stare at the black water and imagine swimming out through the tunnel into the glowing red and silver of dawn.

What I hated most about the hostel was they wouldn't let me keep Sara. I had to leave her with Mikki, a friend from school. Mikki was the only person I trusted enough to talk to about Sara. They got on really well. Usually Sara was very cautious with anyone except me, but she settled down at Mikki's house without any problem. Everyone needs a home, I suppose. Me and Mikki had always been close, but the kinds of shit we were going through stopped us getting together. She liked going out with older boys who had jobs and motorcycles and things. They kept dumping her or getting her pregnant. She was a year older than me, dark-haired, with strong cheekbones and a spider-web tattoo on one side of her neck. I knew she got on really badly with her mum and dad. When she was fourteen, she'd gone round the house and broken all the windows. To let the truth in, she said. Her mum had told her, "You'll end up in a mental home." She'd answered, "You'll have to get me out of this one first." Then her dad had beaten her. She never broke anything in the house again.

When I turned sixteen, I started making plans to find a job and move out. As soon as my school year ended. Then Mikki turned up on my doorstep with Sara and a big suitcase. Told me she'd been thrown out. I blagged some cans of lager off a neighbour who owed me a few favours, and we had a long talk. We also slept together, for the first time. When we woke up in the morning, Sara was lying curled up between us on the blanket. It was like a sign. The family.

But neither of us had jobs. We stayed with some friends of Mikki's on the top floor of a house in Balsall Heath for a few weeks. I managed to get some casual work in the Bull Ring Market, cleaning up the stalls at the end of the day. We were caught in the usual trap—no job without a home, no home without a job. At least the school wasn't after me anymore. Once you're sixteen, they don't give a fuck. You don't even qualify for benefit. It's like you're not the innocent anymore, you're the problem. By now it was late spring, so we weren't that worried about keeping warm. Sara was used to fending for herself by now.

There was only one way we were going to find a home of our own. In the backstreets on the town side of Balsall Heath, the red light district, there were some old terraced houses that had been boarded up for ages. Probably whoever owned them couldn't sell them and hadn't bothered to get them done up for renting. So we broke into one of them at the back, where a concrete yard was half-full of loose bricks. Inside the floorboards were rotten, and the paint was flaking away from some wallpaper that was streaked with damp. We moved in candles, a mattress, some bedding, our suitcases and boxes. The water supply was still connected. There was no electric, but Mikki got some batteries for her radio. From the front, you'd have thought the house was still empty.

That was the best and worst time. The best because it was so different. We were finally in what I'd always dreamt of as the cat world. No need for talk or money or daylight. We used the showers at the local swimming baths. A lot of homeless went there. Mikki got some cheap paints and covered the walls of our room with trees. Big, muscular trees with tangled branches. And in between them, some thin buildings that looked shattered and empty. Heaps of dead leaves on the ground. The nights were best. We'd huddle under the blankets and make love in the dark, staring with our mouths. Or go for long walks in the city, holding hands, with Sara stalking along behind us. There was a built-up housing estate on the edge of the city centre, a ring of tower blocks around an empty car park and a children's playground. Just beyond that was a massive construction site where they'd almost finished pulling down a line of houses and were starting to plan out some new buildings. First there was just a lot of wooden posts and trenches in the mud, then they brought in metal troughs full of new bricks and sand. The tower blocks were half occupied, half empty. Lots of smashed and boarded-up windows. We got to know a few squatters from there who were around at night. In the middle of the night, me and Mikki used to go down there and play about in the small concrete playground. It was like a black-and-white film. We'd ride on the swings and the seesaw, hang upside-down on the climbing frame. That was best of all.

The worst thing was the mornings. What had seemed so mysterious at night became dirty and worthless. Dust glittered in the air and made a skin over everything. Sara was asleep or off somewhere, and I didn't have her eyes anymore. On my own I could have coped, but me and Mikki just snapped at each other and forgot how to talk. That was the only time we needed to drink, the early mornings. Daylight was a threat. But not just daylight. Every contact we had with the outside world, we came off worse. The DSS told us our families were the only people responsible for our welfare. And that was the office on Moseley, where you didn't need a fixed address to sign on. By this time, we were both having sex for money. I coped with it better than Mikki did, but she got more work. Balsall Heath was full of teenage prostitutes, hundreds of them. They stood around in little groups, wearing T-shirts and tight jeans or miniskirts. Like me, Mikki learned to avoid the drunken punters. But she still got raped a few times, once by a policeman. And one guy beat her up and didn't even pay extra for it. I tried to comfort her when she was upset, but it wasn't in me to say, *let me take you away from this*. It was like violence was a part of life, you couldn't rise above it. I've felt that way since I was a child. Kind of numb. If you learn early enough, you don't need morphine.

One morning, Mikki told me she'd met a guy who wanted her to move in with him. "So I'm going to," she said. I laughed, but she just looked at me and I realised she meant it. We sat down together on the mattress and she put her arms round me. "I can't stay here," she said. "It's nothing, it's like dying. We'd freeze to death in winter. You'll do better on your own, Sean. You'll get a room in a hostel, no problem. This guy—he's ok, he's got money, he wants me. There's no choice, Sean. No choice at all." She tried to kiss me, but I pulled away. She started packing her suitcase while I thought about the "on your own." Mikki knew what I was thinking, she always did. "I'm taking Sara," she said. "I can look after—"

"Are you fuck. Sara belongs with me. She's not property." At that moment, I felt so weak and lonely that I started to cry. Sara was curled up in a corner of the room, asleep. Like a child. But also like a wise woman who was older than either of us and had seen every kind of betrayal. I put my coat on. "See you." Outside, I couldn't believe the sun was shining. The city felt so dark, full of empty spaces where nothing could live. I walked for hours and fell asleep on a park bench in Yardley Wood. When I got back to the house, Mikki and Sara were gone. I had some money from a trick the night before, so I bought four cans of Special Brew and drank them. In the dark it felt like the room was empty. Like I wasn't there.

A day later, Sara came back. She was waiting for me in the yard at the back of the house, and she had that strange obsessed look in her eyes that I'd seen outside the toy shop. When I picked her up, she was purring. Sara never used to purr. I brushed some bits of dead leaf and twigs out of her dark fur. And a few days after that, I saw Mikki waiting on the street in Balsall Heath. She was on her own. It was nearly midnight. As I got closer, I could see a freshly healed scratch down her left cheek. She hugged me. "It's good to see you," she said. "Won't be here much longer. He's sending me to London."

"Sending you?" I looked at her face. New make-up. A new perfume. The scratch.

"Yeah. I work for him. There's two kinds of men, Sean. Bastards and more bastards."

I squeezed her hand. We kissed goodbye—gently, the way you kiss someone you care about. I touched her cheek. "Did Sara do that?"

"What?" Mikki laughed. "God, no. That was him. James." She tensed up suddenly. "Here he comes now. Checking up on me."

He was a chubby middle-aged man with short hair, like Friar Tuck in the *Robin of Sherwood* TV series. I walked up to him and said, "See you've got a new pair of legs opening this week." He didn't get it. That was the last time I saw Mikki. A couple of days after that, the owner of the house I was living in got someone to throw out my stuff and brick up the windows and the back doorway.

I was on the streets a few nights. Even in summer, it's cold. All that concrete stores up cold like a massive fridge. Made me think of my mother and finding her dead. I really wanted a safe place to stay. Not another squat. So I went to the Salvation Army hostel in town and they gave me a room. Simple rules: no drink, no drugs, no pets. Everyone broke the first two rules and got away with it.

I thought Sara could manage for a couple of days while I found someone to look after her. But I was getting drunk all the time. The past was blowing into me like dead leaves. My sister. My mum. All those men. Mikki. I was getting Valium off one of the guys in the hostel, in return for the usual things. It was all blurred. Then I went back to the flat where me and Mikki had stayed when we were together at first. Two new people had moved in, but one of Mikki's friends was still there, Janice. I talked her into looking after Sara for a bit. Gave her some money to buy cat food. It was all ok. But Sara was gone and I couldn't find her.

I searched all that day and all that night. And just after dawn, when the traffic noise was starting up again, I found her. She wanted me to. It was in Nechells, that housing estate with the children's playground. As soon as I got there and saw the cold sunlight flashing from the top windows of a tower block like a distress signal, I knew. Sara was on the low wooden fence at one side of the car park. She'd been fixed to it with nails through her neck and paws. There was a shadow of dried blood on the fence, almost black. Flies were crawling over the stiff matted fur. Her eyes were gone. But I could see them inside my head. Close up, the smell was unbearable. I started retching and had to walk away before I could stop. The car park was empty. No one with any sense would park there.

It was a while before I could make myself go back to the fence and pull out the nails. Her legs stayed in place, stretched out like she was flying. She was cold. A stuffed toy left at the back of the cupboard. Flies crawled over my hands, and I wanted to scream but couldn't open my mouth. I took Sara to the building site just beyond the flats, dropped her in one of the trenches and pushed some earth down over her. Then I went back to the playground, sat on a bench and waited. It was cloudy that morning. Every now and then the sun came out and lit everything up, so bright it made the streets unreal.

Some time in the evening, a group of kids came out of the nearest tower block and started playing football in the car park. I counted eight of them. The youngest would have been about five, the oldest about nine or ten. As it started to get dark, one of them went indoors. Then two more turned up and joined in the game. The bigger kids were getting most of the action. They were a scruffy bunch. All white. Several of them with plasters or bruised faces. I wondered how many of them had been beaten or fucked by the adults they lived with. How many useless tears had crossed those pale, empty faces. Then I stood up, walked over to the wall between the playground and the car park, and climbed onto it. The kids stopped playing and turned to look at me. I stared back at them. Then I sang, in a high thin voice I'd heard only once before. Like a scream from a long way off. A place where the crying never stops.

They came towards me. Slowly, like they were moving underwater. I walked along the edge of the wall, jumped down and started to back away, still singing. They followed me between the tower blocks. Their faces were blank. Their eyes were dull, like they were watching TV. I walked up ahead of them onto the building site and jumped the nearest trench. There were mounds of sand and earth on the far side, and a stack of loose bricks. I stood there and kept my mouth open for the sound to come out. The children looked right into my eyes. The youngest came on first. I'd already removed the wooden barrier. They were silent. Nine children. Nine lives.

When they were all in the trench, I started chucking bricks down onto them. They didn't struggle, most of them didn't move at all after they were hit. I felt like crying but I didn't, any more than they did. I just sang. Then I pushed earth and sand over them until they were all covered. It felt like part of me was being buried with them. I went on throwing in dirt until it was more or less level. Then I walked back to the hostel and slept all through the next day.

There are patterns. You have to finish what you start. Make it level. Even. Scratch.

I left the Midlands after that. Hitched a ride to London. There's a whole town of homeless kids down there, but I'll get by. You know how the Red Indians would each have a special animal as a totem, a spirit being? Sometimes a family would be under the same totem, sometimes a whole tribe. How many lives are part of me? Will I end up splayed out on a bed or the roof of a car, with a knife in the back of my neck? I can seek out food and keep myself clean. I like people, but I don't need them. And I'll never trust anyone. My claws are sheathed. They're deep inside me.

COMING OF AGE

A violent death made waves, Rajan thought. The image of a shattered body, a torn mouth, hung around like a tattoo on the daylight. But the disappearance of an adult, or even a teenager, left no mark. The only images that haunted you were normal ones. There was a gap, a missing face, like a door that wouldn't shut. A violent death left a scar. But a disappearance wouldn't ever close. With time it became a mouth, a vortex into which your entire world gradually fell.

He had no specific memory of the last time he'd seen Ashok. Just one evening among many. He'd not even told the boy to take care—he was nearly eighteen, after all, and such reminders made him uptight. And being home by twelve was a given. But not this time. It was only after midnight that a typical evening had become *that night*. The coach of normality had become a pumpkin, with a candle flickering through carved teeth. By two, they'd phoned all the hospitals. Then the police. Not Ash's friends. Kavita was sure they'd ring if they knew where he was.

Over the bare weeks that followed, the August sun had scoured the inside of their house like bleach. The air was so bright that shadows became impenetrable, pieces of dead space. Somewhere in the shadows outside, Ash was hidden. The police had spoken to his friends, the school, the community centre where he sometimes worked. Rajan thought they were doing what they could. But they had nothing to give.

Ash's possessions had yielded no clues. Even searching through the compacted chaos of his bedroom had felt like an admission that he wasn't coming back. The lost have no secrets. Not that much was uncovered. A packet of condoms, still wrapped. A single copy of *Mayfair*. Some letters from his former girlfriend, Tara, mentioning the fact that they'd slept together. Rajan didn't bother pretending to be shocked. What struck him most was that nothing was missing. You didn't leave home without ID or a passport. Unless you wanted to stop being yourself.

Even the boy's diary was no help. The police were very struck by the fact that in March, when he'd broken up with Tara, Ash had written: *I wish I was dead.*

41

Rajan remembered him being quite down for a week, then developing an obsession with the maudlin albums of Pearl Jam—who even Rajan knew were truly lame. He was more bothered by a recent entry: *Think I might join the business.* The police assumed he meant the family business; but, as Rajan explained to them, there wasn't one. He was a designer, and his brother worked in sales. Ash was hoping to make films.

Kavita thought he was dead. "He wouldn't just disappear. We're hearing nothing because… there's no one to speak. He's in a canal or an empty building, or under the ground. We should mourn him, not torment ourselves with a voice we'll never hear again." Rajan wasn't ready to accept that. He didn't think Kavita was either. But where was he supposed to look for his son? There was no other world for him to explore. No secret life. Only the life he knew, which was over. Burned like cellophane in the bright August sun.

Ash's friends had no idea where he was. They were looking for him too, all over Birmingham. He'd gone to the Arcadian Centre cinema with two friends, had a drink with them afterwards, then gone to Snow Hill to catch the bus home. Maybe he'd decided to walk. It was only three miles. Something had happened. His friend Vijay remembered Ash had been quiet. "Not really down, just thoughtful. Staring into space, maybe looking for someone, I don't know." They'd been to see *Cruel Intentions*, which had featured an actress with whom Ash apparently had a slight obsession.

Vijay didn't know what *the business* might be either. "Films? TV? He used to talk about that sometimes… I don't think he was into anything… you know, dodgy. If he was, I'd tell you. Ash always seemed kind of innocent. Sometimes he'd say, *When I'm rich and successful*—but it was kind of a joke. He didn't talk about money." Rajan recognised that as a trait of his own.

Ash's picture appeared in the local papers and on *Midlands Today*. Rajan avoided looking at the photograph. He didn't want the living face to harden into a fixed image in his head. As the weeks went by and the searches began to tail off, it seemed less and less likely that what was found would be recognisable.

The muggy heat of late summer began to thin out. The terrifying stillness in the house had become something else, a gradual decay that at least made time real. Answering the phone was so painful they were discouraging friends and relatives from calling. And they made excuses to avoid letting people visit, because the house was in chaos. Neither of them could face cooking or housework. It was as if they needed to make their grief visible, but had to keep the result a secret. Kavita's acceptance of the situation was slowly unravelling, leaving her empty and silent. Rajan couldn't talk to her, or to himself. He'd never experienced despair like this. Not something inside you, but something you had to live inside.

The only relief came from walking. Night after night, he paced aimlessly around Handsworth and Hockley, looking for any trace or sign of something unusual that might explain how a boy could disappear. The whole process of searching was an elaborate kind of prayer. It reminded him of his own teenage years in Birmingham, when he'd tried to get out of the house every evening to avoid his parents' arguments. Of course, he'd been leaner and fitter in those days. Now, walking for miles made his legs ache and darkened his shirt with sweat. But there was the same feeling of wanting to believe that the city could give him what he needed.

The industrial part of Handsworth hadn't changed much in the last twenty years. There were still the same foundry and metal works, the same jigsaw of iron and concrete. The barbed wire had become razor wire. But along the Soho Road, the shops had changed beyond recognition. Even ten years before, they'd been mostly grocery shops selling cheap tins and stale vegetables. Every facade was whitewashed, and half of them were boarded up. Now, the street was a major shopping centre for the Asian community: imported fabrics, clothes, videos and books were displayed alongside DVD players and mobile phones. The more bourgeois the customers became, the more they bought in the commodities of their parent culture.

Kavita worked there, assistant manager of a clothes shop that became more fashionably retro every year. Rajan hoped that her career would help to get her through what was happening now. Complications with Ash's birth had meant that they couldn't have any more children. Perhaps they'd overprotected him, kept him from becoming streetwise. Or perhaps they hadn't protected him enough.

Near the top of Soho Hill, a new Sikh temple stood in a cloud of blue light. Its flawless white and gold structure drew Rajan's reluctant admiration. Beyond the crest of the hill was the shallow curve of the Hockley flyover. There were usually kids underneath it, smoking or skateboarding. A few times, Rajan had shown them the photo of Ash he kept in his wallet. They always said they'd seen him, then described someone who worked in a local shop or was going out with a friend's sister. Was it stupidity or malice? Or did most teenagers really live in a world where what they didn't know couldn't exist?

Hockley was a patchwork that made no sense. Jewellery workshops, empty warehouses, Yuppie restaurants, beat-up housing estates, vandalised graveyards. Rajan felt sure that something had happened to Ash here. Maybe he'd been involved in some kind of criminal deal. Maybe the film had turned him on and he'd gone looking for a prostitute. Or maybe—and this, in a way, was worse—he'd just been walking through and been jumped by a gang of skinheads. Ever since their brief success in Tower Hamlets, the neofascists had been on the lookout for trouble. Any incident they could provoke, they'd claim as a vindication of their hatred. What had happened to the Dunkirk spirit they went on about? The root of the whole problem, Rajan thought, was that people couldn't stand to be reminded of their own failure.

It wasn't easy to assimilate into a culture so full of ghosts. The English couldn't adjust to the fact that they could no longer help themselves to whatever they felt like. Colonial rule had turned in on itself, like a cancer. Rajan remembered a recent TV programme about the British regime in India. A retired soldier reminiscing about how his squadron had enticed a village girl into the barracks with promises of money. She'd been gang-raped by "about twenty" men, and in the process her neck had got broken. She'd been thrown out with the empty bottles the next morning. And the English wondered why there was anger.

Hockley was linked to the city centre by Livery Street, a long straight road that always seemed to be in shadow. One side of it was a solid block of thin office buildings, at least a hundred years old. The other was a viaduct, through whose arches you could see white light reflected on the motionless surface of a canal. Near the end, close enough to hear the roar of traffic on the expressway, there was a nightclub called Subway City. Maybe something had happened there. But Rajan knew better than to hang around outside a nightclub, asking questions. He wasn't suicidal yet.

The more he walked around these parts of North Birmingham at night, the harder it became to separate what he was seeing from memory. If there was a part of the city where Ash still lived, perhaps his own teenage self lived there too. In those days, he'd found the city frightening and his own place in it chilly. Yet in the happier moments—his first girlfriend, his first job, leaving home—he'd wanted to be young forever.

In September, the catalogue company Rajan worked for increased its productivity targets after a time and motion study. Rajan found himself working longer hours, often skipping breaks, just to keep up. Needless to say, the workforce got nothing from the increased profits. Kavita was putting in a lot of overtime as well, trying to recover herself through work. The time they spent together began to improve a little. They started making love again, more out of loneliness than anything else. It was only a matter of time, Rajan thought, before they split up.

One cloudy evening, he walked from the office in Aston to the jewellery quarter. The clock at the top of Vyse Street indicated midnight, but it was about seven. The graveyard was littered with Special Brew cans. Along Hockley Hill, several of the ground-floor shops had recently changed hands; the upper storeys were the same as before, their elaborately carved windows framing wooden boards or darkness. Only the obsolete had staying power. The flyover was streaming with rush-hour traffic, all heading out of the city. In the shadows underneath, pigeons were tugging at shreds of naan. Three pale youngsters were standing by one of the concrete supports. They gazed coldly at Rajan as he approached them.

Two boys and a girl, all with bleached hair. He couldn't even see any colour in their eyes. They looked about fifteen. "Excuse me," he asked. "Have you seen this person? Any time in the last few weeks?" He held out the snapshot of Ash. The three kids looked at him with a kind of distant curiosity, as if he were something on a microscope slide.

One of the boys took the photo and passed it to the girl. She looked at it for a few seconds, then gave it back to Rajan. "I don't know his name," she said. "But I've seen him. He went to the business."

"What business? Where?"

"You'll find it." She turned away. The other two followed her.

"Wait," Rajan said. "You've got to tell me..." They'd gone into the underpass, which had no light. He stumbled after them. His feet splashed in a pool of rainwater. Their pale heads flickered like distant lights.

They were distant lights. He was standing in the open square under the middle part of the flyover. The grey stone above his head was singing. There were four other passages back out to the streets, each one flanked by stone panels with abstract carvings. No one was there.

Later, he tried to explain what had happened to Kavita. "They were completely white," he said. "I don't mean Anglo-Saxon. I mean they had no colour at all. If you cut them, they'd probably bleed white. Like correction fluid." What had bothered him most was the way they'd just dismissed him. Their attitude of complete indifference. "If they know what *the business* means..."

"It's some teenage slang," Kavita said. "Probably just means going to school, or behaving like an adult. Kids like that live in a different world. You should take no notice." She reached across the table and touched Rajan's hand. "You're not doing yourself any good with these questions. How can it help?" He looked into her eyes and couldn't explain his need to believe.

It was a fortnight before he saw them again. He'd spent hours drifting around Hockley, through the park and the graveyards. The police had said "the business" might refer to crime, but that wouldn't help them much. Rajan wondered if they'd given up. He'd stood in the concrete square under the flyover, praying. It was no use. And then he saw three pale kids on the canal walkway, in the shadow of a bridge. They were staring into the dark water, which didn't reflect them or anything else.

Instead of calling, he ran down the metal steps to reach them. They looked at him and didn't move. He wanted to grab one of the boys and slam him against the bridge wall; but their blank stares made him wonder if he existed at all. They must be drugged, he realised. Even in shadow their faces had an unhealthy sheen, like mould. "Where is he?" Rajan asked. "You said he'd gone to *the business*. Where is it? I'll give you money..."

The girl smiled. Her teeth were dead white and very small. "Try looking some time." She reached into a pocket of her tight jeans and took out a card. "It's here." She gave the card to Rajan; her finger touched the edge of his palm. The card was black, with white lettering: THE BUSINESS, then an address on Factory Road. That was only a mile away, he realised, off Soho Hill. Was it a club of some kind? When he looked up, the teenagers were under the next bridge, only just visible. He didn't pursue them.

Factory Road, as you would expect, ended in a factory. The only other buildings were thin terraced houses, some of them boarded up. The address on the card was number 74. He paused at the door, breathless. A thread of nausea crept into his mouth. It was one of the empty houses. Boards were nailed over the windows. On the first floor there was a small balcony, the kind where you'd stand a potted shrub or hang some washing. The railings in front of it were twisted to leave a gap, like the outline of a face.

There was nothing here. The card was a sick joke. Rajan slipped it back into his pocket. The edge of his right hand felt cold. So did the inside of his skull. The children were playing somewhere. In empty houses, on a different street map. He wanted to find a pub and drink until the pale brightness in his head went away. But he couldn't go home drunk. Alcohol was one of the few things on which Kavita had fairly traditional views.

On the bus home, Rajan thought he needed to go back to his faith. It would protect him against humiliations like this. Give his life a frame that wasn't this city. He'd drifted away from the Hindu religion as a teenager, trying to rebel against his parents. Hidden somewhere in that thought was a connection he couldn't make. Like a gap between curtains that he couldn't reach to look through.

The third of October would have been Ash's eighteenth birthday. It was a Friday. Too depressed to stay in the house, Kavita had gone to her sister's in Coventry for the weekend. Rajan decided to stay in and do some work. Then he decided to stay in and pray. Then he bought a half-bottle of whisky and drank it, sitting alone in the dark. At some point, he heard Kavita's voice on the answerphone saying she hoped he was all right.

Later, he woke up and switched on the light. It was nearly two A.M. His glass had fallen onto the pale carpet, staining it gold. He didn't care. In his mind was the image of the house on Factory Road. It was the house where he'd been born. Not the same road, not the same city. But the same house.

His parents had come here from Gujerat in the fifties. They'd lived in Sheffield for nine years, then moved to Birmingham when Rajan was five and his brother Ajay was eight. That was when the problems had started: lack of money, lack of friends, his parents arguing bitterly over everything. By the time Rajan was sixteen, his parents weren't broke anymore. But they still argued, because it had become a habit. And because their love had died.

Rajan picked up the slim briefcase he took to work and slipped a screwdriver, a hammer and a torch into it. As an afterthought, he added a small kitchen knife. If the police stopped him, he'd have a lot of explaining to do. His vision was blurred from alcohol and memory. He'd looked down through that gap in the railings and seen a world of stillness and peace. He turned out the lights and closed the front door behind him.

The sky was cloudy; the city's light hung like a translucent dome over the quiet streets. There was no one about in Factory Road, though the factory windows were all lit. A song from the early eighties echoed in Rajan's head: "The Dreams of Children" by The Jam. It took him only a few minutes to prise away the board from the front window of number 74. The nails were rusty. Underneath, the glass was mostly gone. It was lucky he'd lost so much weight.

The room was full of rubble: boxes and broken furniture. His torch cast a fragile web of light. Near the door was a bookcase filled with rotting volumes of some encyclopaedia. In the hallway, cobwebs and wallpaper hung from the ceiling like ruined lampshades. There was a small pram near the foot of the stairs, with a doll in it. A wreath of blonde hair framed its waxy face. Its eyes were missing. Rajan touched its cheek, and his fingers sank into cold flesh. Not a doll. But not long dead. Where the fuck were they hiding?

The staircase had fallen through; it didn't look climbable. Then he remembered the cellar. His mother had kept jars of pickle and tins of condensed milk down there, as well as some old trunks from Gujerat that were never opened. He stumbled through the mess of cobwebbed paper and fabric to the door at the back of the stairs. The handle was coated with rust and grime, but it turned. A faint red light came from the room below, and a sound of metallic throbbing. Carefully, he began to walk down the steps.

The cellar was full of rusted machinery. Hulks of metal held together with chains and bakelite-covered wires. Yet he could see wheels turning, pistons moving back and forth. A light came on behind a dusty pane of glass. Rajan's feet made no sound on the rotting floorboards. There was a narrow doorway in the far wall. He passed through.

Lit by a thin red light that had no apparent source, two teenagers were lying side by side on a filthy sofa: a boy and a girl. Their heads were shaved, and they were horribly thin. The boy was fucking the girl from behind. Their faces were expressionless. They didn't notice Rajan as he walked past them to the next doorway. It led into a hall or corridor, where a number of half-naked youngsters stood in alcoves. They were cooking up some fluid in spoons over gas burners, then injecting it with dirt-flecked syringes into their breasts or genitals. Water dripped from the ceiling, like the ticking of a clock.

The next room contained two baths. In one, a girl was using a kitchen grater on her buttocks and thighs. A trickle of water from the taps rinsed the blood from around her feet. In the other bath, a boy was slowly pulling a strip of flesh from the inside of his left arm. His face and body were half-flayed, but Rajan recognised him. The boy looked up and stopped moving. The slow pulse of machinery came through the walls.

They stared at each other. Rajan felt sick with exhaustion. "So," he said. "What kind of time do you call this?"

There was no answer. Ashok stared at him until he backed off, then picked up a razor and resumed his work. Rajan touched the black wall. It was covered with a thin layer of disinfectant. His throat swelled, but what came out was only laughter. An empty laughter. But there was some relief in it.

Slowly, he walked back through the red-lit basement rooms to the steps. The shuddering of a hidden engine made his legs buckle, and he almost fell. The next thing he knew, he was back outside the house. He'd left his briefcase somewhere in the cellar. And he'd left the baby. It didn't seem to matter.

A van drove past. Daylight was filtering through the blue-grey clouds. The streetlamps were looking paler. At the end of the road, men in working clothes had gathered outside the factory for the start of the morning shift.

MINE

Night was falling as he found the place. He'd have liked to wait until dark, but there wasn't time. He had a gig that evening. It was a ritual: the first night of every tour. Once that had meant small towns in the Black Country; now it meant cities scattered across Europe. But always, for him, it started with this visit. His songs needed it. His voice needed it. He supposed most punters told themselves something similar. And it was always the same time of year: late autumn, as the trees burnt themselves out like cigarettes and dropped traces of frost on the pavement.

It was the same in every town, in every inner-city district. A shuttered window with a sign above it, lit up so as to be visible from the road at night. Always on a main road, close to other shops: being discreet was less important than ease of parking and access. The front door open, leading to a short entry passage; then a hermetically sealed inner door with a bell. As Mark got out of the car, the fading daylight made the buildings seem older: a modern street became grey and close-built, like the terraces he'd grown up in. He shivered and pulled at the collar of his black jacket.

The door was opened by a thin, pale-faced woman in a mauve gown. "Come in, darling," she whispered. The sodium light caught her cheekbones for a moment before she turned away. Her hair was tied in a long ponytail. Her feet made no sound on the vinyl floor of the hallway.

The reception lounge had two sofas, a table with a cash desk, and a blue mercury strip light that was just beginning to flicker. Another three men were waiting, their faces blank with a studied anonymity. "Have you been here before?" the receptionist said. Something in her voice and her blue-lit face made him realise that she was a man. He wondered if he'd come to the wrong kind of place.

"Yes." It was always easier to say that. He leaned forward. "Is Carole here tonight?"

The receptionist's sleeves rustled as he flicked through a leather-bound diary. "Yes, darling, she is. And she's free just now. That'll be ten pounds for the room." He tucked the note into the cash-box with a movement like striking a match. "I'll take you to her."

Beyond the fringed curtain of the reception room, stairs led down into a basement corridor with several doors. The thin man walked a pace ahead of him, his slipper-clad feet and long gown making him almost seem to float. It was evidently a bigger place than the frontage suggested. They walked on to the end of the corridor, and down another set of stairs. He could smell incense and smoke in the air. It was colder down here, and the wall-set lights were the dead white of a smile in a magazine. These places were rarely strong on ambience. A draught made the receptionist's sleeves tremble as he stopped at the last door.

The room inside was clearly not a bedroom. It had bare stone walls, and a ceiling that glistened with moisture. Mark couldn't see where the light was coming from. His own breath was a pale smoke in the air. He could hear a distant echo of a woman's voice crying out, only the rhythm allowing any distinction between pleasure and pain. So faint, it could have been an overdub from his own memory.

The receptionist gestured to an alcove on the left-hand side. Carole was sitting on a narrow white bed, wearing a silvery dress. She was brushing her long, dark hair. The light of a smoky oil lamp picked out the individual strands like the strings inside a piano. The thin man went up to her and bent to whisper something in her ear. She smiled at Mark, then held out her left hand. "That'll be sixty pounds, please."

He fumbled with his wallet as the receptionist made himself scarce. As Mark placed the three twenties in her perfectly white palm, he noticed that the gash in her wrist was still open. Ice crystals were forming in it. He cupped his hands to his mouth and breathed into them. Carole stood up and pulled off her dress. He stared at her like a peeping Tom as she unfastened her bra and slipped off her black knickers. She smiled. "Are you going to undress as well?" His hands shook as he unbuttoned his shirt, unable to look away from her.

They lay on the bed and caressed each other. Mark remembered the first nights they'd spent together, in her basement flat on the edge of the park. She still looked about nineteen; only her eyes were older. The skin of her face was pale and neutral, like scar tissue. His mouth crept across her body, kissing the bony ridges of her shoulders, then moving down to touch her injuries. The cuts she'd made on herself, where the ice had formed like salt. The bruises he'd given her long ago, still blooming like ink blots on the white skin. His tongue made her shiver. She turned in his arms to face the wall, and he spread her legs gently. The voices in the wall cried out to him, trapped echoes of need and release. The rhythm track. His fingers probed her, stirred warmth in her passive flesh.

It was time for the bridge. Carole turned again, reached down by the lamp, tore open a foil packet. Her thin fingers sheathed him, then guided him into her. Just as it had always been. There'd be no need to change positions. He kissed her lightly on the mouth, then pressed his lips to the side of her neck. His fingers gripped her ribs, pressing hard where the bruises were. She cried out with pain. "Sorry," he whispered. There were tears in her eyes. He reached up and stroked her forehead, running his fingers through the soft, dark hair. It felt dry, almost brittle. He bent over her and placed a slow kiss in the hollow of her throat. She moved against him and dug her nails into his back. The final chorus.

Submission wasn't enough for him: he needed her response. It always took time to get her warmed up. Her soft cries rang in his head, where all the lights were going out. His back arched, and he stared at the side of her face. She looked peaceful. She could almost have been asleep. He'd found her like this.

Still out of breath, Mark pulled on his clothes. The sweat glued him to his shirt; but it didn't matter, he'd be changing soon enough. Carole sat on the edge of the bed, putting on her underclothes, then stood up to pull on her dress. The flickering oil lamp made the silver fabric look grainy, like ash. He reached out to take her hand. "Come with me."

She stepped towards him, hesitantly. He looked into her eyes. "Will you follow me?" She nodded. He felt a quiet pang of joy, a tenderness mingled with the November ache of loss. Fire in the dead leaves. He gripped her hand, feeling the bones under the smooth skin. Then he let go and slowly walked towards the doorway. He thought he could hear footsteps behind him.

As he climbed the dark stairs, fatigue began to tug at him. It would be easier to stay down here, sleep for a while. Never mind the gig. But he kept walking. In the hallway, the cries of pleasure from behind the closed doors were a coda to accompany the two of them into the starlit night. He shivered. The moisture in his eyes blurred his vision. He stumbled up the second staircase to the lounge. There was no one there but the receptionist, who looked at Mark, then looked at the doorway behind him. He seemed about to say something, but instead just waved them on.

Mark took a deep breath and turned the handle on the inner door, then stepped through. The night was a blue-black curtain at the end of the passageway. He walked on until he could feel the cold air on his face, then turned around. His parting gesture was almost a wave. It could even have been a touch, if she'd been close enough to feel it. But she was already backing off, her face a mask the funeral parlour had been unable to make lifelike. The inner door closed behind him, and Mark was alone on the narrow street.

He waited to cross to where his car was parked. A line of vehicles was crawling past in both directions. Somewhere in the distance, a siren was caught up in the rush-hour traffic. The air was stale with exhaust fumes. Mindful of the time, he began to walk between the slowly moving cars. It would be disastrous to be late on the first night of his tour. If you wanted to build a life in music, you had to observe these superstitions. They were part of what it meant to belong.

PRISON SHIPS

Coming back for a visit made her realise she'd never felt at home here. They'd knocked down a couple of the roadside blocks, clearing the view across the flattened Lee Bank intersection. The taller buildings seemed to float in the shaky winter light, staring blankly at each other. Some other buildings had been cleared for demolition, or looked like it. But the north edge of the estate was looking better: frontages repainted in white and beige, the concrete panels on balconies glistening like a child's teeth. Sarah had come back for the New Year weekend, to stay with her sister Rachel. They still had a spare room because Rachel's two kids didn't want to sleep alone. Sarah thought she knew how they felt.

It was nine months now since Andrew had got the job in Telford and she'd gone up there to live with him. There'd not been much to take with or leave behind. Telford was strange, like somebody's dream of a town that had been left unfinished when they woke up. There were pale shopping arcades as long as roads, and all the buildings looked the same. People had more money there than round here, but they didn't go out. They worked and bought things and went on holiday and lived in debt. The streets were always empty. Which was okay for Sarah, who didn't like meeting people or going to pubs. She liked being with Andrew, but she didn't get on with his arrogant friends from the sales office. Lately, towards Christmas, she'd started getting low again. If she went back on medication, or if she didn't and got worse, she didn't know what would happen. Maybe they wouldn't have a child after all.

The first night she was back, Rachel told her what had happened in Stone House. Only a bare outline had appeared in the *Evening Mail*, to protect the victims and not interfere with the trial. The police had been crawling over the estate like worker ants for weeks in late summer. There'd been a party of some kind. Schoolkids on their own in one of the upper flats. Maybe it had got out of hand, but Rachel thought it had been planned to happen the way it did. Five girls in their early teens were gang-raped by eight boys. It went on all night. Some people had heard screams, but no one had done anything. The paper said the boys were aged between twelve and fifteen. What it hadn't said was that two of the girls were badly hurt, and one became pregnant. "One of the neighbours said she thought it was just a couple fighting. I don't know. Some people, if they can't see it, they don't think it's real."

Now that it was empty, Sarah's room felt smaller than before. Pictures and books had given it a kind of depth. Now there were only a couple of boxes, stuff from her childhood and school that she hadn't bothered to take with her. She drew the curtain across the barred window. Earlier today, she'd seen the rags of a floral curtain hanging out of a shattered window, soiled by the city centre rain. She undressed and climbed into the narrow bed. A few minutes later, the couple upstairs made the ceiling shake. The legs of their bed vibrated against the floorboards like a synth drum. A female cry broke out of the percussion—not loud, but involuntary. A few minutes later, she cried out again. Then silence flooded the air like a recording of sleep.

She hadn't told Rachel about her birthday party in November, the real reason why she'd opted to come back to Birmingham for the New Year. She'd got very drunk, and just before midnight five of Andrew's mates had decided to give her the bumps. She'd said no, but been too disorientated to resist. It felt like they were pulling her apart. Their strong hands on her wrists and ankles, one of them gripping her neck to stop her throwing up. Then she was on the floor, two of them lifting her up, taking the opportunity to paw at her skirt and blouse. Andrew was looking away, just so he could tell her he hadn't seen anything. She'd screamed the place down, then curled on the floor with her face in her hands and vomited. That night was when things had started to go wrong for her and Andrew.

The thin, morning light made the estate shiver. Unbroken windows were dazzled. While Rachel went to five ways with the kids to do some shopping, Sarah walked sleepily through the trees and the children's playground at the end of Rickman Drive. A poster selling Peter Andre unpeeled from the side of the pub, then jumped back: face, blank, face. It was colder than she'd expected. At the back of one of the ten-storey blocks, exposed to the sunlight but sheltered from the wind, was a row of flattened shops. Newsagent, off-licence, hardware, chemist. She'd worked at the chemist's for a while a couple of years back.

Jean was still working behind the counter. She looked heavier than before, her face pale and swollen. A male assistant Sarah didn't recognise was arranging a display of painkillers. As Sarah approached the counter, Jean stared uneasily at her, then smiled. "Oh, it's you. Thought you'd moved away."

"I have. Just back for a visit. How's it going?"

"Fucked. It's all closing down round here. David's trying to get a lease on the Pershore Road. Selling condoms to prostitutes. Makes a change from selling inhalers to schoolkids on glue." Jean cast a sarcastic eye over the cramped shelves.

"Things that happen round here, you wouldn't believe. The *Mail* won't print the truth, in case some local businessman complains it's putting off tourists."

"I heard about what happened in the summer. Those girls."

"What's going on, Sarah? This place is a factory of crime. I don't believe in coincidence, do you?" Her mouth twisted in a mime of broken illusions. "The boys who did that. Even if they're convicted, they'll be out in a year or two. It'll make all the other ones think there's nothing to it. Tell you what *should* happen. It's not just me, ask any woman around here, they'll agree with me. Those boys should not be released unless they agree to be castrated. They won't do it again, will they?" Laughter swelled in Jean's mouth, but didn't emerge. Her eyes cut across Sarah's face. "Don't tell me you think they're not to blame."

She didn't need this. "Jean… look, I don't believe in cutting people's bits off. It makes them less than people."

"They're already less than people. Do you want them out on the streets? Or living in the same block as you? That's like sharing your house with them." Sarah thought of Nash House, her years of feeling unsafe, and smiled. "You think it's funny? Let me tell you something. The government pretends it's anti-crime. But it won't castrate rapists. You know why not, Sarah? Because that would slow down the race mixing. Doesn't matter which lot's in power. Michael Howard or Peter Mandelson, it's the same thing." She tapped her nose.

Jean hadn't changed. There was no point arguing with her. What she needed wasn't political enlightenment, it was a life. Sarah bought a few items and left. Going back up Rickman Drive, she realised she'd forgotten to invite Jean to the New Year party. Never mind. Across the Lee Tavern car park, two kids were playing swingball with a ball attached to a piece of scaffolding on a traffic cone. Envelopes of brown metal were riveted across flat windows, turning buildings to dead hulks. From the past until completion. Well, she was out of here. The city could fuck itself in all its unfinished redevelopment projects.

As she crossed the pitted courtyard towards Nash House, sunlight flared in the upper windows. Sarah felt trapped and exposed at the same time. She decided to phone Andrew before tonight, promise him… what, exactly? That might put him off. *I miss you* would do it. She noticed the patterned metal guards over some of the ground-floor windows. And like a parody of a suburban street, the cluster of brick garages with their windows boarded up. They were only used for storing junk and valuables; they were more secure than the flats. Some day she'd have to decide between security and freedom. But when you had neither, they seemed like the same thing.

An hour into the party, Sarah began to wonder if her sister knew all these people. Were they friends of friends, or pure gate-crashers? Rachel was locked in an intense discussion with her new man, Carl, their mouths separated by a gauze of words. Guests were blocking the hallway, drinking in the kitchen, dancing slowly in the dim living room where Rachel had put in a red bulb. Tricky was snarling his way down the long, twisted passages of *Pre-Millennium Tension*, Martina struggling to hold the thing together. It made Sarah think of her parents' half-concealed rows. Earlier, Andrew's voice on the phone had sounded so close and yet so far away, like her own thoughts in the night. She wondered what state he'd be in by the New Year.

The children were stopping over with friends in Bordesley Green. Sarah drifted between the kitchen and the living room, saying hello to people she knew but hadn't missed. The music changed to a dance compilation featuring Blueboy and Mark Morrison; the tempo quickened. Sarah was drinking Pulse cider spiked with large shots of Tesco vodka. Her body was dancing, but her brain was trying to hide. *Remember me.* The glass was cloudy with water droplets, like a bathroom mirror. She needed to lie down, but her bedroom was occupied by four teenagers sharing out pills. Maybe Rachel's room was clear. But Carl was following Rachel into her room, his hands on her waist. The door closed behind them.

Sarah hid in the toilet for a few minutes while her head cleared. It was 11:30. There was blood in the washbasin, she didn't know why. When she came out, a man she'd slept with before Andrew gave her a bottle of White Dragon cider and started dancing with her. She rested her hands on his shoulders. Soon they were leaning against the wall, her face pressed into his neck. If he let go of her, the crowd would pull her apart. She felt his hand lifting her shirt, fumbling with the button of her jeans. "Wait, wait." He looked at her face and backed off. She rushed down the hallway and he tried to follow her, but more bodies stumbled between them and he either lost her or gave up.

The staircase outside the flat was chilly and grey. The only light came from weak security lamps set in the walls. Sarah fell to her knees as a metallic edge of bile cut her tongue from inside. Only a few drops trickled from her open mouth. She gulped the cold, damp air. As her vision cleared, she realised that she was not alone. Couples were pressed against the wall on the staircase and the landing, blurred together like knotted shadows. She could hear the sounds they made. As she walked past them down the stairs, they went on blindly struggling. A family of partial ghosts: hands, breasts, voices, hair. At the foot of the stairs, a small child was waiting.

It was a girl, maybe seven or eight. "Will you help us?" she said. "There's no one around. Please. You've got to come now." In the dim light, her face was a mask of shock.

"What's happened?" Sarah asked. But the child turned away, leading her out of the building into the moonlit courtyard. Broken glass twinkled from the ground. Vertigo caught her as she glanced up at the windows of the opposite block, rising from the splintered trees. She was too drunk for this. Ahead of her, the girl was running along the line of garages. The door of the last one had been forced open. Inside, a light flickered.

The girl pointed. "In here. Quick." Sarah pushed herself sideways through the narrow gap. At once, a torch beam dazzled her. Someone pushed her knees from behind; she fell hard onto the concrete floor. The garage door screamed as it was pulled shut. Alcohol dulled the pain in her kneecaps and hands as she climbed back to her feet. The torch beam played slowly over her body. Five or six lighters wavered in the narrow room, like aircraft in formation. The garage was full of children. At least a dozen of them, boys and girls, no older than ten. All staring at her. They all had knives. From somewhere outside, Sarah heard a muffled cheer and some kind of singing. It must be midnight.

Sarah backed towards the door. Pale light flickered on steel. This would find its way into someone else's nightmares, via the local paper or the TV news. The hopelessness of it would become an image. She could feel the vodka in her gut struggling for release. The little boy with the torch stepped towards her. He raised a black-handled kitchen knife to her throat. Sarah stepped backwards, felt a brick wall imprint her with dust. Her head struck the ceiling and she had to lean forward. The children closed in, their eyes and mouths empty.

The boy dropped the torch. He touched her breast, then stepped closer and said, "Comfort me." She didn't know what he meant. He stared at the hollow of her throat. Sarah put her hands on his shoulders; they were as hard as metal. She drew him closer. *It's okay,* she whispered. *It's okay.* His fingers scratched at her shirt, with nowhere to go. She held him tight. Then she pulled him under her left arm and drove his head into the wall. The knife clattered between her feet. A crack of light showed in the doorway. Sarah kicked at it and forced her way out. No one followed her. She walked across to Nash House. The doorway was still open.

On the dark staircase, she felt herself come apart. Unable even to find the door and knock, she huddled on the first landing. His face had cracked like a shell. She sat with her arms around her knees, listening. The silence drowned her own breath. All the couples had gone.

LIKE SHATTERED STONE

It happened in the early hours of the morning. After he'd gone to bed. He'd spent a frustrating evening in his studio, chiselling nervously at a new block of granite. The shape he wanted was fairly well-defined in his head, but the stone wouldn't listen to him. And it was too expensive to waste; so as usual he'd chipped away without committing himself. When his hands had begun to seem as strange and difficult as the stone, he'd given up and gone through to the next room, his bedsit. It was nearly midnight. Two or three hours later, he'd woken up in the dark. He was naked, and shivering with cold. There was a hammer in one of his hands, and a chisel in the other. His elbows were resting on the table in his studio. A vague light from the street outlined the curtained window on the far side of the room.

Peter hesitated, trying to remember where the door was. This was worse than being alone in bed. He rubbed his arms together, trying to warm himself. Then he stood up and walked away from the table, groping almost randomly for the light switch. There was a click, and the room became familiar again. He rubbed his eyes. The block of stone on the table had been intended to represent a collapsing building. But now, most of the top third of the block had been chipped away. Crude, jagged chippings were scattered on and around the table. And sticking out from the top of the stone was a perfect replica of a child's forearm. The hand was half-closed, its muscles tense. Peter stepped towards it and, without thinking, took hold of the rigid fingers.

He couldn't believe what a good likeness it was. Even when fully awake, he could never have carved something this convincing. Human figures weren't his line. The arm ended between the wrist and elbow, in a rippled surface of granite. He knew there was no way he could develop the figure: the rest of it was lost, hiding inside the stone. That was a strange way to think about it. Wasn't it Michelangelo who'd talked about finding the body in stone? Whatever. He'd just have to complete his distorted building, with the hand reaching up through the roof. The image disturbed him. He'd better get back to bed, before he died

59

of exposure.

At dawn, he was still awake. He wished he could afford a place with central heating. *Get a proper job*, he told himself angrily as he drew the curtains and touched the thin crust of ice on the window-ledge. Across the narrow yard, which was littered with empty bottles, he could see part of the General Hospital: lighted windows and plastic signs beyond a grey wall that was mouldy with frost. The dawn chorus of city-centre traffic pressed in through the fragile glass. It was February. If there had been any trees, they might have shown the onset of spring. *The green shoots of recovery*, he thought grimly.

The morning post brought a cheque from the Ikon Gallery. They'd sold two of his wrecked-car sculptures (based on things he'd seen by the disused railway in Harborne when he was a child). Well, the money would help to keep him going until the end of the month. He was working part-time as a designer for a correspondence course publisher. The salary was more reliable than what he earned from his art, but it didn't give him the little shock of joy that made him feel able to keep going. Some people got by on money alone. Or love. Or nothing at all except the will to survive.

He couldn't face going back into the studio, after last night. Perhaps some exercise would help to wake him up. And he had to deposit his cheque in the bank; it wasn't just an excuse for not working. Outside, the chill took him by surprise. The sky was as white as a freshly painted wall. His lack of sleep made the buildings seem insubstantial, like a stage set. The pavements were slippery with frost. Near the Salvation Army hostel, he was stopped three times by beggars. These days he couldn't tell who was sleeping rough, who might be starving, who just wanted money for drink. The dividing line between "deserving" and "undeserving" cases was invisible on the street. He tried to give something to those who looked sick, or very old, or very young. The alcoholics never pushed their luck; it was the mothers with ragged children who took your coins and followed you, begging for more. They knew it was never the rich who gave. A few years ago, there hadn't been anywhere near as many of them around here.

He was stopped twice more in the shopping precinct along New Street. Guilt made him hand three pounds to a young girl in white, whose staring, bloodshot eyes suggested heroin addiction. Her arm was so tense she almost dropped the coins. He didn't want those eyes burning inside his head all day. By the time he reached the bank, Peter was in a foul mood. The new design of Victoria Square was still hard to believe. It had been grassy once, surrounded by trees that shaded benches from sunlight and rain. Now, an entirely redundant semicircle of steps led down from a bored-looking stone goddess in a fountain, attended by two Enid Blyton sphinxes. The entire square had been paved over. The effect was of a mass-produced artifact, like something found in a cereal packet. The restored statue of Queen Victoria looked on approvingly from the steps of the Town Hall.

In the distance, the mirrored bulk of the new Hyatt hotel complex glittered above the stores and office blocks of a four-acre boom town.

If any city centre could get it together, Peter reflected, it wouldn't be Birmingham. But was it possible anywhere, with public spending crippled and communities scarred by a decade of neglect? Only the owners of hotels and restaurants, catering to visitors from outside, were investing in the "new" city centre. While conditions in the poorer residential districts got steadily worse: Newtown, Aston, Shard End, Castle Vale, Smethwick, Nechells, Kingstanding, Castle Bromwich. As the circle of poverty widened, the inner city spread through the suburbs of Moseley and Edgbaston. There was nothing "inner" about it at all. But of course, there was nothing there for commercial interest to invest in. Apart from cheap property rental, which was a vicious and exploitative racket. Still, as long as the *Birmingham Post* could go on printing pictures of the new Convention Centre and advocating moral crusades against lawlessness, all would surely be well.

Back at his flat, Peter worked carefully at the base of his collapsing tower block

The hand was real, and he avoided doing anything to it. After a while, fatigue began to overwhelm him; it felt as if tiny flakes of stone were lodged under his eyelids. But he was afraid of going to sleep. Eventually he gave up, made some coffee and put a record on. The Hüsker Dü album *Candy Apple Grey* seemed to echo his mood. Second post had brought him a letter from Rachel. It was relentlessly cheery, as usual. She hoped he was coping financially, was in good health and wasn't drinking too much. He made a mental note to write to her when hell froze over. Though from the way this morning had felt, it already had.

The music was atonal, bare nerve-endings and fragments of bone without the skin of melody. He remembered the last evening he and Rachel had spent together. She'd come round for dinner; he'd asked her to stay the night, and she'd refused. A tense and bitter ending to a relationship that had lasted nearly two years—a year of which they'd spent living together in a house in Handsworth. She'd left him for someone who hardly seemed to want her, who had a lover already and would never commit himself to Rachel. She and Peter had been proud of the openness that allowed them both to sleep with other people. It was a measure of how much they trusted each other, and a freedom which they very rarely took advantage of.

Then Carl came along, passed through their lives and took Rachel with him. He'd told her that she was bound to leave Peter someday. No doubt that would make him feel better about himself when it no longer suited him to be with Rachel. *I gave you all I had to offer a person*, Peter thought, *and it wasn't enough*. He felt like stone: cold and exposed. *Carl didn't even have to love you, did he? It's just as well.* The house where they'd lived probably had new tenants by now. *You swore you wouldn't leave me for him. Oh shit, drop it. Let it go.* He punched the side of his face until his jaw felt numb. For months he'd been swinging between apathetic misery and a kind of frantic, wild joy that had nothing to do with happiness. The few women he'd tried to get close to since Rachel had sensed his lack of balance. They'd given him sympathy and affection, but been wary of anything more serious. So was he. Sex was a comfort, but love was a confusing threat. That was the worst thing of all: his own loss of depth, loss of need.

Now that he'd started thinking about Rachel, it was hard to stop. They'd split up nine months ago. The sensible thing to do was to put it behind you, get on with your life. But sometimes reality wasn't sensible. There was something inside him that was waiting to tear its way out. Something as vacant and hungry as an infant. He shivered; it had suddenly turned cold, though nightfall was still an hour away. There were spots of frost on the window. No, not frost. Snowflakes. He'd never seen them so big. They drew whiteness from the sky, flocked together above the buildings, clung brightly to the glass. They were the dead skin of angels. Behind the falling snow, the view trembled and started to dissolve.

The phone rang; it was Graham, an old friend from the laboratory where he'd worked a few years ago. Was he coming out to the pub this evening? Peter said yes. It would help: he'd sleep better and have a more normal day tomorrow. By the time he left for the pub, it had stopped snowing. The roads were grey and tacky with slush; but fresh white scars marked the edges of pavement where no one walked. The trees by the cathedral dripped light, melting like chandeliers in a firestorm. Peter rubbed his arms and watched his breath making knots in the air. The snow gave way underfoot, too light to survive. But it was cold enough.

The White Lion on Bristol Street was crowded, though it was only mid-evening. Graham and his wife Jane were in the lounge at the back, away from the main bar. Peter recognised a few other faces, including three of his former colleagues. Stu the warehouse manager, whom Peter had never liked, was there with a much younger girlfriend. The sound of his jarring South-East London accent made Peter suddenly recall hours spent counting and sorting tiny bottles in the stock room, which was kept at sub-zero temperature and had no windows. You were only meant to stay there for up to ten minutes without a break; but it was easy to find yourself going in and out all day, looking for missing items as discrepancies arose between stock records and actual supplies. He remembered the quilted jackets and gloves they'd worn for that work, and how your face went numb after a few minutes among the metal shelves.

As he started getting drunk, Peter realised how tired he still was. People's voices seemed to drift in and out of focus like wavebands on a car radio. Graham touched his shoulder. "Are you ok? You're shivering." Peter nodded. It wasn't cold in here, was it? He smiled at Graham, who still looked worried. Jane was at the bar, and Stu was relating some loud and humourless anecdote to his other colleagues. "By the way," Graham said quietly, "I've been made redundant. I've got three months left. They've dropped five people. I'm the oldest." Most of the staff were young, because inexperienced workers could be paid less and were easier to dominate.

Peter stared at him. "God, I'm sorry. That's dreadful." He knew Graham detested the company; but he liked the job, and was good at it. "Did they give you a reason?"

"Falling sales figures. Need for restructuring, all that." Graham shook his head. "They'd been going on all year about how the company was expanding. But they've taken on three new publicity and marketing guys. You know the type. Clean-cut boys in Armani suits, with floppy disks where their brains should be. If you pushed them against the office wall and fucked them they'd say, *Hey, loved your input*. The company's paying them huge salaries to talk trash on the phone. Meanwhile, they'll probably replace all the people they've sacked with kids on Youth Training Schemes or work experience." He drained his pint angrily. "Don't worry. It's not the end of the world. If nothing else turns up, the redundancy money should keep me going until early autumn. I hope Jane won't have to support me. Any more than she does already."

Suddenly Graham looked puzzled. "What's that? Outside." His mouth formed the word *shit* as they listened. From behind the pub, on the corner with Thorpe Street, someone was shouting. *Help. Help.* Was it genuine or part of a drunken argument? *Oh my God. Help. Please help.* "Come on," Graham said. A number of people at the back of the lounge area had heard it and were starting to head for the door, which was in the main bar. Graham and Peter followed them, moving as quickly as possible through the crowded space. Somebody shouted something to the barman. As they broke out into the frozen street, Peter felt a sudden tension deep in his chest. The screaming had stopped.

Two men were standing in a circle of yellow light, just out of view of the main road. One of them had backed against a high brick wall, his arms flung out. He was wearing a light grey suit; the jacket and shirt were torn into thin strips, held together by threads of blood. The other man was leaning towards him, waving a broken bottle in a hazily deliberate way, as if trying to hypnotise his victim. Both men were about forty; the attacker had a crew-cut, bomber jacket and DMs. The sound of footsteps behind him made him pause and draw back. Still clutching the bottle, he began to stagger away, then to run. Nobody followed him.

A police car turned off the main road, its roof light flashing, and braked with a crunch of broken glass. The man against the wall didn't move; but he was shaking. The sweat on his face seemed about to freeze. "Are you all right?" someone said. Peter thought he couldn't be seriously hurt; there wasn't enough blood. It looked as though the attacker had been trying to terrify him into giving up his money. Or else to cut away the pockets of his suit. There was no snow on the ground, or in the air. It had vanished as suddenly as the peace.

Two policewomen got out of the car. One took the injured man's arm and helped him forward. After a few steps, he fell to his knees. "The wall held me," he said clearly. "The wall. Holding me." He was evidently in shock. The other police officer asked the group from the pub what they'd seen. By now, the attacker had disappeared into the backstreets of the Chinese quarter. "He followed me from the pub," the injured man said. The policewomen exchanged looks. Helped to his feet, the victim stared as if wondering where he was. "My glasses," he said, sounding confused. "In the road. They fell off." A few people started looking. On a hunch, Peter examined the ground under the police car. Just behind the front right-hand wheel was a crushed wire frame and a few fragments of thick glass. He picked them up, feeling a painful and senseless urge to laugh. The car driver was apologising as Peter followed Graham back into the pub, where people were drinking and talking and playing pool as if nothing had happened.

At closing time, snow was falling thickly onto the roads; the sound of traffic was muffled. Jane and Graham gave Peter a lift home, their blue Metro crawling in a slow procession of cars and taxis. He remembered saying goodbye, blundering drunkenly through the flat, making coffee which he forgot to drink. It seemed only a moment later that he woke up in darkness, reached for the duvet and bruised his hand on the edge of the table. The smell of dusty floorboards and split stone told him he was back in the studio. At once, his mind filled with the images he'd planed to sculpt: smashed cars, burnt-out buildings. Nervously, he stood up and turned on the light. On the table, cut from a fresh block of stone, was the head of a child.

He sat looking at it until the morning, unable again to believe how perfect it was. He'd never been that good at representational sculpture, hadn't really seen the point in an era when computer design and synthetic fibres made it possible to replicate any shape you wanted. His sculptures were symbolic in an obvious, external way. But this head was different. There was something within it that made it a symbol, not just an imitation of life. The eyes were shut. The short hair could belong to either a boy or a girl. Hair that looked soft, even though it was made of stone.

Outside, everything was white. It was like being still asleep. He walked to the office in Hockley where the correspondence course publisher was based, and spent a few hours designing the pages for a new booklet. The computer was an old IBM, and its software was both pirated and out of date. He left the proof pages on the production editor's desk. One of the subscriptions people asked him how his sculptures were going. He said something noncommittal. How could he take credit for work done in his sleep? Or predict the outcome? It scared him to think about it. From the barred window of the production office, he could see the rippled surface of fresh snow covering the demolition site where, all summer, heaps of rubbish had been burning. How did the old men and women sleeping on the streets survive weather like this? Being drunk wouldn't help; it only stopped you feeling the cold. It couldn't protect you.

Partway through the afternoon, he ran out of things to do. There was a typical Friday atmosphere in the office: people were exchanging gossip, making plans for the weekend, scouring the job section of the local paper. The old storage heaters fixed to the walls filled each office with a stuffy barrier of heat; employees had long since moved their desks to the areas of more normal temperature. Peter was starting to fall asleep. Fear made him stand up, switch off his computer and say goodbye to the other workers. Outside, it was brighter than he had expected. The snow hoarded daylight, like a sea of broken glass.

Under the Hockley flyover, three drunks were sharing a bottle of gin. Their layers of clothing identified them as vagrants. Unwilling to go home, Peter headed up into the Asian part of Handsworth. Trays and boxes of frosty vegetables were displayed outside grocery stores. Most shops along the Soho Road had cars parked on the pavement to protect their windows. Peter remembered the ram-raiding in 1991, the jokes about the new drive-in branch of Visionhire. He'd been living here with Rachel up until last summer. A few more of the shops and large Victorian houses were boarded up now. On the steps of a Seventh-day Adventists church, an old woman crouched in a nest of plastic bags and newspapers.

Up ahead, the yellow lines of a box grid marked the crossroads close to where he and Rachel had lived. Peter reflected that you always noticed road markings when it was too late to act on them. Rather than turn left and pass the house, he crossed at the lights and walked along the number 11 route. One of the side roads, a cul-de-sac which ended in wasteground, was now wholly derelict. The narrow terraced houses had been exposed by vandals or squatters: the window-panes and front doors were broken or missing. A grey blanket nailed across one doorway indicated a definite attempt at occupation. So many empty buildings. So many people without shelter. It wasn't necessary for vagrants to die on the streets, any more than it was necessary for someone to get bottled because of his choice of pub. It just happened, and if you said it was inevitable you were helping it to go on.

The light was fading. Peter turned right, onto an oblique sidestreet that would take him back up the Soho Road. By now, traffic and pedestrians had left marks on the layer of snow: it was bruised with slush, crusted with broken ice. It wouldn't last. Then he stopped. Across the road was a large, dark building he didn't recognise. It was at least three stories high; the windows were all boarded up. The walls weren't brick, but something like granite: huge grey blocks that were smeared with frost. Peter stared at the building; he felt sure that something had led him here. Was it a school? A church? A hostel? No insight came to him, apart from a sense of being used. After a few minutes, he walked on.

More snow fell before midnight. He slept badly, disturbed by the silence outside. Waking up in bed was both a relief and a disappointment. The flat was cold, but he couldn't really feel it. He dressed, though it wasn't yet daylight, and went into his studio. The child's head was unchanged. From the other block by the wall, the hand was still reaching upward as though trapped in the process of birth. Was this as far as it went? Because there was nobody to witness these miracles, they were lost. He could feel the empty nights moving over him like a chisel. The need for contact screamed in him; he sat down and put his hands over the stone face. The slight texture of the surface mimicked the imperfection of skin. Falling asleep, he imagined that he could feel the eyes opening, biting into his palm.

When he woke, a colourless daylight had soaked through the curtains. His shoulders and arms ached from the position he'd slept in. His hands were numb. There was blood all over the stone face; it had run like a shadow onto the bench, around the dull chips of granite. The blood had dried on his hands, but he could see a whorl of tiny cuts in each palm, like a tattoo without ink. He got up and washed, then rubbed TCP into his hands. It was only then that they started to hurt.

The crowding in the White Lion made him feel more alone than ever. Newcomers shook fresh snow from the hoods and shoulders of their coats, their faces clouding in the sudden heat. Towards closing time, an inertia swept through the bar. The jukebox changed its tune, regressing from Madonna and Kylie Minogue to the Eagles, Chicago, the Walker Brothers. The scarred words of "No Regrets" were still falling through Peter's head as he walked out onto the street. *Just behind the dawn.* A pack of late-night buses came up Bristol Street into town, all empty and staring white.

In the flat, he sat with a bottle of gin and watched the snow falling past the window. The drifting flakes seemed to cohere into a pattern just before they reached the glass. If the window-frame were an inch further out, would he be able to see properly? By now, he was beyond crying, beyond the compulsive emotion that came with being drunk. He felt—what was the phrase?—*out there.* Everything was new and irreversible. The bottle was empty, but he knew he wouldn't sleep. Stumbling a little, he pulled his coat back on and went out into the night. Invisible lips brushed against his face.

On the Soho Road, most of the shops had metal shields. It was like a row of garage doors on a housing estate. Someone had sprayed YOUR DEAD on one of the grey screens. He wondered if it could be the end of a message: *Bring out your dead.* Outside a pub, a few aging drunks were slumped against the wall. The snow painted their faces. Two were fighting in a slow, confused way, pulling at each other's coats. Peter carried on towards the crossroads. The image of his own footprints weaving from side to side occurred to him, making him smile. Lamplight glistened on boarded windows and edges of broken glass. But the snow had cleaned the district as easily as correction fluid. No more hedging of bets, he thought. No more going from winter to spring and back again. It was going to be winter.

When he reached the sealed building, his exhaustion caught up with him. The only movement was in the snow that made a blurred thumbprint across each streetlamp. And something on the steps, in the shadow of the doorway: a pile of rags and newspapers, shaking, trying to form. It was the same old woman he'd seen outside the church. Flakes of torn paper fell from her shoulders. She stood up, growing as she moved forward into the light. Rachel. The same pale skin, bruised eyes, long streak of dark hair. Or it wasn't Rachel, but it was very like her, and that was enough. She recognised him. They embraced slowly; he gripped her arms and felt her breath on his face. By now there was no sensation in his hands at all.

Then she pulled away and began walking along the side of the house. Reaching up, she gestured at the boarded window. Her hand mimed the tearing out of nails. What did she want to get in for? Peter examined the wood; it was firmly secured. He needed tools. "Wait," he said. She seemed to understand. It didn't take him long to catch a taxi on the Soho Road. Entering his flat, he felt like a burglar. There wasn't time for him to recognise the place. On the taxi back into Handsworth, he fought to stay awake. The taxi cost nearly all the change he had. The small hammer and chisel were in his coat pocket.

Working by sight alone wasn't easy, especially in the poor light at the side of the building. He couldn't risk being seen from the street. Rachel stood beside him, silently touching the window-frame with her thin hands. Eventually, the board shrieked as he worked it loose. There was no glass in the window. Inside, the room was cold and bare. Rachel felt their way along the blank walls to the bottom of a flight of stairs. There was some light here, though he couldn't see where it was coming from. It seemed to float, like mist. He sat down on the stairs with Rachel and held her. When she kissed him, his lips went dead as if the nerves had been cut. Her arm was torn, the white flesh gaping open under a flap of cloth. As he watched, crystals formed in the wound and became opaque. There was no blood.

At the top of the stairs, they reached a hallway. The walls were covered with messages and drawings. Not sprayed: carved into the surface. People were sitting in corners, on steps, against the wall. They pressed themselves to the stone, as if for warmth. Nobody moved or spoke. The faint light from the walls shone through them and made their faces seem alive. Peter stopped and tried to speak, but the words wouldn't come. He was thinking about the things people did to keep their feelings warm. How the senses came to life when imagination died. And vice versa, sometimes. Rachel stumbled and fell against him. They sat down together, holding each other as if unable to let go. Though he couldn't feel it,

Peter saw Rachel begin to come apart.

When all the flesh had melted, it refroze over his jacket and hands like a white skin. He looked upward, and saw more people huddled on the next staircase and landing. Briefly, he wondered why they had all come here. Perhaps they were just looking for shelter. Perhaps they believed this was a place where they could be looked after, where they would find comfort. Or perhaps (he thought with a growing sense of calm) it was the city itself, trying to restore the balance between flesh and stone.

AMONG THE DEAD

He woke up with an unpleasant taste in his mouth. The air was dense with heat and filtered early morning sunlight. He reached to silence the alarm, and hunger twisted in his gut. There was no time to recapture his dream: clean youthful limbs entangled with his own, eager hands gripping his shoulders. The train wouldn't wait for him to touch up the past.

He'd taken his breakfast out of the fridge last night. It was on the sideboard, cooking with the slow heat of decay. He ate fast, washing the food down with gulps of black coffee. The morning post interrupted him. A brochure from a new funeral service and two letters from the bank—one threatening to foreclose his overdraft, the other offering him a new credit card. He cleaned his teeth, noticing the crimson threads in the water he spat out.

Outside, the sunlight was flecked with ash. Smoke was rising from office buildings that had been torched in the night. Wrecked and burnt-out cars littered the pavement along the Moseley Road. Whoever had the contract to clean up the south part of the city was evidently working standard hours only. David wished he'd thought to go out before dawn. Never mind. There'd be more chances tonight. He'd be out with the boys, though, which would mean sharing whatever turned up. A social life always had its cost.

He'd expected to spend the working day on the next issue of *Children As a Market*. But Tony wanted some new promotional material put through ahead of schedule. By lunchtime, David had roughed out a new web page with the heading: *Neotechnic—quality edutainment for children of all ages.* The heavy red and black logo made him think of violence and loss. There was an odd contrast between the cosiness of whatever the company put out for public consumption and the hard aggression of its internal memos. He liked to think of the logo as a covert statement of the truth.

At lunchtime, they had a union meeting. No time for him to get anything to eat. He hoped his stomach would keep quiet during the meeting. Lorraine and Katie, the MoC and Deputy, reported that management was stonewalling on redundancy terms. They'd also refused to accept the union's guidelines on stress and workplace health, on the grounds that levels of sickness absence were already unacceptably high.

"They view sickness absence as a disciplinary issue, not as a health issue," Lorraine said. "But I'm hoping to arrange a series of regular meetings with Tony to discuss staff issues. If we can appeal to his better nature…"

"What better nature?" David said. "He's a director of the company. End of story."

"He's still a human being." Lorraine fixed him with her dark, watery eyes. He felt rage building in him like indigestion.

"Excuse me," he said quietly. "Are we talking about Tony Eden the cunt? Or some other Tony Eden I haven't yet encountered?"

"Cynicism is not going to get us very far."

"I just wish you'd stop thinking that if the bosses and the workers get together over a plate of choccie biccies, things will magically be ok. As far as you're concerned, the union's only role is to get the kettle on."

"Fuck off," Lorraine snapped. David smiled, then remembered that his teeth these days were stained. No wonder no one had kissed him in years.

Katie gave him a furious glance. "I don't know what you're trying to prove," she said. "All this aggression is getting us nowhere, David. I mean it. You're becoming what you claim to be fighting against."

The meeting dragged on to another lame conclusion. Afterwards, David went into the Gents' and stared at himself in the mirror. The red eyes and the colourless skin were a dead giveaway. His breath probably stank worse than the company's health and safety policy. Why did he even pretend to be like the others?

This part of the city had been ruined for years now. The contract for rebuilding had gone to a company owned by the son of a leading local councillor. He'd siphoned most of the money into another business, sold off the building equipment and sacked his entire local workforce, but due to a legal technicality the contract was still his. Meanwhile, the district—once famed as the Jewellery Quarter—supported a thriving population of rats, prostitutes and junkies. It also had most of the city's graveyards.

David was the first to arrive at the pub. Matt, Gary and the others joined him in a twilight corner of the lounge, where cigarette smoke threaded the air like sperm in water. They were just in time for last orders. Over the mosaic of conversation, he thought he heard Gary say: *What do you call a fridge full of organs?* He racked his brain fruitlessly for the answer. *A donor kebab.*

By the time they reached the graveyard in Vyse Street, no one with a legitimate reason for being on the street was still there. The main reason for coming as a group was security. They hung around, pretending to be drunk, until the old green clock at the top of the road clasped its slender hands together. David could hear the wail of sirens from the city centre, not close enough to be either a worry or a temptation.

The graves were Victorian or older, huge granite slabs and crosses like the pieces of an alien board game. The accumulated deposits of polluted rain had sleeved their messages. A few pale angels hovered in the moonlight, waving. This part of the graveyard was on a steep hillside, overgrown with shrubbery and distorted trees. Half-decayed leaves from the previous autumn made the ground soft and treacherous underfoot. Low walls protected the bricked-up entrances to family vaults and air-raid shelters.

They came this way mostly for atmosphere, though you did stumble across the occasional junkie or murder victim in the hours before dawn. The silent headstones and the weeping trees made you feel calmer about all the other stuff. Rituals were important. But they were headed for the new part of the cemetery, where graves were evenly spaced in the fresh turf. Bunches of white flowers declared the presence of the living. That was the place where they had business.

Two new graves had been dug since last weekend. The party divided into two working groups. They produced trowels from the inside pockets of their coats and began to dig in the moist soil. A kind of cold mania was on them, so that they hardly paused for breath but wasted no energy. David felt sweat trickling through his hair, stinging his eyes. As the hole grew they crept into it and burrowed like moles, crouching low over the black surface. They made no sound. Loose soil fell like rain onto the turf above them.

Both groups achieved their target at roughly the same time. David gazed at the dark wood of the coffin lid, still unblemished. An earthworm writhed blindly in the light of Matt's pocket torch. The pedant in David reminded him that "the conqueror worm" referred to maggots, not annelids. He picked it off and dropped it into the loose soil. Together, the three diggers forced open the coffin lid. The familiar smell of formaldehyde rose into the still night.

They hadn't bothered to look at the headstone, David realised. The body was that of a young man, eighteen or so, with dark curly hair and pale skin. A few freckles marked his bony forehead. Whatever had killed him had left his face intact. The eyes were closed, but David felt his calm stare. This could have been himself, twenty years earlier. He reached out and brushed the cold cheek with his cold fingers. *What happened to you?* he thought.

"Do you want him?" Gary said. "It's ok, we can come back later. Just clean him up afterwards. I don't want your mess on my breakfast."

"What do you think I am," David snarled, "a fucking pervert?"

"Keep your voices down, girls." Matt looked around anxiously. "There isn't time to say grace."

Using penknives and their dirt-streaked fingernails, they tore off strips from the face and began to eat. The viscera had been removed, of course, but there was plenty of muscle on the arms and legs. David reached in his trouser pocket for a Sainsbury's mini-bottle of red wine. The evening meal didn't feel civilised without it.

He went on eating long after his physical appetite had been appeased. This was a hunger that grew out of rage and disgust. The more nauseous he felt, the more he needed to eat. He gagged and belched, but didn't throw up. A soft breeze cooled the air, mingling the smell of formaldehyde with smoke and petrol fumes from the ruins of Hockley.

Gary cracked a rib and sucked out the marrow carefully. "Bet this one was a car crash," he said. "The pelvic girdle's shattered. Best way to go. Live fast, die young, leave an edible corpse."

David looked at him. It was like looking in the mirror. The only humanity left in them would trickle from their bowels in the morning. How much longer would this go on? "We were young once," he muttered. "We were human too. What's happened to us?"

"I don't know." Gary dropped the fragments of bone and wiped his mouth. "And I don't give a toss. This isn't a fucking therapy group, Dave. If you want to wallow in existential angst, you should have been a vampire."

"Time to clean up," Matt said. "Save the after-dinner conversation for later, ok? We've got a ton of soil to shift." They picked their fingernails, climbed out of the trough they had dug and began restoring the scene to normal.

On the way to New Street, their mood lightened. Matt produced a half-bottle of gin and they passed it around, sharing its colourless fire. In role as drunks, they staggered in front of cars and made obscene gestures at the half-naked girls waiting for taxis outside the nightclubs. Then they split up, with only token attempts to say goodbye.

The night bus to Perry Barr passed over the Hockley flyover and through the charcoal sketch that was the Heartlands district. The only expense invested in the area was the erection of a huge electronic noticeboard, like a cinema screen, to advertise local attractions such as the NEC Arena and the Spearmint Rhino club. Further north, the view dissolved into fragments of wall, blank windows with teeth of glass, twisted hulks of cars. Nobody walked on these pavements. Missing people sometimes turned up here, in skips or bin liners. What had been a city was now a cost-effective mass grave.

The next morning at work was hotter than ever. The company that owned the building had said that the reason the air conditioning wasn't working was that staff were opening the windows. Perhaps it worked if the windows were shut, but no one in the airless offices was willing to find out. The heat from the computers didn't help either. David worked opposite Lorraine, who was looking very pale. She kept pausing to wipe her forehead with a tissue.

They'd just received an internal memo warning them that the company would no longer tolerate uncertificated sick leave. All employees returning to work after sick leave, even if for a single day, would face a formal "return to work" interview with HR and would be required to produce a doctor's note. David had just e-mailed Lorraine with the query, "Should the union respond to this?" She hadn't replied. Then a "new message" icon appeared on his screen. The e-mail was from Lorraine. It said simply: *help.*

He looked up. Lorraine was on her feet, but seemed unsure which way to go. She turned towards the door, stumbled and fell heavily. David rushed over to her. Some other staff looked away from their screens, began to move forwards. Lorraine was lying face down, rigid. David gripped her shoulders, turned her onto her side. Her face was turning blue. He looked up into the panicked faces of three of his colleagues. "Ambulance," he said.

By the time the paramedics arrived, the tension had gone out of her. She was no longer breathing. Katie had tried mouth-to-mouth resuscitation, but without any effect. Lorraine had suffered with heart problems for years. The paramedics tried again, then took her out on a stretcher. It was ten A.M. Janine, the head of department, made a cup of tea for everyone. David remembered his sarcastic remark of the day before. He felt sick.

Janine went up to talk to Human Resources. The rest of them sat in silence. Katie was crying, but no one tried to comfort her. David logged out Lorraine's computer and switched it off. It felt like closing her eyes.

After half an hour, Janine came down. "We've heard from the hospital," she said. "Lorraine didn't recover. HR says you can have a break until lunchtime if you want. Go out and get some fresh air. We have to carry on this afternoon."

The air outside wasn't fresh. David walked through the park. The colours in the flower beds seemed too bright to be real. Waves of nausea shook him. He'd never seen someone die before. The stillness that came when the heart stopped. He knew, now, that the hunger was a cover for something else. A kind of awe. The dead were more real than the living.

When he returned to the office, Lorraine's desk had been cleared. Nobody was in sight. He went to the kitchen for a glass of water. The first mouthful almost made him retch; he poured the rest away. When he went back to his desk, a young woman he'd never seen before was sitting at Lorraine's desk. She'd switched on the computer. "Are you from HR?" he said.

"No, I'm from Media Temps. Emergency cover. They said I'd be here until the end of the week." She gave a nervous half-smile. David just nodded.

The HR manager, Alice, was at lunch. He waited until she came back, clutching a bag of sandwiches. "I need a quick word with you," he said.

"Ok, fine." She followed him into her office and closed the door. "Sit down. I'm very sorry about what happened to Lorraine. You know she had a history of heart problems. Could have happened at any time."

Maybe, he thought. *But it happened in an overheated office, chasing an impossible deadline, with responsibility for seeing through a hopelessly under-resourced project.* What he said was: "There's a new girl at Lorraine's desk. A temp. Couldn't you have waited at least until tomorrow? Her computer had barely been switched off. There are still biscuit crumbs in the keyboard from this morning."

Alice smiled. "IT has pulled Lorraine's profile. If you're worried about her personal correspondence, it's all been deleted."

"No, I wasn't." *She thinks I was having an affair with Lorraine.* "I just feel… How can you just send someone in like that, the same day?"

"We have a commitment to maintain productivity. Missing targets is not an option. And to be honest with you, what difference will it make to Lorraine?"

David felt the nausea coming back. The office was close and too bright. The mercury light reflected off the computer screen, Alice's glasses, the polished surface of her desk. "The point is the difference it makes to the rest of us. If you can't respect the dead, at least—"

"Neotechnic is fully committed to maintaining staff welfare and morale," Alice interrupted. "Section Five of the *Staff Handbook* makes it clear—"

"Fuck the *Staff Handbook*." David pushed himself to his feet. Biting his lips, he stepped around the desk and pulled the door open, then stumbled out into the corridor. He made it to the Gents' just in time, gripping the edges of the washbasin as his gut twisted and clenched. His jaws opened wide, as if he were screaming.

What came out of his belly, splashing into the basin and staining its white curve, wasn't meat. It was something hard and metallic that came out in discs, each one the diameter of his throat. Coins. Coated in bile and mucus, they flashed silver as they struck the enamel. He was crying. More and more of them came out, a nest-egg voided from somewhere deep inside him. He didn't remember consuming them. Nobody ever does.

At last he was finished. The air stank. He ran the cold tap, splashed water over his face. His eyes were still bloodshot and his skin was still as pale as a fish's belly, but he recognised something human in the face that stared at him from the strip of mirror above the taps. At least he didn't feed on the living. The nausea was fading now. He considered taking the lift, but instead walked down four flights of stairs to the reception desk. And carried on, straight out of the building.

THE WINDOW

It wasn't until their third date that the boy asked Richard to behead him. He'd been asked for similar things in the past, but had never taken it literally. What people tended to want was to hear themselves ask, and then to go through some kind of ritual that took them close. So close that a careless or vicious twist of the garrotte or jerk of the harness could end it. Edge games. But somehow, he was sure Ian didn't want to play a game. The boy had probably been born in role.

It had started a fortnight earlier, in Subway City. Richard had been window-shopping. He was too old to stand a chance with that crowd, but the images helped to renew his desire for the other things he did. Imagination couldn't run without fuel. He watched the pale, speed-driven teenagers shiver around the dance floor. Droplets of light sprayed onto their faces and T-shirts. In alcoves, couples were frozen in the trance of foreplay. The beat was too quick to dance to, almost too deep to hear. It was like the roar of water in an underground cavern.

Wearing a black T-shirt and matching jeans, Richard crept from bar to bar. Frequent body contact was unavoidable, but nobody gave him a second glance. That was fine. He sipped chilled vodka, the ache in his side barely noticeable. For now. He began to imagine some of the lithe bodies twisting in pain, their mouths open in a silent awestruck grimace. He'd seen enough. Any later, and taxis would be hard to come by. A friend of his had been half-killed outside here; it wasn't a good street for hanging around.

First, he needed a piss. Bypassing the club's famous paired urinals, he made his way to the main toilets on the ground floor. Various shattered youngsters were slumped against the wall, shirts dark with sweat, hair reduced to thorns of chaos. The petals of their skin. He stumbled inside, wincing at the scent of violets, and relieved himself. As he was rinsing his hands, a face appeared in the mirror beside him. A teenager, brown spiky hair, eyes so dark they were like holes. The face rang a faint bell, but he couldn't place it. He rubbed his hands under the dryer, which wasn't working. Then the boy's pale hands took hold of his and stroked the water from them. He could feel the tension under the skin.

"Batman." The boy's face was low, breathy. His mouth twisted into a question.

"Shh. I'm here incognito. What do you want?"

"I've been watching you. At the Basement. And the Nightingale. You punished me in a chatroom, last Friday."

Richard laughed. What on Earth had the boy's messages been like? *Bruise me. Cut me in half with your sword.* A blur of one-handed typing. "Ian, yes? If I'd known you were a local boy, maybe we could have…"

Ian nodded. His eyes were fixed on Richard's. There was a bleak stillness in his face. Now that he thought about it, Richard did recall seeing him in the shadows of the Basement. But he'd been otherwise engaged at the time. He touched the boy's neck, gently but with a firm hand. "Look, that Internet stuff is just day-dreaming. Ok? The things I do for real, they don't just happen. I have to get to know someone. Train them. I can't do it overnight."

The boy leaned against him. "So what *can* you do overnight?"

"This." He took Ian's arm and drew him out into the dim hallway that led to the cloakroom, then pushed him to the wall and pressed their mouths obliquely together. They kissed desperately. Richard filled his lungs with air and blew it into the boy's open mouth. He drew a finger across the back of Ian's neck. His other hand traced the outline of a stiff cock through denim.

"Taxi. Come on." They joined the cloakroom queue. Richard had his trademark leather jacket with the Bacardi bat logo; Ian had a white ski jacket that made him look even younger. Instead of waiting outside the club, they walked together up Snow Hill to the city centre. It was surprisingly warm for an October night. Maybe autumn was a thing of the past now. Cars and lorries raced along the expressway; on the other side, yellow lights shimmered on patches of canal glimpsed through Victorian stone arches. For a moment, Richard didn't feel like Batman, an invisible creature of the night, or a master about to initiate a new servant. He just felt like a middle-aged man who was grateful for some company.

Back at the house, he poured Ian a Cointreau and himself a Bacardi, unobtrusively necking a couple of paracetamol and codeine as he did so. Ian admired the sombre living-room: black leather sofa, prints of symbolist paintings, wooden masks. He told Richard he was seventeen and worked in an electrical goods shop. They shared a joint. Then Richard undressed Ian on the sofa and fucked him slowly in front of the coal-effect gas fire.

Afterwards, they lay tangled together on the rug. Richard kept his face in shadow, so Ian wouldn't see how tired he was. Sex seemed to put years on him these days. He was about to suggest they moved to the bedroom when Ian started putting his clothes on. "I'd better go, mister."

"You're welcome to stay for breakfast."

"It's ok. Sorry. I don't like to stay over. Feel strange in the mornings."

"If I'm going to be your master, that'll have to change."

"Then, yes. But not now." Ian's face was blank, masklike in the fire's orange glow.

"Shame. I love the smell of melted KY in the morning." Richard struggled back into his tight jeans with as much dignity as possible. "I'll call you a cab. Don't want you to come to harm, do we?"

"When can I see you again?" The boy's tone was low, deferential. But he seemed oddly sure of himself. That was Richard's cue to be difficult. But he wasn't in the mood.

"Give me a call on Wednesday night," he said. "Seven o'clock. Five minutes late, and you've blown it."

When the cab arrived, they kissed slowly in the dark hallway. Then Richard opened the door and let the teenager out into the quiet suburban street. "Take care." Fine wires of rain slashed through the yellow light. He shut the door, poured himself a final drink and stood in the kitchen, watching the rain scar the full moon and disappear into the black undergrowth of his hopelessly neglected garden.

Their first date was a week later. They met at Boots, a new leather-and-denim bar on the edge of a Digbeth housing estate. As the dimly lit bar area filled up with skinheads and ugly trade whose only hope of intimacy was the backroom, Richard explained what the duties of a servant were. Talking through the details was important: it established the relationship. Ian was quiet, attentive, a quick learner. But hopefully not so quick that he wouldn't need the occasional correction.

When the bar became too crowded for talking, they went on to the Nightingale. Richard made Ian stand motionless and silent, holding Richard's glass while he chatted with his friends in the members' bar. As a reward, he was given a sip of beer every half-hour. He seemed to find it easy to switch off. Maybe he didn't know anyone here. Eventually they caught a taxi to Richard's place in Solihull, Ian maintaining the required silence. It was colder than the previous week. There was hardly anyone out on the streets.

Back at the house, Richard poured them both a large whisky. Then he told Ian to undress and led him into the black room. It was a spare bedroom upstairs, overlooking the garden. The walls and ceiling were painted black; there were black velvet curtains. Richard dimmed the light until Ian was only just visible. He directed the boy to lie down on the table, face against the wood. "What do you want me to do?"

The reply was almost a whisper. "Whatever you desire."

"What's your name?" He began fastening the clamps to the boy's tense arms and legs.

"Whatever you choose to call me." Ian winced silently as Richard tightened a wrist clamp.

"Listen carefully. From now on, you call me only Master. If you call me Richard, this will stop. But it won't start again until it suits me. Is that clear?"

"Yes, Master." Richard applied the neck brace and tied the chain around Ian's ankles so that he was bent back from the table. Then he went and poured himself a drink, took it into the black room, and stood by the window. He drew back the curtain. The garden looked alien in the bleached light: broken flagstones, rotting shrubs, patches of spiky grass. A cat darted across the muddy path, paused and leapt. He didn't see what it caught. When he turned back, Ian's eyes were closed; he was sweating. Richard unlocked the trunk he kept under the table and took out a bamboo cane.

An hour later, he rubbed Savlon into the boy's wounds and carried him into the bedroom. They made love with a tenderness that was almost unbearable. Richard always tried not to get involved in ways that could undermine his control. But somehow, Ian was different. There was a kind of purity in him, a distance in his thin face that made him hard to possess. Richard had been careful not to mark that face.

While Ian lay asleep, Richard went back downstairs and finished off the whisky bottle with some ice. The pain in his right side was sharper now, as if a rib had broken free and was tearing something. It was only justice. If you stole the fire of the gods, they'd send an eagle to peck at your liver. He tried to be a good boy most of the time. But sometimes he'd rather have the fire.

Something flickered outside the kitchen window. Surely it couldn't be snowing this early? He looked out at the ruined garden. For a moment, something pale and bright seemed to cover the ground like frost. Then there was nothing. He blinked, drained the glass and rubbed the stiffness from the back of his neck. Still nothing, except the first grey hint of dawn over the built-up skyline.

He spent the week attending to business. He was a landlord with a dozen tenement houses in the Shirley area, and an investor in several bars and nightclubs. His actual income wasn't huge: he'd only be rich if he liquidated his assets. All through the week, images of Ian hung at the edge of his vision and confused him. The still, intense face; the pale, curved back; the scarred buttocks and thin cock. He was so wrapped up in Ian that, one evening when he ran into a similar-looking boy in the Nightingale, he'd bought him a drink and was about to kiss him when he realised it wasn't Ian.

Night after night, he told himself he should finish it. There were too many risks, legal and emotional. But even as a part of him mechanically added up the dangers, another part knew that he needed something like this. It gave him a window onto humanity. Maybe just for a few weeks, until the feeling wore off and he could go back to what he knew.

On the second date, he insisted that they go back to Ian's place. "It's too easy to command you on my own ground," he said. For a moment Ian seemed reluctant, but he was in no position to refuse Richard anything. They left the Jester's claustrophobic, over-lit basement bar and caught a taxi to Northfield. It was on the south edge of the city, a cluttered overspill district of steel-grey housing estates and shops fenced in with wire netting. They stopped in the concrete triangle between three tower blocks that shut out the moon and the city's light. A few windows shone high up in a wall of nothing.

The lift stank of ammonia. Ian unlocked his door and switched on the light, then held the door open for Richard to go in first. The flat looked surprisingly comfortable: a new red sofa, black rugs, a small TV and computer. A shelf of videos; framed photos of film actors. Where had he got all this stuff from? It didn't seem to go with Ian's stark, empty character. Maybe a legacy, or some gifts. Richard felt a blackness wavering in the air. He closed his eyes. The chemicals in the lift must have got to him. Feeling less than masterful, he stumbled to the toilet and knelt over it. Nothing came up.

Ian touched his shoulder. "Is there anything I can do for you?" Richard wiped his mouth and stood up. "Would you like something to drink?"

"You have vodka?" The boy nodded. "And I'm cold. Put the fire on." While Ian sorted out the drinks, Richard stared into the gas fire. Behind the blue sparks of flame, the ceramic grid was cracked and grimy.

The vodkas were large, triple measures at least. They drank quickly, together on the sofa. Ian's face flushed. He knelt before Richard and sucked him off with heartbreaking skill. Richard's climax reminded him of the convulsions of nausea.

"Have you got a balcony?" he asked. "I need some fresh air." Flecks of darkness were swirling in the light, like ashes in the heat-haze over a bonfire. They wouldn't go away. Ian opened the left-hand curtain, revealing a small door and a black-railed section of balcony. "Stay here," Richard said.

The city's lights hung like a firework that had stalled. Richard zipped up his leather jacket. He could smell traffic fumes in the damp air, and vomit in the back of his own throat. So many separate lights. So many bars, restaurants, bedrooms, vehicles. And the pattern they all made. This was his garden. From this vantage point, all of it was close enough to touch. The frames of stone and metal, the bodies they held, and the cave of night that surrounded them. Smiling, Richard turned back to the window, and stopped.

The inner surface of the glass was streaked with dust. Through it, the moonlight caught on blank floorboards and scraps of rubble. The two halves of a shapeless piece of furniture were joined by some kind of pale stuffing. Where Ian had been, there was nothing. Just some clothes pulled out of shape. The window had no curtain.

Richard stood with his hand on the door for several minutes. Finally, he pulled it open. At once, the room was full of electric light and fluid, pulsing music. He drew the curtain shut and felt the sense of dereliction fade, settle behind the walls. "Ian?" The boy was nowhere in sight.

The bedroom door swung open. Ian was wearing a green rugby shirt, white shorts and plimsolls. "Are you ok?" Richard said.

"Yes, sir. Just twisted my ankle. I thought I'd get an early shower."

"Let me see you do some exercises first. You don't get off that easily."

They ended up in the shower, Ian's face pressed against the immaculate white tiles. Clouds of steam filled the room like dust. As his fingers gripped the pale flesh of his pupil's shoulders, Richard felt sure of who he was and where he was. Nothing else mattered.

The next night, he stayed in and drank his way through a bottle of dry Martini. Some phrases from a song kept drifting through his head. A student party in Leeds in the late seventies. They'd been sitting in a circle on the carpet, passing round a huge joint that probably wasn't just hash. Leonard Cohen was singing about a man standing by the window, weighed down by pain and remorse. Then something about kissing the moon. Leaving the ruin for a new holy city. The word becoming flesh. He sounded so tired, so uncertain, so desperate to lose himself. Outside, dawn was rising between the thin houses.

He couldn't remember the words. At nineteen, he'd found the voice impossibly old and bleak. Now, it felt like a comfort. But he'd left all his records behind when he'd left Leeds, gone to Frankfurt, then The Hague, then Birmingham. A trail of empty bottles and empty boys. Looking for something to take away the feeling of powerlessness. He'd never got close... The phone rang, blocking the thought.

Ian. "Master. How are you?"

"Tired, boy. I wore myself out correcting you."

"I've been bad. You don't know how bad." He could almost feel those lips whispering in his ear.

"Do you need to be punished again?"

"I need to see you." There was a pause. "I need you to do something. Please."

"What is it? What do you want?" Another pause.

"I want you to cut my head off."

Richard put the phone down. Then he picked it up and dialed back. "You've got to be fucking kidding."

"No." The voice in his ear came from darkness, from a cold outside the city.

"I need it."

He put the phone down again. Filled a tall glass with ice and vodka. Gazed down over the unlit garden. Now he was thinking back past university. The house in Stockport, with its roses and hollyhocks. The red books, hardbacks, tales of adventure and magic. The bedside lamp.

Where had he read it? The rose elf. The jealous madman who killed his sister's lover, buried the head in a flower pot. The rose bush that grew with its roots in the dead man's skull. The elf in the rose who told the bees, so they flew into the murderer's chamber and stung him to death. Jesus, why did they give this stuff to children?

Why did they give this stuff to children? Why wasn't it on the top shelf, out of reach? Along with the drugs and the dirty books and the truth.

Maybe he and Ian could start again. Get to know each other as people. Talk through all this shit. Come through the night. Richard stood with one hand pressed against the damp window, and the other gripping his right side in a posture that was becoming habitual. It was too late, he realised. They couldn't get out of role. The safety words didn't exist.

Their third date was on Friday night, in the Basement. A petrified forest of leather. Ian was perfectly obedient, fetching drinks, speaking only when spoken to. He was shivering a little—from tension rather than cold, as the crowd of black-clad bodies kept the Basement sweaty and airless. His eyes were lowered, searching the floor. There was nothing there but cigarette butts and fragments of glass.

"Tell me something," Richard said. "Were you a happy child?"

"Think so. Don't remember it much."

"Nothing you hold onto? A perfect time?"

Ian's mouth twisted. "Before I was born. You know how, when you're a kid playing in the park, you want to hit the ball so hard it's never seen again? So it ends up somewhere that nobody ever goes? I wanted to be the ball."

Richard's hands began to explore Ian's torso. He could feel the heartbeat, the slow breathing. "How did you get to like pain? How did you get used to it?"

Ian shrugged. "I don't remember. There wasn't like an abusive stepfather or something. I'm not a professional victim."

You're more than that, he thought. "Tell me about the first time."

Ian bent his neck, looking rather like James Dean. "I'd rather not," he muttered. "Please don't make me."

The music was industrial techno, a pulsing echo that made the room seem vast and empty. Vodka was smearing the lights across the black walls. Richard slipped a hand inside the boy's shirt and teased his nipple ring. Ian gasped silently.

"What do you want?" Richard said. "Are you trying to get back to something, or become something new? What would make you happy?"

The boy's face was a pale, damp mask with holes for eyes. His teeth caught the molten light. "Just imagine, Master. Imagine a moment so perfect that you'd spend the rest of your life reliving it. So true it would never end."

"What you asked me to do. I can't."

Ian looked back at the ground. He let Richard pull him close and kiss him. They stumbled together through the webbed curtain that enclosed the backroom. "Don't move," Richard said. They stood for a while, listening to the sounds of pleasure in the dark. Richard fended off other men's hands from them both. Gradually, his eyes adjusted until he could make out the contorted figures. Or perhaps he was imagining them, building images from the sounds. He and Ian were silhouettes a few inches apart, not touching. The air was thick with the odours of sweat, amyl nitrite and semen.

Eventually he touched the boy's arm, then pushed his way out through the webbing. The main bar wasn't much brighter, though a blue strip gleamed above the optics like the nightlight in a hospital ward. Ian followed him to the cloakroom. "Hang on," Richard said. "I need a piss. Wait here."

There was a queue at the urinal, which stank of bleach. It took him a long time to empty his bladder; he was aware of being drunk. Instead of washbasins, this place had holes in the wall that dispensed soap, water and heat. The chipped mirror had a crack in it. No, not a crack. There was a mark across his throat. He lifted one wet hand and felt a ridged scar. He rubbed it, but it didn't go away.

When he got back to the cloakroom, Ian hadn't moved an inch. Probably hadn't even breathed. They walked out into the dim backstreet, overshadowed by defunct warehouses, and up to the pale, vomit-spattered pavements of Paradise Circus. Unsteady teenagers were emerging from the clubs: boys with their shirts open, girls with white bellies and thighs exposed.

Back in Solihull, the air was tinged by the bonfires of early November. There was no one about. Richard made two cups of black coffee. When he opened the kitchen drawer to find a teaspoon, he let his fingers slip over the edged knives. The steel was as cold as the air. They drank their coffee in silence. Then he took Ian's hand and led him up to the black room. "Time for a change, Boy Wonder." Ian stripped and lay on the bare table, face down. Richard tied him in place: first the ankles, then the wrists, then the neck.

He stood like that for a while, then reached out and touched the hair at the back of Ian's head. "How many times?" he asked. There was no response in the dark eyes. Richard began to shiver.

In the kitchen, he poured himself another vodka with the last of the ice. His right hand nervously massaged the pain in his side. A mouth opening, dark with blood. He thought about locking the door and never going back in. An end to the black room and all that happened there. It was like the old joke: the masochist saying *Beat me* and the sadist saying *No*. An end to roles, an end to the moment of forever. Perhaps, much later, a burial. It was all he could do.

As he turned back to the fridge for the last of the vodka, a glitter of fragile white caught his eye. He stared at the window. The garden was nearly covered with rose petals. They were scattered evenly, as if they had fallen from invisible shrubs. The wind made them rise and fall. They had no trace of colour. He stood there, watching, as condensation dripped from the glass onto his hand.

The only implement he had for digging was a rusty trowel. He'd expected the ground to be hard, but it wasn't. Not the first time, anyway.

THE QUIET HOURS

Sometimes his wife seemed like a stranger to him. It wasn't that she'd changed. He was just losing it. In the mornings, he felt like an under-rehearsed actor without the script. At least when he was working, the words seemed to hold together of their own accord. It didn't matter who was writing them. And in the evenings, there was enough familiarity around him to keep him going. Or if not, he could plead fatigue. It was no hollow excuse these days. He felt so tired he wondered if he'd been leading a second life in his sleep.

That was why he'd got lost on the way into work. Street names getting mixed up in his head, the way they did in a bad dream. There must have been some higher self that took care of driving, the way it took care of washing and shitting, so he didn't have to work out each task from first principles every day. He'd needed to use the map today when driving to the TV station, a journey he'd made a hundred times in the last few years. And strangely, what had seemed more important the whole time was trying to remember the opening lines of a new song by Neil Diamond that he'd heard on the radio. Something about the night being *just like a friend.*

Being thirty-three made him think about records. The scratches, the dust. How the faults in the heavy black vinyl eventually became part of what you expected to hear. A character in a story or a script was like a record: the identity was in the grooves, the memories. The plot was just the mechanism that kept the record spinning round. Which was why he'd been pissed off when Jackson had told him this afternoon: "You've quite literally lost the plot. Nothing you've written for this episode connects with what happened before or what's supposed to be happening next. It's just an isolated story, and not much of one at that." He'd been ready to argue back, but then he'd realised that in fact he didn't know what had happened in any recent episode. It had just felt like he knew, the same way he always felt. Because he always did know.

Sitting at home in his favourite chair, a glass of brandy in one hand, things felt almost normal. The vagueness that had clung to his typewriter all day began to float away, like smoke when you opened a window. Jean was watching TV, some programme he didn't recognise. *Jean is my wife*, he thought. *We've been together five years. We have a daughter… who is sleeping. These facts are true.* If he stuck to what he knew, the rest was connected to it. Like another room that was behind a curtain: it might be unlit, but it was still part of the house and there was nothing keeping you out of it. *I can't remember my daughter's name, but she's still there. I could go and see her if I wanted to. I am still young.* He raised the glass, but his hand shook and the liquid missed his mouth.

"Are you ok, sweetheart?" Jean was looking at him over the back of the sofa.

"Yeah. Just… I don't know. Tired."

"You look worn out. You're working too hard."

The news started on TV, but seemed to refer to some other country he didn't know about. He ached for the familiarity that had slipped away. When had everything changed? It was like a story, a *Twilight Zone* episode. Like one of his own stories, even. The normal giving way to the alien. Or time rising up against a society that exploited it. Time taking back control, breaking up causes and effects. No more calendars, no more schedules, no more past, present and future. He smiled. "The Revolt of Time." Would Jackson go for that as a half-hour episode? Or would it need a whole schedule to itself?

He poured himself another drink and sat watching the ice cubes dissolve in the pale liquid. Soon, Jean turned off the TV and motioned him to join her on the sofa. Her face was tinged with shadow. "Mark, are you all right? You don't seem yourself."

"Oh, I am," he said. "It's everything else that's changing."

Jean laughed, but stayed tense. "I think you need a holiday. We both do. Looking after Deborah is wearing us out." *See?* he thought. *The name didn't go away.* "When are you due to see the doctor?"

He frowned. "Doctor? Hang on." His diary was by the phone. The appointment with Dr Williams was this afternoon. He wondered why it hadn't been with the family doctor, whatever his name was. "It was today. I missed it."

Jean mimicked frustration. "What am I going to do with you? You're in a world of your own, Mark. I'm worried about you. Make another appointment, ok?" He nodded. She moved against him, kissed his mouth, her face blotting out the light. His hands traced her body through her clothes, letting her need shape his own. This was who they were. Names and passports didn't matter.

They fucked in the smoky light of the African floor lamp. He thought it had been a wedding present, but it could have grown there out of the ground. Carved wood and painted eyes. It could have crept into their house like a charm, a curse, an omen. Anything was possible. Jean's silhouette on the creaking sofa, holding him against her, was all the reality he needed.

Afterwards, they shared a cigarette—a ritual that went back to their first night together, when they'd both been so nervous they'd forgotten to buy a new pack. Jean shook her dark hair over his chest. It smelt of perfume and sweat and dreamless sleep. She kept a band around it in the daytime. Suddenly he wondered who she was.

"Are you feeling better?" she said.

"I guess so. How did we come to be here, like this?"

"Mark, are you really awake? We agreed to stay down here, so as not to wake up Deborah. Just use the bed for sleeping. Don't you remember that?"

"Sure," he said, though he didn't. "That's not what I meant." He reached out and stroked her hair. The texture of it between his fingers calmed him. "It was… about you and me. About time."

"Well, you didn't seem to feel like it last night. Or the night before. Too tired. But it was worth the wait." Her hand moved on his cooling skin.

"No, no," he said, confused. "I meant… out of all the fragments of time. All the chaos of things happening. For us to be alive, to be together. There's no story to anything. No plot. But when you hold me… the fragments connect up. Your face, your hair, our bodies wrapped together. Our child. It all holds together. Nothing else does but that. Time sleeps when you kiss me. It's like when we first shared a cigarette, breathing smoke into each other's mouths. The smoke is life. Do you know what I mean?"

Jean held his face between her hands and stared at him. "Yes," she said after a while. "I know what you mean. I just don't quite know what you're talking about."

Later, in bed, Jean lay curled away from him. He could see her dark hair spread over the pillow, though the curtain hardly let in any light. He thought of their sweat and cigarette ash on the sofa, the fragile ghosts of their tangled limbs, like multiple exposures. When the light was gone, the heat remained. And then there was only the taste of smoke.

The dawn woke him in a strange room, next to a woman he'd never seen before. He slipped out of bed as quietly as possible and went in search of the bathroom. Behind the first door he tried, a baby was sleeping in a cot. It stirred but didn't wake. In the next room, the light was reflected as angels in the frosted-glass windows. He stumbled to the washbasin and stared at his face, bewildered. It was the face of a young man, his cheeks and neck barely shadowed. There was no grey in his hair. But the stubble had collected in his eyes: they didn't look capable of seeing.

As he splashed cold water over his face, some familiarity came back to him. His home; his wife; his child. But the face in the mirror was still a stranger's face. He wished he'd been able to go on sleeping forever. Without daylight, there would be no sense of loss. No mark, no record; only the ocean of darkness. Two heartbeats in a bed.

But it was too late for that. Time had taken over the house. He stepped into the shower and closed the glass door. Steam enveloped him like a mist. He stood there for a long time, watching his skin redden and drip, hypnotised by the moment. Then he dried himself, got dressed and went downstairs. None of it looked the way he expected.

There didn't seem to be a fridge in the kitchen anymore. He cooked some toast and burnt it, then sat gnawing at charcoal and sipping black coffee until he heard the alarm clock ringing upstairs. Footsteps sounded in the hallway. He hoped she wouldn't come down. He didn't want her to realise that he knew she wasn't his wife. His only chance lay in behaving as normally as possible.

"What's wrong?" Jean said when she saw him at the kitchen table. "You look like you haven't even slept. How long have you been here?"

"I don't know." Looking at her made him realise how much his eyes hurt. "Can you live through a night more than once? The same night, I mean."

Jean gripped his shoulders and let him press his face into her neck. "You've got to see Dr Williams," she said. "Make an appointment today." He wanted to tell her that he couldn't face seeing the doctor. He didn't want to know what was wrong. He gripped her with his shaking hands, and perhaps she understood. He traced the curve of her throat with his lips—not from desire, but like a child or a blind man. Trying to fix her in his memory, something too real to slip away.

While Jean was getting dressed, he went up to see the baby. She was lying in her cot, wrapped in an oatmeal-coloured blanket. She smelt faintly of sick. *Do you know who we are?* he wondered. *Does time have a story for you? Or is it an ocean, gently rocking you to sleep? Are you capable of forgetting?* She opened her round, dark eyes and stared at him, silently. He stared back at her. Minutes passed. She went back to sleep, and he went downstairs feeling renewed, given a new life by her sight of him. The phone was ringing.

"Hi, is that Mark?" He said it was. "It's Alan. How are you?"

"Not so bad." Who was Alan?

"Good. Look, I read your story." Was Alan an editor? "It's good, of course. But somehow it didn't... seem like you. I wanted to check you were ok."

"Been very tired. No time..."

"Well, you've got another month till the deadline. Your story's... well, it's like a fever dream or something from childhood. The fragments of memory—really strong emotions, quite painful... but the details are hazy. There's no structure. It's like the narrator is in great pain, but he doesn't know why."

"I don't know why either." He remembered now. The anthology. The sleepless night he'd spent trying to come up with a story; the hot Sunday he'd spent writing and drinking water, as if the typewriter keys were draining something from him. He felt sure he'd known the story, but he hadn't known how to tell it, and now it was lost.

"Look, if I send it back to you, can you have another go at it? Keep the feelings, the grief, the anger. But try to fill in the gaps. Weave it all together. The way you always do. Okay?"

"Sure." Maybe when he read the piece, the story would come back to him. And his own story with it. The opposite of catharsis. It was strange that he could remember a word like that when he couldn't remember his wife's name.

The hallway was in shadow. He stepped behind the coats, just inside the door. Grey fabric covered the lower half of his face. He wanted to see what she did when he was out of sight. Would she look for him or revert to her real self, resume the life she led without him? Her footsteps sounded too regular, mechanical, on the stairs. She didn't look towards where he was standing. The living room door closed behind her. Suddenly he felt like an intruder in this house. The feeling made him walk out onto the doorstep, shut the door behind him. It was suddenly cold.

Some of these houses were no wider than their own doorways. Gaunt, rusting terraces from the start of the century, standing like old men in the harsh light of their own remembered sins. This part of the city had been scheduled for demolition for more than a decade; some of the buildings had been adapted into short-stay accommodation, some housed elderly loners or couples and some were derelict. He'd been walking here for hours, looking for something he wasn't sure was even here.

The first four years of his life had been spent in this part of the city. He could only recall isolated images, like pieces of a torn photograph: a low wall, a staircase, fresh tarmac, apple blossoms, a cracked paving-stone. A sick dog that had crawled all the way along the road in midsummer, leaking from its bowels. Perhaps if he found evidence to prove one single frame, his memory could start to heal itself. Was that charcoal sketch of a school, with its high wrought-iron railings and twisted playground surface, an image from his past? It looked unreal enough. His throat was dry and his legs ached, but he couldn't stop walking.

Around the next corner, the tall houses gave way to a strip of parkland with a children's playground at its entrance. He walked through, vaguely reassured by the feel of turf under his feet. Late-afternoon sunlight filtered through the trees like burning dust. He thought he could hear water trickling in the ground, somewhere ahead. A black dog raised its head from the rank shrubbery and barked. This place seemed more familiar than anywhere he had seen all day. He walked on between the trees.

The undersides of the leaves were shiny with moisture. The light was shifting, breaking up, like paint on a waxy surface. He could smell the decay of wood and human flesh. Feel the pain of a twisted ankle after an hour on the playing field.

Taste the vomit that had filled his mouth after some drunken fool at a party had given him sherry when he was five years old. See the cracked plaster and the smear of blood in the hallway where his father had punched his mother in the face. Hear the shuddering crash that a stolen car had made outside their house in the middle of the night.

The blank light that filled his mother's dark eyes as she died. The needle of broken glass, sharpened by whisky, that bit his hand as he passed out. The yielding curve of a girl's breast. The cries of his newborn daughter, mingled with the cries of his wife in a shared agony. The smell of freshly dug soil. The taste of cigarette ash and red wine in a kiss. The sweat on the back of his neck. The pressure of bile in his throat. The threadbare darkness of the world just after sex. The sound of a dripping tap.

None of it meant anything. He could remember all the things that mattered: the feelings, the sensations, the secret moments of truth. But he couldn't recall the names or the stories. He couldn't make any of it link together. The shadows of the trees were starting to blend, and he couldn't see the buildings anymore. He was no longer real. He belonged with the lost.

It was dark outside now. He poured himself another drink and squatted by the record player, searching through his albums. What was he looking for? Eventually, more or less at random, his hand settled on a jazz record with a musician's face lit up in blue. The musician was biting his finger, as if trying to remember something. He tipped the black vinyl disc out of its sleeve and held it up to blow the dust from the grooves. Then he put it back in the sleeve, back in the box. The record had been perfectly smooth: no grooves, no tracks, nothing but the fluid reflection of light.

The clock hands were drawing together, like the blades of a pair of scissors. He'd found a new hard-backed notebook, unstained by any notes or outlines from his past work. This was his last chance to recover the thread. This was what he did for a living. Now he was doing it to save his life. He didn't know what the story would be called, but he knew how it would start. *The people he knew had become strangers to him.*

He sat there for another hour, trying to remember how to write the letter "T". He thought it looked something like the shape of a hanged man. The clock's ticking grew louder in the small room. His hand was sweating; the pencil lead felt as soft and grainy as charcoal. Somehow he felt that it wasn't the story that had taken him over. It was the blank page.

EXPOSURE

The phone call had come out of the blue. I hadn't heard from James in five or six years. "Just thought it would be nice to get in touch," he said. "Fancy meeting for a drink before Christmas?" I suggested the Duck, which had been our regular haunt in the old days. "We'll catch up properly then," he said. It sounded like he had things on his mind. But James was never the most easy-going of people.

We'd been friends in school, back in the seventies. A kind of geek solidarity thing, UFO stories and Goth music and occult paperbacks. He'd hinted a few times that he'd like to sleep with me, but I'd managed to keep my distance. Ironi-cally, he'd gone on to get married and have a child, whereas I'd drifted through several inconclusive relationships and ended up the archetypal loner. Perhaps that was why he'd always come to me for advice on critical matters: his marriage, his career, his divorce, his decision to stop buying Cradle of Filth albums. No doubt this would be another time for the wise old monk to offer guidance.

My first impression was that he looked calm, if a little tired. He'd lost weight, but that was all to the good. As we'd passed forty he'd continued to look young, whereas I'd become Max von Sydow's understudy. But as we sipped our pints of Old Speckled Hen, I realised that his appearance of calm was due to his barely registering the outside world. He was just going through the motions.

The Duck had changed little in twenty-odd years. It was still an old man's pub. Darts, racing papers, and a cloud of smoke so thick that you weren't sure if you were looking at the barman or seeing a vision of Christ. As teenagers, we'd enjoyed the chance to get away from football chants and broken glass. Now we looked like we belonged here.

We talked a little about work, music, the final season of *The X-Files*. James drank faster than usual, trying to mask his rather cut-off emotional state. When I asked him how his son was doing, he looked away and said, "I want to talk about him later." That didn't mean outside the pub, it just meant when he was drunk enough to get onto the subject.

91

Near closing time, when we'd graduated from pints to double gins, he sat back and gazed at me thoughtfully. I waited. Finally he said, "Vic, I need your help."

"Has something happened?"

"I need you to help me talk to my son."

I'd only met his son once, a decade earlier. The boy would be—what, nineteen now? "Well, I'm flattered, but why have you asked me? I hardly know your—" The pub wavered, as if the optics and wall hangings were a mirage and only the smoke was real. "Oh, no, James. I'm sorry. Oh, my God."

"Terry was at college in Stafford. No problems I was aware of. They found him in a car park. He'd been beaten to death, probably by more than one person. It was six weeks ago now. We haven't had the funeral yet, because the police are still trying to establish what happened. There's nothing… I mean drugs, money, sex life, whatever, there's nothing to explain it. How can they find out who when they don't know the reason?"

I reached out and gripped his hand. "James, I'm so sorry."

"Carol's as much in the dark as me. We're trying to help each other in spite of everything. But it's impossible. We can't even start to mourn him when we don't know how he died. I can't make sense of anything." He took a deep breath, then drained his glass. "Can you help me?"

"As a friend, James, yes. Of course. But that's not all you're asking, is it?" He shook his head. "I don't do that anymore. To be honest, I don't think I ever really could. It was just… other people's despair."

"People like me." I could see now what his calmness and the beer had disguised before. A single, absolute need, like a dying man's need for water or oxygen. Nothing else was real for him.

We stared at each other for a while. Then I went to the bar to try for another round. It was just a minute after eleven. The barman was wiping glasses; he shook his head at me curtly. I sat back down. James hadn't moved a muscle.

"It's been over twenty years," I said. "I left the Spiritualist church while I was at college, remember? Part of growing up. I felt my family had used me. They'd taken advantage of my need to belong. Just as I took advantage of yours. It made me feel special. But in the end, it was all fake. Not a con-trick, but fake all the same. Because all there was to it was belief. And need. It was like being a Goth. You put your trust in the darkness, but the darkness never gave you anything back."

"But you used to say… the lights, the voices. Faces. So much evidence. Are you saying that wasn't real?"

I paused for a while. The glass-collector asked us to be on our way now, gentlemen. We ignored him. "No," I said at last. "It was real. But it came from the people around the table. Their need. It didn't come from another place."

"Are you really sure?"

I stood up and put my jacket on. The same leather jacket I'd worn since the sixth form. We left the pub together, and I walked with him to the bus shelter at the top of Lordswood Road. In the distance, the streetlamps touched the drifts of leaves with a misty fire.

When the bus appeared at the bottom of the hill, I turned to James. "All right," I said. "Call me at the weekend. I'll do it."

By the time he called, I knew I couldn't go back to the church. It would have to be at my house. I did what I could by way of preparation: cleaning, tidying, reading some of my old books. I even threw out my porn magazines as a gesture towards purity of spirit. I didn't know what would be needed of me. It was frightening. At that point I'd much rather have slept with James than done what he was asking.

"I can't promise anything," I said on the phone. "If it really is the dead speaking from the other side, they're not good with explanations. Whatever they've been through stuns them. They don't remember the death."

"I'll take my chances," James said. "Anything at all will be a start. A reason to go on. I can't live feeling that it's all just over." *That's what they all say,* I thought. But I said nothing. We agreed to meet the next Friday night.

All week, I could feel something draining my energy. Mystical forces preparing the way, or just fear? It seemed cold even for the time of year. On the Friday afternoon, I could feel a storm building. The sky was hidden by layers of murky cloud, and the rain came and went like nausea. When the storm broke, the thunder seemed muffled but the lightning was piercingly bright. It was hard to believe that something so intense could burn through the shell of gloom and confusion. I wanted to believe it was an omen.

James was punctual. He'd brought a bottle of wine, but I didn't open it. We sat in my living room, listening to a CD of monastic chants that reminded us both of Fields of the Nephilim. I lit a few candles. Around midnight, I repeated the standard words for a spiritualist religious service. I don't like the word "séance," it makes me think of professional occultists. Spiritualism is a faith, like any other. You can drop out of it, but you never really leave it behind.

I didn't really expect anything to happen. My adolescent career as a medium had been patchy, and I'd felt more power coming from the gathered people than from the other side. This time it was just me and James. Was his grief powerful enough to guide my shaky mystical steps? I didn't know if I believed or not. I only knew that he did.

We clasped hands across the tabletop, rather as we had done in the pub. I wondered if it would have helped to drink the wine. The room smelt of burning wax and the mothballs in the curtains. The silent display on the VCR numbered the passing minutes. Wisps of smoke crept up the wood-chip wallpaper from the pale candles. I thought of other kinds of smoke, in the local pubs where resin was secretly crumbled into roll-ups and brown powder was heated over tinfoil, and I wondered if what we were doing was really so different.

After an hour, I repeated the opening of the service. A train went past on the line at the back of the house. Passenger or freight? I didn't know. My legs were stiff with cramp. James rubbed his eyes, trying to keep awake. I needed some coffee, and a piss. Nothing was coming through. With a sigh that was meant to express patience rather than frustration, I stood up. A sudden wave of vertigo made me reach out to steady myself. My hand touched the wall. It was so cold my fingers stuck to it.

I don't know how long I stood there. Something was passing through me, but I didn't feel any kind of presence. I just felt empty. I could still see the two candles on the far wall, but their light seemed to be spread in a layer of ice. I could see regular crystals, ripples on water. The scattering of a meteor shower in the blackness of space, where depth could be seen only by the fading of light. I seemed to be cut loose, separate from any world—not travelling, but drifting. I felt the pain of intense cold, and then a kind of numbness.

The dawn light gradually brought me back to myself. I was crouching by the wall, making a cradle with my hands to breathe into. The wallpaper was flecked with black mould. The candles had gone out. My own breath was a veil over my face. I felt like a vagrant waking up on the street. My legs ached as I struggled to stand up. Then I saw James. He was lying by the far wall, curled up as if trying to disappear.

His eyes were open, but there was no light in them. His bearded face was pale and clammy. I touched his lips and felt a trace of breath. Still confused, I phoned for an ambulance. While I waited for it to arrive, I used the toilet. There were a few woodlice on the bathroom door and a fly in the window, all dead. The bell rang and I opened the front door to let the paramedics come in. I noticed that the hedge and rose bushes in the front garden were grey and brittle, as if they had been dead for a long time.

James didn't recover. The cause of death was recorded as "exposure." I said he'd spent the night outside, and I'd found him on my doorstep. There was no way they could have understood the truth. I didn't understand it myself. For the next few weeks, I could feel death clinging to the house like black ice on a motorway, a cold breath in the timbers and bricks. The back garden was dead too. The young couple living next door were expecting a child; the mother had a miscarriage during the night. The house on the other side was empty. I found a dead cat in the gutter the morning after they took James away. But nothing much else happened in the street or the district that weekend. The effect seemed to thin out, like gravity.

Did he get his explanation? To be honest, I don't think so. What he got was a glimpse of what's on the other side. I don't know why it killed him and not me. Maybe because he believed in a way that I didn't. He was the passenger and I was just the track. I suppose the train took him where he wanted to be, in a manner of speaking. But words aren't worth much. That was the first time I'd reached the other side, but surely not the first time anyone had. If you found out the afterlife was no life at all, would you rush to tell everyone? Not all secrets are personal.

THE OUTSIDE WORLD

Sometimes there was a visual clue: long sleeves in summer, wristbands or strategically placed bracelets. More often it was just a kind of air they had, a fragile energy. The people who shone brightest on their good days were usually the ones living under a black cloud. He'd got used to watching people's faces and gestures for evidence of the hidden darkness, and the slight bravado that came from having touched the underground river but not crossed it.

Maybe there was some real existential quality, or maybe it was just trial and error on his part. Nobody could affect him in the same way as failed suicides. He'd been drawn to them for as long as he could remember wanting anyone. And there was always the question. Somehow, even if it cost him their friendship or the chance of intimacy, he had to ask. These days, he'd get as close as he could before trying.

Sometimes the circumstances of his life—moving from one city to another, working in bars, some low-profile drug dealing—brought him close to what he was looking for. But not close enough. The real despair wasn't found in short-stay accommodation, but in council flats: people locked into families and relationships that destroyed them. People who lived alone tended to be good survivors, and not to be very deep. As for drug users—well, they didn't count. If you could remember a heroin OD, you weren't there. Not that Martin ever dealt in narcotics. It was too likely to get you a third eye, and not in the Tantric sense. Pills were easier to get and sell.

It was a Friday night, the second week in April. Outside, there was frost on the ground. But the Canary Club was hot and sweaty, as usual. Cigarette smoke hung in the air like the grains in a newspaper photo. Martin was serving in the upstairs bar, the only quiet part of the club. People came up here to talk and pick each other up, away from the dark crucible of the dance floor. It was nearly two A.M. and he'd been working since nine, but he wasn't tired. Filaments of quiet music drifted between the wall speakers. Martin rang for last orders, but no one came to the bar. The Northern lad who'd been drinking rum and Cokes since midnight looked up at him. Martin reached for a fresh glass, then realised the boy's glass was still full. Their eyes met and held. "You ok there?" Martin said. The boy nodded, then smiled. "What's your name?"

"Kerry." The last syllable was like the flourish at the end of a signature. Mancunian, possibly. His face had a kind of waxy sheen, pale but not unhealthy. His black hair dropped in a fringe across his left eyebrow. There was a sardonic twist to his mouth. Martin stared into his eyes for an unguarded moment and saw a flicker of unease, a shadow behind the hazel iris. They talked for a few minutes; whenever Martin broke off to serve a late customer, Kerry watched him. The tape playing through the speakers reached its last track, "Don't Turn Around."

Martin switched it off before it could start over again. Kerry reached up towards him, a cigarette in his hand. "You got a light?" Martin reached for his lighter and flicked it on, leaning forwards. The boy's hand was trembling; Martin took hold of his wrist to keep the cigarette steady. His thumb traced the thin scar just inside the cuff. Kerry's shirt was a deep red with threads of black.

When they left the club, the sky was the clotted blackish-grey of old injuries. Flakes of sleet drifted around them, freezing on the roadway. Kerry pulled his denim jacket tight around himself, shivering. In the small car park across the road, a huddled group of youths were exchanging banknotes, pills and packets. All they'd want, most likely, was an E or some speed to get them through a night's dancing. The junkies tended to avoid the city centre and go to districts like Newtown or Alum Rock: the dead-eyed housing estates where no one cared what you looked like. Martin found his blue Metro, got in and put the fan on to warm the interior. Kerry got in beside him; they kissed. His mouth tasted of rum and cigarette smoke.

Driving through Sparkbrook with the Rolling Stones' "Let It Bleed" playing on the car tape-deck, Martin thought about the way things had changed since he or his parents had been young. People knew the risks of everything now, and they didn't care. What had once been tried for the sake of excitement or image was just a neutral fact. The garden had been paved over. A generation of free-market economics had not only killed off the revolution, it had killed the idea of change. Instincts were mortal. He reached for the warmth and tension of Kerry's hand. Sleet fell across the windscreen, tinged with dirt from the upper air: ashen feathers from burning wings. Even now, the Stratford Road was busy. It would be clogged with traffic all through the day. Running down public transport was another way of isolating people, breaking up the sense of anything being shared. But then, Martin knew all about travelling alone.

Kerry's flat was on the top floor of a cuboid block set back from the main road, behind a fringe of poplar trees and a narrow tarmac-laid car park. Those poplars were a generic element, Martin realised: the run-down districts of South Birmingham holding onto their suburban past. It gave them a lost, ghostly feel that was quite unlike the concrete mosaic of the north Birmingham estates. The trees were as stiff and regularly spaced as black railings in the yellow light.

They walked quietly up the angular spiral staircase. The interior of Kerry's flat (or rather flatlet) was sparsely furnished, impersonal. There were bookshelves full of tapes; a pile of magazines; posters of Nirvana, Tim Roth and Suede. A fold-out bed occupied most of the living room. "Want a drink?" Kerry said. "Tea? Coffee? Whisky?"

"Whisky'd be great," Martin said. "I couldn't drink in the club." Kerry poured them each a large measure. He didn't seem drunk at all, which suggested long experience of this kind of thing. They sat together on the bed. Kerry's arm and shoulder were hard with tension; Martin caressed him gently, muttering, "Relax, take it easy. You're safe here." Kerry smiled in that bitter way of his.

They talked about their jobs, their backgrounds; nothing too serious. When Martin admitted to his pill-vending activities, Kerry laughed. "Who needs that? It's all in your head. To feel up, down, crazy, turned on, whatever. It's all there. I don't need pills to keep me awake. Need them to sleep, like. When I'm on my own." He embraced Martin and kissed him, nervously, his mouth widening like oil on water. Then he drained the last of his Scotch and lay down on the bed.

They made love quickly, while the alcohol rush was still on them; before it could slow them down and blur their perceptions. Martin licked Kerry's inner arm from elbow to wrist, gently brushing the ridged scar with his tongue. He adjusted his own actions to match the closeness and sensitivity of Kerry's movements. Just as there was a darkness in Kerry's eyes that seemed older than his face, so there was something that cried out from within Kerry's body—an emptiness that had to be filled, not with flesh, but with something Martin couldn't define and couldn't provide. Rather than enter Kerry as a stranger, leaving him even more alone, Martin worked on the boy with his mouth and hands. When Kerry shuddered in the moment of climax, eyes shut and teeth gritted, Martin came in sympathy. Kerry pressed his face into the hollow of Martin's throat and lay still. For the hundredth time, Martin wondered if he was some kind of vampire feeding on other people's pain. But he didn't cause it. And if he couldn't help, at least he wasn't making it worse. But what if, in some hidden and terrible way, he was?

Kerry opened his eyes. In the pale, shiny mask of his face, their darkness was unnerving. "Want some more whisky?" he asked.

"Drink really doesn't get to you, does it?"

"Oh, it does. But it doesn't show, like. Sometimes I've walked home completely off my face. Woken up here, not knowing how I found my way back."

"Amazes me, the will of instinct." Kerry smiled. "Have you ever really thought about instinct? How it works?" Kerry shook his head, reached for the bottle of Scotch. "It's like this. Animal behaviour is all instinct, right? But some German psychologists watching animals a hundred years ago decided their behaviour was based on what they called the *Umwelt*, the outside world. If you had a map of the outside based on how you lived in it and what it did to you, that map would be your instinct. It's a part of you, but it can change. Do you see why that matters?" Kerry frowned and shook his head again, swallowing a mouthful of whisky. "When the environment changes, the instincts have to change too. So if the outside becomes destructive, the instincts become destructive.

"I don't know what's going on these days, but I think that's part of it. People don't learn from each other anymore. It's just the individual and the outside world. The more crowded and polluted and senseless the environment becomes, the more distorted the instincts have to be. So when people *do* join together, they only pool their madness. The result is… gang warfare, massacres, mass suicides. The future's a blank. Like it happened last night and we're too drunk to remember. And the only way to go on living is…"

"Is what?" Kerry said, pressing himself against Martin. His body was damp with sweat and seemed insubstantial, as if he could melt away. "I know what you're getting at. How can you put something right when it's wrong everywhere? Draw a new map, like?"

"I think you have to go outside life." Kerry didn't react. "Tell me something. When you cut your wrists, what happened?"

"You mean why did I cut them? Or what happened when I did?" Martin nodded. This was the moment he'd been waiting for, as always. The whisky in his gut felt like a bright ribbon of fear. "I don't know," Kerry said quietly. "It was like… I was just my own blood. My own breath. The bathroom where I did it. Then I was the flat. Tom's flat. Never mind about him. It was like a jigsaw coming apart. Then I was the hospital. But not awake, not really there… Do you understand?" Martin couldn't answer. Kerry drew his fingernails down Martin's back. "Kiss me. Now." The meaning of the boy's words was in the darkness of his mouth. A strangely blank aftertaste. "Hold me." They started to make love a second time.

"What you said," Kerry whispered in his ear. "The outside world. That was me. I just came apart. And then… they put me back together. It was really bad. It was like that poem by Sylvia Plath. She says *they stuck me together with glue.* Yes. Go on. Slower." He crouched over Martin, his thin body a nest of secrets. "Why do you want to know?"

This was crazy, talking about death while making love. But he had to say something. "I'm not sure, Kerry. When I was nine, my brother died. He was thirteen… He went swimming in the sea near Minehead, one evening. Never came out. Nobody knew if it was suicide or an accident… I wanted to go after him, be with him out there or bring him back. But I was too fucking scared. It's always too late." Kerry was rocking above him, every muscle tensed. "Why *did*

Orpheus turn round? To check she was following him? Or to test where she really belonged? Maybe he needed to come back alone. We can't join each other. Only touch. Like this…" Kerry stared at him, silently. His mouth framed an unspoken word as his come flowed over Martin's hand. Then, as if someone had switched him off, he lay down and turned his face away.

Martin's sleep was uneasy and crowded with transitions. A curtain over a wind tunnel. A hailstorm beating on a window. The ocean around some kind of boat: churning, white with froth. He could see himself beyond the divide. But he couldn't reach out of his stillness, through the barrier. He had to watch himself caught in the storm. When he woke up, the bed was cold. Dried sweat had painted him with a film of salt. Kerry was lying close to him, very still. So the alcohol had caught up with that one at last. There was something in Kerry's hand: a small glass bottle.

Martin reached over him, tugged at the bottle. Kerry's hand wouldn't open. The bottle was empty; its screw-top cap was missing. *Keep out of the reach of children.* He looked at Kerry's face. A small whitish trail of saliva had dried on the pillow under the boy's mouth. Very carefully, Martin licked a fingertip and placed it against Kerry's lips. Nothing. The body was still warm. Martin lay there, holding him, for another hour. Beneath the smell of whisky and sweat, he could detect the cold stale odour of the sea.

It was still early morning when he left the flat. He didn't feel able to drive. Traffic was jostling and crowding its way along the Warwick Road. He could hear a police or ambulance siren, up towards the city centre. Shreds of yellowish cloud gleamed around the steel-grey chimneys of the Tyseley industrial estate. *A jigsaw coming apart.* He could feel his own life inside him, barren and strange. But for the first time in twenty years, he didn't want to die. Something had changed. He waited at a bus stop; got out a cigarette, then realised he'd left his lighter in Kerry's flat.

When the bus came, it was already packed. There was a seat on the upper deck, at the front. Near the ring road, police on motorbikes were directing traffic around the scene of an accident. More sirens; lights flashing like cameras, unreal in the daylight. As the traffic picked up speed, Martin realised he was crying. He didn't know where the tears came from. It was too cold inside him. As the bus accelerated through the amber lights at a traffic signal, he heard a woman talking a few seats behind him. "Have you heard the news?" Then the driver braked suddenly. Martin was thrown against the window. In front of the bus, five or six children had run out into the road. As the bus came to a halt, there was a terrible soft bump under its left wheel. Somebody downstairs began to scream. The engine stalled; its silence went through the passengers like an icy wave. Nobody moved or spoke. Then a voice said, "Please clear the bus."

There was nothing Martin could have told the police. Or nothing of any use.

He started walking back out from the city centre. Traffic was blocked solid; even ambulances were trapped. Martin couldn't shake off the feeling that it was all somehow his fault. Maybe the city was taking on his memories. It couldn't work the other way, he knew that much. As the sirens faded behind him, he realised there was no point in going back to his lodgings. Maybe he'd take his car from outside Kerry's flat; maybe he'd leave it there. All directions seemed the same. He didn't have a map. Nobody did.

THE COUNTRY OF GLASS

At the age of forty-seven, Matthew Lang stopped being an alcoholic. It had to do with a bottle of mescal that his friend Jake had brought back from a trip to Mexico. They shared the bottle one evening in Lang's flat, over a meal of spaghetti and wood mushrooms. A calm Latin silence, underscored by the chirping of distant cicadas, drowned out the mechanical fugue of traffic along the Alcester Road. They were more than halfway through the bottle when Lang noticed the worm: a pale, dragonlike creature drifting inside the glass. Jake explained that the worm flavoured the mescal, and was meant to be eaten. An hour later, they finished the bottle by sharing the worm. As he bit into the soft, drugged flesh, Lang realised something.

He floated it in his mind that night, letting the insight flavour the murky dregs of his consciousness. Being an alcoholic was like refusing to eat the worm. It was a denial of the essence. Just as a fetishist created false challenges through his inability to deal with sex, so an alcoholic created his *drink problem* through fear of alcohol. The truth would admit no compromise. Whatever conflicted with drinking had to be set aside. Lang stared at his thin curtain, seeing the contents of his bedroom by sodium light and by the liquid-crystal lucidity of distilled alcohol. He didn't know it, but that night had brought him to the ragged border of Vitraea.

It had been coming for a while, of course; or rather, he'd been travelling unconsciously towards it. The social pub and party drinking of his thirties had given way to lonelier practices. Regular drinking sessions with a group of friends had fizzled out after he'd thrown up in a friend's car twice. For a long time, he'd felt trapped in a vicious circle: loneliness drove him out to pubs, where the presence of young and possibly available women awoke in him a mixture of desire and fear that he had to drink to overcome, until he was too drunk to do anything except go home. His only affairs were with women who drank, and their self-hatred tended to evolve into resentment of him. Lang refused to be tragic about alcohol. In retrospect, the taste of the worm had always been in his mouth.

Solitary drinking means never having to say you're sorry. For Lang, rearranging his life around alcohol had given him a measure of control and even of artistic vision. The way last night's vodka remained as a slowly melting icon in his gut through the afternoon at work; the way sweat crawled lazily over his skin in the first light of morning; the way ice chilled the flame of malt whisky without putting it out; these were at once reliable and startling, the painful treasures of his life. Sometimes he'd go to an unfamiliar district and comb the off-licences for exotic bargains or obscure links to the drinking lives of other cultures. Wine was an occasional delight, liqueurs a sentimental journey, strong cider a dose of cold realism. Spirits were the truth: cynical vodka, melancholic gin, turbulent whisky, furious rum, erotic tequila, devout cognac. He'd gone to great trouble to obtain a regular supply of the Dutch spirit jenever, which was like gin with more juniper berries and less essence of razor blade. On special occasions, Lang would go into a quiet bar in Digbeth and drink his way along the row of optics, including doubles of his favourites. He was a connoisseur of jukeboxes, able to define a pub's clientele and district from a glance at the list of selections; but he disliked pub-rock bands, and hated karaoke almost as passionately as he hated fascism.

Just as a brilliant summer creates deep shadows and pockets of decay, Lang's drinking had its unpredictable dark moments. He tended to glimpse a kind of wavering or rippling in buildings, like the effect of a heat-haze. It included, but wasn't caused by, the crawling of beetles or ants. Sometimes he'd see them on bus windows or people's shirts, though he managed to control his reaction. He shaved thoroughly, though he often cut himself, because stubble was a perfect hiding place for them. Worse, sometimes he'd look along a tree-lined avenue or a sunlit canal and see images from his own past clotted with dust and dead leaves, abandoned: his junior school, his parents, his first girlfriend, the black ornamental railings of the tenement house where she'd stayed with him that summer. All of it blurred and corroded, but still there. The past was not biodegradable.

One still evening in August, Lang decided to go to the Triangle Cinema in Aston. He'd not seen a programme in months, but there was usually something good on. And if not, they had a quiet café with film magazines and old posters. He caught the bus into town and walked up through Corporation Street, past the red sandstone buildings of the Law Courts and through the disinfected subway to the university. He found the cinema from memory, but it had recently closed down. Through the tinted windows, he could see tarpaulins over shapeless furniture. Angrily, he walked past the back entrance into the sloping terraced streets of the student quarter. The sky ahead of him was marked with dark bruises of pre-rain. He chose the smaller and older-looking of the two pubs within sight.

The interior was desiccated and smoky, dark wood hung with old photographs of railway bridges in the Black Country. The husk of Shane MacGowan's voice was drifting over the tense piano chords of "A Rainy Night in Soho". It was still too early for the main evening crowd; but a handful of after-work drinkers on their way home, students preparing for a night out and soberly dressed couples on adulterous dates were scattered around the heavy, unvarnished tables. Lang was into his third glass of Smirnoff Blue with fragmented ice when a voice spoke in his ear.

"Matt, how are you? Haven't seen you for months."

It was Jake. He looked greyer, more angular than before, unevenly shaved; but there was a youthful fire in his dark eyes that Lang didn't remember.

"Good to see you." They sat down at one of the smallest tables by the railings above the cellar steps. Lang realised they hadn't met, only spoken on the phone, since the mescal evening in April. "How have you been?"

Jake didn't immediately answer. He was drinking malt whisky, neat, no ice. "I've been looking for something," he said. "I think we both have. But I know its name." He lifted the glass to the light, watched a star dying in a twist of smoke. "Do you remember what you said about the worm in the mescal bottle?"

Lang didn't recall telling him about it, but then he'd been a little drunk. He nodded.

"Well, that's only the start. Have you ever heard some of the old farts in places like this talking about Vitraea?"

Lang stared. The name didn't so much ring a bell as strike a bass chord somewhere underground, causing reverberations in parts of his memory he didn't know were there. He was sure people had been talking about it when he'd thought they were talking about something else. But what did it mean? "The country of glass," he said without thinking.

"Have you been there?"

Lang shook his head, blushing. He felt foolish.

"Don't worry, not many people have." Jake sipped his malt whisky thoughtfully. "It's a region, but not necessarily a country. The wine district. The house of spirits. Its location has to do with some kind of secret geography. Lines and borders created by alcohol. There's only one thing that's widely known about it. Lager louts and beer monsters have no key to its gates. Vitraea is definitely Latin rather than German, Sephardi rather than Ashkenazi. It's the place where the bottle is never empty, and the drinks are so pure that hangovers are unknown. Imagine drinking rough blended whisky all your life and then discovering single malt. In Vitraea, the whisky is to single malt what Isle of Jura malt is to the Claymore."

Lang shuddered, recalling low-budget trips to Moseley off-licences in recent years.

They finished their drinks; Jake bought another round while the pub filled up with students and Brett Anderson's voice crept uneasily through "The Wild Ones," yearning for the celluloid kisses of ghosts. When Jake returned from the bar, he was in a sombre frame of mind. Lang was used to his mood shifts, and waited a while before asking him, "You said you've been looking?"

Jake nodded wearily. "It started in Mexico. Then Amsterdam. Lately, Glasgow and the west coast of Scotland. Maybe it's within myself. The distillation of the soul. When I started to think of it as a religion, I realised that I already had one. It was buried, but still there. The skullcap under the skull. You were brought up an atheist; maybe you've got a better chance of finding it." He lifted his glass and stared at the pale liquid. "Tell you something, though. It's a quest you don't come back from. Whether you find it or not, there's no way back." His troubled eyes met Lang's as he tilted the glass back to his mouth. "Cheers."

Waiting at the bus shelter in Dale End, Lang marvelled at the things people came out with when drunk. Especially when friends drank together, building a card-house of delusion on the table between them. Jake had walked on through Aston to his home in Gravelly Hill, near the concrete forest of Spaghetti Junction. Up here in the city centre, the dense air was curdled with traffic fumes; the threatened rain had failed to materialise. Lang could hear the faint muttering of people in the shelter: drunks asking for cigarettes, lovers saying goodbye. The sound intensified into a consistent rhythm, a chant. He turned around. They were all staring past him at the approaching bus. All their faces were deformed by madness. When the bus stopped, Lang threw himself onto it. Nobody followed him. All the way to Moseley, he sat on the top deck and watched his hands shake.

His flat was warmer than the street outside. He could smell the remnants of food in the kitchen, the used plates and the full bin liner. Swaying slightly, he walked through into the bedroom. He'd not changed the sheets in a month. Behind his alarm clock, an unfinished nightcap of vodka was cloudy with mould. He'd never known that spirit could decay, let alone that it could decay so fast.

In September, Lang was offered voluntary redundancy. He'd been with the same company for nine years, and they knew they weren't going to get any more out of him. What kind of person *would* put their heart into computer systems analysis, Lang didn't like to think. Alcohol was a factor in his lack of ambition, if not in his actual performance. He never drank before work or even at lunchtime, because he didn't want his drinking to be tainted by the unwholesome vibes of the office. The redundancy would allow him to take an extended holiday, maybe until Christmas, before drying out and looking for freelance work. If he was ever going to find the country of glass, it had to be now.

His new life started awkwardly. Years of suppressed fatigue dropped their black leaves inside him. He lost the will to go out of doors for anything but essential supplies, and even then waited until it was dark. By day he kept the curtains shut, sometimes pulling the duvet over his head, as he listened to records and drank neat Scotch. The stillness frightened him, but he was afraid to break it. Without vision, light could only bring pain.

When he began to go out again, the nights were longer and colder. Instead of going to pubs, Lang started hanging around with the older drunks in Moseley's graveyards and car parks. Some of them were homeless, but most lived in bedsits on the cheap side of the district and came out for company. Lang was quite happy drinking alone. What he needed was some kind of information about Vitraea, however distorted or speculative. Most of the piss-artists he approached seemed to know nothing. A few said they'd heard the name long ago, but didn't know what it meant.

One very old man said to him: "It'll find you while you're looking for it. You won't have any way out." Lang tried to make him explain, but he was barely conscious and just muttered again and again: "I swear to God, I once fucked a woman with three tits."

Desire was never far from these conversations. Prostitutes also hung around these places, and drunken couples hid in the shadows. Lang would store the occasional glimpse of an exposed breast or buttock in his memory, for use on those occasions when he woke up with an erection. Like the sentimental songs that people wept over in pubs, the sexual desire evoked by alcohol had no real substance or depth. The permanent light of Vitraea dispelled the need for sex, just as it dispelled the need for tears.

One night in October, Lang was walking past a row of derelict houses on the edge of Balsall Heath. Lamplight glittered from the teeth of broken windows. Rain was beginning to fall, smearing the rear lights of passing cars. Lang had bought some fish and chips and been unable to eat them. He felt choked with emptiness, as if he might throw up a void. The Old Moseley Arms was still open; but instead of going in, he stood gazing down at the city centre. All you could see was the lights: blue and gold and white, a mass of buildings reduced to points in a man-made constellation. As he watched, the rain made the city's lights blur and waver. The pattern rose towards him and began to spin gradually, like a Catherine wheel starting up. What did it represent: a flower, a symbol, a face? It trailed a pale fire below itself, reducing the buildings to meaningless rubble.

"Got a light, mate?"

It was someone who'd just come out of the pub, his white face luminous with sweat. Lang shook his head. When he looked back at the city centre, all he saw was the familiar view. He stared at it for several minutes, but it refused to change. The rain was soaking into his collar. Moving slowly, as if underwater, Lang walked back towards the off-licence on the corner of Mary Street. He passed the children's playground behind the pub; nobody was there, but the metal roundabout was revolving slowly. The cold air wavered and shimmered around him as he walked on.

Autumn ended in a feverish cluster of bright days and frozen nights. By then, Lang had given up dreaming of Vitraea. He was too drunk. The honeymoon was over. Too many nights spent out of doors had given him backache and severe rheumatic pains, but he felt nothing. His breathing had grown thick and deliberate, a monologue silenced only by complete inaction. His laundry basket resembled a compost heap. What he would do when the money ran out didn't concern him: he couldn't imagine living that long. For now, as long as his fridge and coat pockets were full of cheap vodka, it was ok. He could manage without the ice. It was cold enough inside him.

On the last day of October, drawn by a nervous energy that felt more like sleepwalking than conscious action, Lang revisited the district where he'd grown up. It seemed appropriate: a way of saying goodbye, of making the ghosts unreal. His parents had long since moved on. The High Street was very different; but much of the suburb had hardly changed in thirty years. It was part of Edgbaston, neither wealthy enough nor run-down enough for redevelopment. As the afternoon light flickered through trees like a distant candle, Lang walked through the park where he and his brother had played cricket with a tennis ball. Clouds of midges hovered over the pond like a belated heat-haze. He pulled his coat tight around his shoulders; every few minutes, he took a quiet sip of brandy from his metal flask.

His primary school was still there, its flaking red-brick mass surrounded by paler new buildings. It had a different name. Further downhill, the second-hand bookshop had gone but the fire station was unchanged. Here was the railway bridge where two eleven-year-old girls, twins, had exposed themselves to him one summer evening; he'd not been aroused, though the memory seemed erotic in retrospect. The house Lang's parents had owned was still there, but painted red over the black; recognising the porch and the leaded windows, he felt a wave of disorientation pass through him. As if he were a tunnel with a train running through.

It was getting dark; the streetlamps pulled curtains down between the tall houses. Around the corner was a crossroads where one road came over a hill and another came out from under a bridge. Apparently it was still an accident black spot, since a crashed car had been dumped on the pavement. The whole of this block had been demolished in the late fifties; it was still wasteground. A few apple trees were scattered at the lower end, close to a ruined brick wall; their fruits were blackened, mostly unfallen. Across the road, an off-licence shone its message of promised glory. Lang went to investigate.

Later, clutching a discounted four-pack of Special Brew, he sat in the shadow of the wall and drifted between sleep and waking. In his experience, being inconspicuous was the best way to evade trouble. It worked so well that when, later on, a group of children in luminous Hallowe'en masks started playing some complicated game of tag involving passing on a broken doll, none of them noticed him.

Fibres of rain twitched in the yellow light, tangling the air. He felt as unreal as a charcoal drawing on stone. Some more children had come from behind the wall, carrying something. Through the acidic ferment of Special Brew, he could smell petrol. A beetle or an earwig crawled over his hand.

As Lang watched, the children formed a ring around the wrecked car. Its front end had been torn back and sideways; the windscreen had a hole the size of a fist punched through it, sheathed in white. One of the children, wearing an expressionless ghost mask, threw the doll inside. Another spilled petrol over the roof and tires, as if pouring brandy over a Christmas pudding. The children backed off, masks glowing faintly with the reflection of a secret light. One of them lit the end of a rolled-up newspaper and threw it. Lang shut his eyes; the wave of heat touched his face like an angry wound. When he looked, the wasteground was on fire.

All around him, the smell of burning leaves was mingled with the smell of alcohol. Small knots of fire were pressing up through the soil; above them, insects were streaming through the grainy air. The car was still burning with a soft blue-white flame. The children, their pale masks sweaty with rain, were dancing. The wasteground was a forest of drowned lights. The rain tasted faintly bitter. Lang put his tongue out to catch a drop. Juniper. He picked up a handful of dead leaves, crushed them and tasted the damp fibres. Then he stood, trembling as his lungs filled with the charcoal-tinged air. Patches of frost drifted in the reddish light, looking for a surface to crust on. The rain was gin, the dead leaves were soaked in brandy, the air itself was vodka. He looked up at the stars; they drifted, hard and bright, making new patterns and symbols across the fluid sky. Then one of the floating scars of frost bound itself across his face, and all the lights blurred into the dark fire of underground.

Much later, he was vaguely aware of being picked up and shaken; of daylight; of something sharp being inserted into his arm. But he didn't want to know. As long as he didn't wake up, he was still there. Eventually he was forced to return by a tense hand on his shoulder and a voice repeating: "Matthew, Matthew." He opened his eyes to the half-light of early morning indoors. A young woman with short, dark hair was leaning over him. She was wearing a nurse's uniform; the name badge on her lapel read *Virginia*.

They didn't keep him long. Apart from some bruising and a painful cough, his exposure to the night had done no real harm. That morning, he was encouraged to eat breakfast and drink a lot of water. The need for a real drink hit him almost at once; but he kept quiet, aware that the next time it could well be a police cell. The ward seemed full of glass: bottles, tumblers, vases, drips, syringes, windows. Outside, trees were swimming in the drowned light. Insects swarmed on the ceiling, where the mercury tubes wept silent trails of moisture. Lang fantasized about breaking into the hospital's medical store and finding bottle after bottle of pure ethyl alcohol. For all he knew, they kept it for scrubbing down the operating theatre.

In the twilight of late afternoon, he fell asleep and dreamed of walking through a forest. The path was buried under layers of dead leaves that were slowly turning to soil. As he walked, the drifts of leaves grew deeper. They absorbed the sound of his feet into a gentle, unbroken whisper. The topmost layer was red and gold. They were letters and photographs, sketches and certificates. The magazines in the garage; the furniture in the canal. They were memories waiting to be recovered, held up and loved in the grainy auburn light of Vitraea.

He was released that evening. Pressure for available beds made rapid patient turnover a necessity. The doctor gave him an appointment card to see a clinical psychiatrist later in the week. Lang stopped at the off-licence on his way home. By midnight he was blind drunk; but the visions didn't come. Only the black specks, the insects crawling between areas of shadow, less phantoms of Vitraea than reminders of the polluted world. Days passed in a drizzle of vodka, washed down with dry Martini. He didn't keep the appointment. As the nights grew longer, he felt their darkness settle inside him. Outside, frost whitewashed the city.

The build-up to Christmas is usually enough to get even sober people drinking. By opting out of the festive mania, Lang gained a certain measure of control. Violent, destructive boozing was unlikely to help him find Vitraea. But he didn't know how to keep his spirit pure, untainted by the world. After months of redemptive drinking, visionary drinking, he'd gone back to merely being an alcoholic. Maybe Jake could have told him what to do; but Jake had moved on, his phone disconnected, his flat occupied by a new tenant. Maybe he'd found what he was looking for; more likely, he was still searching.

On Christmas Eve, the centre of Moseley was snarled up with traffic. The cluster of antique and craft shops had drawn a mass of shoppers, while the off-licences were shifting enough good-quality stock to make the liver of God feel queasy. At the other end of the district's economic spectrum, a restless community of the homeless and destitute were scattered along the Alcester Road: in bus shelters, around the church, in the doorways of boarded-up shops. Lang had already stocked up with enough Smirnoff and Johnnie Walker to see him through to the New Year, and had already bought the few gifts he intended to give. It was loneliness that drove him to wander around the so-called village, coughing quietly from deep in his chest. Loneliness, and a hope spread as thin as frost.

Just off the Alcester Road was another, older church whose graveyard looked frosty even in midsummer. The entrance from the road had a little wooden porch where local drunks often sat and solved the world's problems. This afternoon, as darkness closed in around the ribbon of shops and pubs, two men were staring from the low benches. Lang recognised one of them: an ageing tramp who was an expert on the Biblical Apocrypha. Lang had tried, and failed, to pump him for rumours of Vitraea. The other man was younger, his beard slightly flecked with white. They waved at Lang.

"Hey, pilgrim! Come and join us. Did you remember the myrrh?"

The older man passed Lang a half-bottle of sweet sherry. Lang drank from it, though the honey-petroleum odour made him gag. The tramp looked at him warily, as if deciding whether to trust him. Finally he muttered, "You remember that place you used to go on about? The country of glass?" Lang gazed steadily at him. His eyes were china-blue, cracked and smoked. "I found something from it. Want to come and see? It's not far from here. Me and Barry, we hid it. Too precious to carry around."

Lang glanced at the younger man; he nodded. "Ok." He had nothing to lose. They walked, in no great hurry, down the steep hill of Salisbury Road. To their left, giant trees curtained off an area of parkland. To their right, further down, the lights of a submerged housing estate floated like phantoms of a drowned city. At the bottom, two adjacent roads ended in derelict houses. One house was little more than a façade, moonlight shining down through the roof-timbers and edging the smashed windows with silver. The other house was shorter and more enclosed, its windows boarded up. Lang's two companions walked silently towards it.

One of the side windows, concealed by a low brick wall, was unboarded and shattered. "In here."

The younger man went in first, Lang second. When they were all inside, the younger man opened his rucksack and took out a torch. Lang had a glimpse of stained walls, damp like a giant spider, a few rotting kitchen cupboards. Then, suddenly, his arms were gripped behind his back. The rucksack was opened again, and something small and dark was taken out: a cosh. He was struck three times, hard enough to drain the strength from his arms and legs. Darkness streamed around the torchlight, spilling over his face like water.

They'd lit candles in the four corners of the room. When Lang surfaced, his arms had been spread across a table and tied down with rope. He was lying face up. The other two men were sitting on rotten fabric-covered chairs, one to either side of him. Damp had painted a forest in the walls. Lang craned his neck, trying to see what was going on. The two silhouettes in the chairs didn't seem to notice his awakening. Around their feet, and wherever he could see that far down, the bare floorboards were littered with bottles. Some full and unopened, some empty. Wine and sherry, he thought. Belatedly, he realised that the room stank of alcohol. Had he failed to notice because he was used to waking up in a similar atmosphere? One of the seated figures bent down, lifted a glass and drank. It took Lang several minutes to find the courage to ask: "What the fuck's going on?"

Candlelight played on the surfaces of green and brown light. As if explaining the obvious, the older man said, "It's the only way. We can't get to Vitraea, but it will come to us if we give it an offering."

They're mad, Lang realised. He needed a drink. After a while, he asked for one. There was no response. The presence of booze, in such quantity and of what appeared to be fair quality, was having an effect on him. His eyes and mouth felt painfully dry. Despite the cold, he was sweating. In a corner of the room, he glimpsed the movement of dark insects. If there was a window, it was behind him; no light came through it.

Hours passed. His two captors were almost insensible from drinking. They wove unsteadily across the floor, choosing bottles, struggling to open them. A glass broke; kicked over, a bottle spilled red wine across the thirsty floor. Lang's mouth was so dry he found it difficult to breathe. He'd tried arguing, begging, cursing. His lips were cracked, and the chafing of his tied wrists was like a Chinese burn. The branches of damp in the walls were beginning to waver and swim. The eyes of flame were crying. Little black crabs were scuttling furiously across the dim ceiling, as if it were an intertidal zone.

Silence flooded the room. A faint green light, from no window that he could see, made the bottles invisible. Lang felt a cool wind strip the last traces of sweat from his drying face. The two men were on their feet and stumbling. Or rather, they'd been lifted and their bodies were shimmering, like candle flames about to go out. Waves of soft light crushed all the bottles, and the shattered glass dragged back and forth across the floorboards like sand. And then his two captors were floating, twisted, pulled into vortices of light. The smell of alcohol was so intense Lang could taste it. But he'd never been more sober in his life. The cold air thickened, turning momentarily to glass. Then all the lights went out at once.

The police found Lang the next morning. Someone had heard him crying for help, provoked by the faint shafts of daylight through the boarded window. Two officers forced an entry through the front door. They found him fully conscious, but unable to loosen the ropes from around his wrists and ankles. The room was empty apart from Lang, the table he'd been tied to and a couple of badly deteriorated chairs. And a layer of finely ground glass that crunched quietly under their feet. Lang described his kidnappers, said they were after a ransom.

He and the two police officers had a laugh about that, back at the station. They even offered him a glass of Scotch, but he declined. He didn't tell them that he hadn't really been calling for help so much as crying out in despair. And he never touched alcohol again. There was no need for any pledge or twelve-step cure: he simply couldn't drink. It would have been like screwing a prostitute after losing the great love of your life.

THE NIGHT THAT WINS

In the last generations of the west midland region, the wilderness began to reclaim much that had been built over. As human populations dwindled, rats and wild dogs overran the weed-choked ruins of the cities; and bats flew between the distorted branches of trees growing through broken roofs and the rubble of collapsed stone. The only remaining human settlements were in the valleys where the soil was still fertile. But it is said that a few solitary humans scratched out a bitter living in the remains of the cities. One of these persistent city-dwellers was Sygigh the seer.

Sometimes people from the villages sought him out in his adopted home, the ruins of a great library. They said that he had built chairs and tables from wadded paper, soaked in the rain and dried in the tepid summers of the red-tinged dying sun. That he spent his days in fruitless contemplation of books rendered illegible by decades of neglect and decay, and that in any case he was illiterate. That he foresaw only the darkest of futures: betrayal, disease, suicide and loss. That he was never wrong. And that the only price he demanded was that those who sought his counsel stay in his infected home long enough to hear his story.

In the last years of the city of Brymygem, Sygigh lived with his aged parents, his young wife and their child in a narrow house in the slum district of Tysli. He made a living by fashioning and selling items of leather, used for clothing and other purposes that are not recorded. Already, at that time, the blight of necromancy and corrupt magic was spreading across the midlands like leprosy. The dead walked on feet of splintered bone, and creatures no longer human had made their lairs in the towers and tenements of the cities. But Sygigh and his family were honest, working people, who had no business with the cold occupants of the night.

One day, Sygigh was engaged on a commission for a wealthy young woman who dwelt in the artists' quarter. She had asked him to fashion a lifelike mask of pale calf leather for her to wear while dancing. Whether this was her recreation or how she made her living, he did not know. He had laboured through the day to make a mask that resembled her thin, fine-boned face, and when he took it to her apartment the red sun was already low in the tainted sky. The young woman insisted that he stay while she tried on the mask.

The drink she poured him must have been drugged, for Sygigh was unable to move—or even to look away—as she began to remove her garments. The mask was all that she intended to wear. The dance occupied some time, during which his glass was refilled. At the end, she convinced him that the streets were too dangerous for him to risk walking home in the dark. Who knew what kind of malformed and deadly life was abroad in the city?

Sygigh did give some thought to the welfare of his family, waiting for him at home. He prayed to Kâlchi'an for their safe keeping before he blew out the scented candle in the young woman's bedchamber. In his arms, she was still wearing the soft leather mask he had fashioned for her.

The dawn light, filtered through a red silken curtain, woke Sygigh from uneasy and formless dreams. Without looking at the still figure that lay beside him, he crept from the house and joined the early tradesmen on their way to work. He still felt drugged; the narrow streets seemed unreal, flickering as the bloodshot sun rose in the polluted sky. As the familiar, decayed buildings of Tysli came into view, he began to fabricate an excuse for his overnight absence.

The house was silent and cold. In the doorway he became aware of a sour odour, like cooking gone stale. Had they left his dinner out on the table to rebuke him? But there was nothing unusual in the kitchen, or anywhere in the cramped downstairs rooms. The embers of the previous night's fire were as chilled and damp as the stone wall. From above, he could hear a faint sound of water dripping. There must be a leak in the roof. But had it rained overnight?

As he climbed the stairs, the smell became more intense. Spoiled meat, or perhaps the leavings of some diseased stomach. It must be his wife Xania who was ill, or she would have cleansed the room. Yet he could not immediately tell from which bedroom the stench issued. It seemed to have claimed them all. He tried the small room of their child first, but no one was there. Something appalling had been left on the floor, perhaps a cat that had been skinned by desperate, nomadic hunters: a spreading mound of tissue already crusted with beetles and other vermin. Who had been here, and where had his family gone?

The next bedroom was the one he shared with Xania. The bed on which their child had been conceived was a stinking chaos of muscle and sinew and congealing blood. The dripping sound was of terrible fluids that had soaked through the fabric of the bed. The floor was alive with drowsy beetles and bugs, swirling in a gradual vortex of corruption. But the bed had preserved the atrocity it held from the insects, so that Sygigh could see the bone structure that held the molten flesh in place. He could see, more clearly than ever before, the narrow cheekbones and fragile eye-sockets of his wife's face.

As he stood there, his throat convulsed with nausea, Sygigh knew that he had fallen through the surface of the world into some realm of Hell beneath. This looked like his house, but it was not his house. The city outside would never be the city in which he had worked and made a home. The world would never again be the world. He did not need to go into the last room and find the two ruined shapes of flesh drying on the infested floor. But he did so, noticing a strange fact: that his mother and father had shed the appearance of age along with their skins.

When he burned the remains of his family, Sygigh burned his house also. The fire spread like plague through the slum district, and many more families died as a result. He did not care. For all he knew, the murderer of everyone he loved was a neighbour. There were no innocents in the city. He rented a room in a pitiful tenement house close to the derelict ruins of Zhal-Yhul, and embarked upon a bitter and determined search for a thief whose treasure-trove was entire human skins.

Years passed, and the search aged him. Grief darkened his eyes like flakes of ash, and the muscular limbs of his youth became unnaturally thin and tense. The young woman who had worn his mask passed him in the street one day, but did not recognise him. He did not bother to acknowledge her. To his eyes, everyone wore a mask now. He had visited basement rooms in which desperate men paid harlots to maim and disfigure them, and the cold smell of narcotics tainted the air. He had waited in cemeteries where the yellow moonlight painted the blood of children, spilt on altars into which no name had been carved. He had stood immobile as the black stone bull of the city's marketplace stirred with unnatural life and charged to gore and trample the bodies of its helpless sacrificial victims. He had watched in ruined theatres as nocturnal plays of debauchery and murder were enacted for an audience of deviates, addicts, poets and the dead.

All this he had seen. But it meant nothing to him. He was no heroic defender of the persecuted and the abused. For him, there was only one crime to be avenged and only one criminal to be punished. But the stealer of skins evaded him. That name was not whispered in the gutters and alleys and dens in which Sygigh pursued his endless quest for the truth. In his grief and his madness, the gift of second sight had come upon him. But he made no use of it. What did he care for the future of those who crossed his path? He lived in a city of the dead. The gift had come too late to wake him from his drugged sleep and guide him back to the house where death was standing in the doorway, looking in at his family. He did not need second sight of that visitor. First sight would be enough.

After nine years of fruitless searching, during which time the city of Brymygem had fallen still further into ruin, Sygigh decided to appeal to the deity whose grim eidolon had cast its shadow over these streets for a thousand years. He gathered together such coinage as he had been able to save from his labours as a stonecutter, and made his way by night to the black temple where the priests of Kâlchi'an carried out their secret rituals.

As the heavy door to the temple swung open, his nostrils were assailed by the cloying aroma of incense; and beneath that, the acrid smell of narcotics; and beneath that, the faint but unmistakable odour of the dead. A bleached face peered out from within a black hood. Sygigh raised the leather purse that contained his meagre offering. The face disappeared, but the door did not close. He followed the black-robed figure into the narrow hallway of the temple. Torches, set in the bare stone walls, gave out a feverish red light. The floor was littered with rose petals that clung to his shoes like fragments of drying skin.

When they stood before the harsh basalt likeness of Kâlchi'an, the priest took the offering of money from Sygigh and wrapped it in the folds of his own robe. The gold was merely the price of entry; the god demanded something else. Sygigh noted, with an odd sense of irony, that the priest was not unlike himself: a small man with a shaven head, thinner than was usual for a priest. His fingers were abnormally long and slender, and his eyes bulged in their dark sockets.

Sygigh knew the ritual, though he had never performed it before. He stood in the shadow of the dark god with his hand outstretched, as though begging. The priest lifted a tiny dagger and struck once. Sygigh felt the steel go though his hand and strike the cold stone beneath. As the dagger withdrew, his blood flowed onto the expressionless face of Kâlchi'an. It soaked into the polished stone; no drop of blood reached the ground. He closed his eyes, grimacing with pain, and prayed silently for a glimpse of the stealer of skins. No vision came to him in the dull red light of the smoky torches.

Then the priest lifted Sygigh's injured hand and began to bind it with a damp cloth. The pale, thin fingers felt cold against his fevered skin. Gently, the priest stroked the edges of his wound as if to assess the damage. The caress was not sensual: it was the measured touch of a craftsman... or a collector. Sygigh drew in a deep breath that tasted of roses and decay. Without a word, he turned and walked back though the hallway and the door, and out into the stale air of the city night.

The priest's home was a tall, shuttered house in a narrow backstreet adjoining the temple. Rats fought over some unidentifiable heap of rags in a waste-heap close to the door. It was strange that a man of wealth chose to live in a place of such deprivation and squalor. Before dawn, Sygigh had gained entry through an upper window at the back of the house. There was no one to see him.

Stealthily, he crept from room to room, using a tiny lamp he had found on the windowsill. The flickering red light showed him canvases painted with bizarre scenes: decaying city landscapes occupied by pale, distorted creatures and their human prey. Perhaps the priest of Kâlchi'an was an artist. The air was chill, and a strange odour clung to the walls: a mixture of incense, natron and charcoal, together with some chemical that Sygigh did not recognise. A light rain tapped on the roof overhead, like fingers brushing a drumskin.

Apart from the paintings and some candle-holders made from the skulls of cats, there seemed little out of the ordinary in the priest's house. Its very simplicity made him feel uneasy. Soon the dawn would come, and the thin priest would return to his house. Years of obsession had made Sygigh an expert in the ways of stealth and concealment; but there seemed no place here where anything could be concealed. Just when he was about to abandon the search as misguided, he noticed a ridge in the crimson rug beneath the kitchen table. As if it had been lifted and hastily replaced.

Beneath the rug was a locked trapdoor. Among Sygigh's many skills was the ability to pick locks; and his skilful fingers soon released the catch and lifted the door. A few bare wooden steps led down into a basement room. The chemical odour was stronger here, and the earthen floor was sprinkled with pale constellations of salt crystals. Sygigh reached the bottom of the steps and raised the lamp to look around him. At once, he had the terrifying impression of having interrupted some kind of gathering or ceremony.

Arranged on the bare floor in various poses were a dozen or more dead people, or perfect likenesses of them. One was drinking from a half-full goblet of wine. Another was crouched on the floor with his head bowed, as if in obeisance to the dark god. In a corner, a young couple were locked in a secretive embrace. Two old men sat over a chessboard, their brows furrowed in concentration. A beautiful woman sat in a chair asleep, a white cat cradled in her arms. Beads of moisture glittered in the low ceiling.

Could these silent figures be real? If so, how had the priest managed to preserve so many corpses against the inexorable ravages of decay and the attentions of rats? Surely they must be structures of wax and paper, nothing more. Uneasily, Sygigh reached out and touched the cheek of the woman in the chair. It was stiff and hollow, like a lantern. The pressure of his fingers made her body tilt. Suddenly his fingernail ripped the fragile cheek, releasing a natron-scented cloud of dust. He touched something beneath the skin: a wooden framework, crafted to restore the appearance of the living body.

In the next room, the figures were naked and twisted into postures of erotic passion, or of violence and torture. Some of the skins were incomplete. In the next room, they were all dressed in black robes like the priests of Kâlchi'an, looking on as a maiden was sacrificed on the altar of night. It was here that Sygigh recognised the lost faces of his mother and father, Xania and their child.

He reflected grimly that they did not look well. Yet the priest's craft and insane magic had preserved their stolen skins with hardly a flaw or blemish. There was another door; but he did not explore any further.

By the unstable light of the oil lamp, he stared into Xania's still face. The skin was as white as bone. Her eyes had been painted on her eyelids, and the priest had used the wrong colour. He tried to say something to her, to make some apology or tell her what he still felt for her, but no words would come. His mouth was as dry as paper. He was still standing there when the priest found him.

Covetous of the intruder's skin, the priest did not attack him with a weapon. Rather, as Sygigh turned around, he began to weave his long fingers through the air and mutter a hasty invocation. The air began to fill with streaks of darkness, like smoke or charcoal. In this twilight, the hollow figures began to move. Sygigh backed away from the sight of their stiff-legged approach, their stretched grimaces of lifeless skin. He felt his back press against the mouldering wall of the basement. A pale hand reached for his throat; and though it had neither bone nor muscle, it had the cold strength of a buried memory. The other figures clustered around, reaching for him. He knew there were too many to fight off. With a final, desperate gesture, he flung the oil lamp at the puppet whose hollow fingers were sinking deep into his neck.

The burning oil streaked across the dead face like a wound. In moments the dried skin was aflame, and the figure crumpled like a moth that had flown into a lamp. Another dead skin, supported by wooden splints and animated by the corrupt breath of Kâlchi'an, stumbled upon the burning remnants; and still the others pressed forward as if guided by one command. Soon the dark flame was raging through the entire multitude. Their disintegrating shapes twitched and jittered in the grip of an insane dance. Hands, faces and limbs melted into grey ash. The stench of burning skin and acrid chemicals made Sygigh nauseous; his vision blurred, and he fell to his knees on the salt-covered floor.

At last the flames died. Sygigh rose to a crouch, and felt in the terrible dust for the lost oil lamp. When he lit it, the unnatural strands of darkness had gone. So had the priest. The dark god protected his own. Slowly, with painful care, Sygigh gathered together the remaining fragments of skin and clothing into a single pyre. Then he set fire to it and watched it burn, intoning some meaningless chant from his infancy. He knew he was completing a funeral rite begun nine years earlier. The search was over. But in his memory, the horror would remain undiluted by either daylight or time.

This time the fire spread to the beams, and hence to the upper rooms. Sygigh escaped the house only moments before it flared into red chaos. He turned his back on the spreading blaze and the smoke, walking through the quiet streets towards the far side of the city. Ahead of him, dawn was creeping like a pale mould across the rooftops. His mind was cold and empty, a house no longer inhabited by the living.

This is the tale that visitors to the crumbling library took with them when they returned from the dead city to those places where clans and families still lived. And with it they took the seer's bitter prophecies, which they knew to be true even as they declared him a liar and a madman. They took away, also, an uneasy memory of the hunger in the seer's eyes. And the way in which, when they took their leave of him, the old man clasped them by the hand. How soft his fingers were, and how his touch lingered for a few strangely tender moments, tracing the ridges and hollows of their skin from wrist to fingertip, until they shivered and turned away. That touch, somehow, told them more than the seer's words. It spoke to them of the last days that were coming, the eclipse of humanity and its fragile world.

AGAINST MY RUINS

The sky was a cracked window. Niall crouched on the pitted roadway, filled a hand with water and pressed it to his mouth. Hunger twisted inside him, doubling the edges of the pale buildings. Three days in the city, and the only food he'd been able to find was what he could have found outside: berries, grubs, winged insects. He'd picked them off cobwebs in the shattered walls. Any stored human food had long since been looted. Yet he didn't feel able to leave.

At least in the city, the rubble and detritus of other lives made him feel less alone. It promised something he might be a part of. Outside, among the crumbling hills and burnt trees, he felt too exposed. There was too much that had been alive: it might harbour diseases or parasites. He didn't want nature. He wanted meaning. A way to decode the language of ruins. And in the city it was all around him, as if the walls themselves were made from layers of printed paper. Every pattern of cracks, every film of dust, contained a message.

This morning must be a Sunday, because he could hear the vague thumping of bells from a jagged clock tower. The clock face was marbled with growths; above it, the spire had collapsed inwards. A few grey headstones were scattered around the building: a tilted cross, a headless angel. They were difficult to pick out, now that the entire landscape was a graveyard. Did that mean everywhere was consecrated ground? Niall hoped so, since there was little prospect of burial for anyone who died here.

Veils of dust blew across the sun, draining its warmth. Niall shivered. Ahead of him, the ruined buildings were taller; chunks of masonry hung from twisted steel girders. He must be nearing the city centre. A square car park was crowned with rusting hulks. A windscreen held up a rose of splinters. In the shadow of a blackened office wall, fireweed trailed the whitish smoke of its seeds. He thought he could see a man down there, walking slowly along the canal towpath, his body shapeless with layers of clothing. But he wasn't sure, and there was no point talking to people. Most of them were insane. Let them close and they'd harm you or themselves.

Not far beyond the canal, he found a huge concrete structure like a collapsed wedding cake. Subsidence had released its windows: a strangely ordered pattern of glass fragments covered the semicircle of steps around the front entrance. The hand of neglect was gentler than the hand of violence. Niall picked his way through the dull shards to the entrance hall. Damp flakes of plaster clung to his trouser-legs as he stepped between heaps of swollen rubbish. The smell of decay was overwhelming. Through broken walls, he could see dim arrays of shelves whose contents were grey with mould.

Perhaps the words could help him. He felt desperate to belong to something. A split in the nearest wall let him pass through to the gap between two bookcases. He reached up and tugged at a large volume. It stuck, then tore free of its cover. The pages exploded around his feet. He reached down. All the pages showed the same photograph. A woman's face, mouth open as if in shock, darkness staring through her eyes. There was no text.

Niall stumbled back out and down the glass-carpeted steps. He leant over the edge of a fountain that held only a dark thread of rainwater. After a few minutes, he realised he wasn't going to be sick. It was just hunger. He spent the next couple of hours searching for food in the remains of the shopping centre. It was no good: human and other scavengers had cleaned out everything edible. But some of the displays were intact. Glass ornaments furred with dust, glowing with their trapped fire when you wiped them clean. China mugs and coffee cups suspended from a rotting wall, like shells embedded in a cave. Nothing to drink.

Later, he found a cathedral fringed by dark railings whose rust flaked off in his hands. Its pearly blue dome was still unbroken. As he approached the dust-curtained rear window, a flock of pigeons exploded from the long grass around his feet. Dust trickled from their wings as they rose into the air. At once, Niall threw the half-brick he'd been carrying in his jacket. One of the birds fell, crashing into the wire grate over the cathedral window. Its wing brushed at the ground, over and over. He lifted it and felt its rapid, struggling heartbeat falter and then stop. Niall tried to recall the painting this moment reminded him of. But the memory was gone with the heartbeat. No matter. He'd burn some wood to cook the pigeon later.

The interior of the cathedral had been stripped: no seats, no curtains, no altar. The tiled floor had partly subsided into a basement flooded by the recent heavy rains. Dark water covered the floor of the nave down the middle; the edges were dry. There was a stench of rotting wood. The pattern of the diamond-shaped tiles was just visible through the water—except in the dead centre, where some elongated object lay just below the surface. Niall reached down and turned it over. Her skin was grey, her mouth open, her eyes eaten by decay. A halo of black hair surrounded the remains of her head.

As night thickened the screens of dust, Niall found a park outside the city centre and broke off some dead wood and bracken to make a fire. The pigeon he'd killed was slow to cook, its skin burnt while the flesh was still raw. Still, he chewed enough of it to keep the hunger quiet. Hollow faces twisted in the smoke, masks over darkness. He threw the bones into the dying fire. It began to rain. The trees would give little shelter. He'd better find an empty building. Rain trickled down his face as he walked, running into his mouth. It tasted of decay.

The full moon became visible through drifting cloud. Niall could see the black trees around him, and the faint outlines of houses up ahead. As he got closer, he saw that the doors and windows were bricked up. He turned back into the moonlight and saw a figure stumbling towards him. Her hair was blowing around her face, as if she'd fallen from a height—or risen from below. He couldn't move. The figure reached him and dissolved into rain, carried on a gust of wind. The impact stopped him dead. For a moment he couldn't see anything. Then the wind dropped, but the moon was fading. He walked on to whatever lay beyond the row of sealed houses.

Were they more houses? They all seemed to be joined together, but there were darker areas below. It was a viaduct. And in one of the arches, a red flame was glowing. Cautiously, Niall approached the fire. Someone was crouching against the brick wall. He froze as she looked towards him. Her hair was cropped short; her eyes were alive. She was wearing some kind of overcoat. He spread his empty hands. "Can I stay here a bit?" She nodded.

Rain tapped the bridge around them. Overhead, pale stalks of lime had grown out of the brickwork. They sat and watched the fire dwindle. Her name was Judith. Like Niall, she'd only recently come to the city. But she'd found food: boxes of sweetened biscuits, stale but edible. She offered him one. He chewed it slowly, willing flavour into the dry fibres. "It's not always food," she said. "Sometimes there are other things in the boxes. Must have been a little shop of some kind. I broke in through a window."

Judith had found cigarettes as well; she lit one in the red embers. Niall found the domesticity of the gesture at once reassuring and threatening. The rain had stopped, and he said he'd better leave. "You can stay if you want to," Judith said. "I don't mind." He lay down with his coat over his shoulders and tried to sleep. Judith lay down beside him in the dark; he could hear her breathing. She reached out and touched his face. Slowly, awkwardly, they undressed each other. Her kiss tasted of ashes and dead cigarettes; but it also tasted of her mouth.

In the morning, everything seemed unnaturally still and bright. Niall could hear each crack of disintegrating masonry, each rustle of shifting litter. Silence lay on the city like a heap of thin blankets, each with its own tiny sounds. He and Judith avoided each other's eyes, but touched occasionally as they gathered up such fragments as might be useful to them when they moved on. Judith thought there might be more food stored in the abandoned shop. It would make sense to take it out into the country, where they'd be safer. They hadn't talked about staying together. If they said too much, Niall knew, his fear would rise to the surface and make him run away. Was it the same for her?

Judith led him through a maze of backstreets where rubbish had been piled up and burnt. Flowers of ash clung to the walls, perfect until you touched them. Rats crept among swollen black plastic bags; a grey-haired man leant through a window-frame to throw pieces of broken glass at them. One alley was so full of brick dust and other rubble that they couldn't walk down it. "I could have sworn that was clear yesterday," Judith said.

Eventually they reached a shop with a metal blind rusted over the front. "This is it." The upper windows were all smashed. Judith climbed up the broken wall of the next building to reach a narrow ledge, then slipped through the black frame as if disappearing into a negative. She reached out to help Niall step onto the ledge. Inside, there was just enough light to see by. Metal shelving units leant to the right along a wall papered with black mould. They were empty, but dust-wrapped boxes and bags were scattered over the rotting floorboards. "Nobody else has been here," she said.

Niall found that hard to believe. But he picked cautiously through the mounds of rubble. Paper flaked away in his hands. A rusty tin proved to contain something like flour, but congealed to a mass covered with threads of fungus. He moved away from the light, and was trying to prise open another tin with a screwdriver when he heard Judith behind him. She was crying.

He turned round. Judith was on her knees, holding a wooden box she'd dug from the rubble. She was staring into it. Niall moved behind her, to where the broken window let him see into the box. It was empty. She was still weeping when he took the box gently from her hands and put it back into the dark mound. They left the shop empty-handed.

If they just kept going long enough, they'd get back out of the city. The sun was low in the sky when they reached an arcade filled with cobwebs that shone like threads of crystal. The strands broke as they walked through; glass splinters pierced their hands. Shadowy figures waited in the doorways, but Niall avoided looking at them.

Beyond the exit, the only unblocked route passed through a great hallway. The roof was in tatters; the red evening light revealed some kind of tenuous growth between the walls. Faces and hands were suspended in a frozen mist, shapes that a breath could destroy. Beside him, Judith began to weep again. *I'm sorry,* she whispered over and over. *I'm sorry. It's too late now.* Niall held her trembling hand and led her through the community of staring ghosts. The dark-haired woman was only one of them, but he kept on seeing her. The cry of her open mouth filled the hall.

At last they were outside, and it was almost dark. Unless it rained, they'd stay in the open. Dust was falling on them from a clear sky; it stained the atmosphere. They had nothing to eat, and nowhere to go. But there were trees in the landscape ahead of them. Some might be alive.

The moon was just short of full. Its scarred face rose as they sat among the dead leaves, holding each other. They talked long into the night, remembering who they were and what they had lost. Neither of them knew how they'd come here. But surely that didn't matter. For the second time, their bodies folded together in the dark. They were still embracing when they fell asleep.

Niall awoke just before dawn. Whatever he'd been dreaming of, the grey light and the silence had banished it. How could he have thought it would be different? He saw the charcoal forest around them, the ruined city ahead of them, the impossibly fine dust trickling over Judith's face. She opened her eyes. "You were right," he said. "It's too late."

At once, her eyes filled with darkness. She knelt on the cold ground, rocking back and forth, holding herself. "Leave me alone," she said quietly.

He couldn't. Eventually, she reached for his hand. Her mouth opened, but she didn't speak. He felt her breath on his face. They sat together, watching the streams of dust that blew like sleet across the blank face of the sun.

THE ONLY GAME

On the last morning in February, Jean died again. I went into the bathroom and she was curled up on the floor, her hands outstretched as if trying to reach something. Or push it away. The door was open. She was wearing her pale blue dressing gown. Before, I'd checked the pulse at her wrist, found her tiny make-up mirror and held it to her blue lips. But this time I just looked at her. There was a stillness in her face—not peace, not tension, just an absence of life. It didn't really look like her. Though we'd spent the night together, I felt uncomfortable seeing her dressing gown half-open and her breasts exposed. It made me feel like a voyeur.

I went downstairs and put on some coffee, got eggs and toast ready for when she came down. The kitchen was cold. When I tried to wash our glasses and mugs from the night before, my hand slipped and I broke a wine glass. The blood streaked through the warm water like red hair in a bath. I was used to it, but I wasn't. Next door's cat was prowling around my garden, hoping to find a mouse or a bird in the long grass. The water cooled; I dried my hands and put a band-aid over the cut. The coffee boiled and I poured myself a cup. I was considering going out for a paper when I heard Jean's feet on the stairs.

She appeared in the doorway, rubbing her long dark hair with a towel. Her face was still pale. She was wearing a different sweater from the night before. These days, she kept a few clothes in my chest of drawers. I smiled at her. She touched my shoulder and kissed me. "Must have gone back to sleep," she said. "You know me. I'm a late riser."

In the afternoon, we went to the Midland Arts Centre to watch a film. It was a documentary about some American revolutionaries who went underground for a decade. I wondered which was worse: to compromise or to know that you would always be defeated. Was being pure the same thing as being right? Afterwards, we walked around the lake and watched the geese stalking through the shallow water. Jean thought the film showed that being right was pointless if you couldn't take others with you. She was always the one to join things. I wondered what my father would have said.

On the far side of the lake, there's a stream with a bridge across it. Jean and I walked through the trees, holding hands. It was quiet there. My house is on a main road, so I'm not used to silence. Jean's hand felt cold. When we stopped on the bridge, I could feel her shivering. "Are you ok?" I said.

"Not great," she said. "Feel sick a lot. Got some pain in my guts, I don't know why. Could be an infection. I'm seeing the doctor tomorrow."

"Why didn't you tell me before?" In natural light, it was easier to see how pale she was.

"Didn't want to worry you. And what will you do if I'm pregnant?"

I put my arm around her. "Do you think that's possible?" She didn't answer. "If that happened, whatever you wanted to do, I'd support you." Jean looked away. I didn't know if that was too much or not enough.

When we got back to my house, Jean said she needed to go home and get some work done. I was slightly relieved. A day like this called for solitude. And I wasn't ready to see her die again. Or seem to die. I asked her to let me know what the doctor said, and to let me know if anything changed. Or didn't change. "Take care of yourself."

That evening, I chopped up whatever I had in the fridge and made a stew. My father's default recipe. The house was cold, but I didn't feel like heating it. I drank some brandy, listened to Coltrane and, for the thousandth time, relived the last time I'd seen my father. It was just over a year ago. He was huddled on the sofa with his feet up, the fire on low. "I just feel tired," he said. "Tired and confused. Nothing makes sense anymore." I would have suggested going for a walk, but it was pouring with rain. An hour in the house made my head ache, and I took off after making him promise to see the doctor.

He didn't answer the phone the next morning. When I got home from work I phoned again. No response. Late that night I decided to go and see him. He didn't answer the door. I went round to the back, through the narrow entry passage where I'd played war games as a kid. Pretending a tennis ball was a hand grenade. In the back yard, I could see the light was on in the living room. He was lying on the floor, curled up. I rapped on the window. Then I hung my jacket over my fist and broke the glass.

The cause of death was carbon monoxide poisoning from a faulty gas heater. Because he was home all day, it had built up gradually. They told me the poisoning was cumulative, so he'd been dying for days without realising it. Even if I'd taken him for a walk it wouldn't have done any good. Like filling up a glass, nothing changes until the level reaches the top and overflows.

Of course I blamed myself. What else could I do? All my life I'd had trouble believing that death was real. My mother died when I was too young to understand what it meant. Somehow I'd stayed like that, as if that death was the only one. There was illness, there was pain, but there was always a recovery. It caught me by surprise every time that sometimes people didn't make it through. And this time, it could have been prevented. By me.

That was quite early in my relationship with Jean, and she was a fantastic support to me. She didn't try to make me "get over it," she just kept things in some kind of perspective. *Other people are part of us. Missing them shows that we're still connected to them, we still need them. It's the love we need to hold onto. The life, not the death.* But I couldn't get past the death. With Jean, I alternated between being too needy and being too distant. If I thought of her needs, it was in terms of brief and particular things: a cuddle, a meal, a night out. Things I felt able to give.

A few weeks before Christmas, I began to see people dying. Or rather being dead. I'd be in the office or on the bus, and someone would just flake out. It only lasted a few seconds, not even long enough for me to try to help. Then the frame would dissolve, the colour would come back into the picture, and they'd be breathing and seeing again. With people I knew, it lasted longer. One of my closest friends pegged out in the pub; I felt his pulse, was about to call an ambulance when he sat up and reached for his drink. I told him he'd passed out, which worried him a lot. But he hadn't been unconscious. He'd been dead.

With Jean, the dead spells were longer and always left me shaken. One day I'd get it wrong, and she'd really need my help. I had to make sense of it. But to be honest, every time it happened I felt like I was the one losing touch. Nothing was human anymore. Imagine your home, the park, the train. Now imagine all the shadows turning to stone, so nothing could be moved. There was nothing warm or soft in the world. Make sense of that, go on.

The lonely horn blasts at the end of *Blue Train* faded into the crackle of the worn-out final groove. Which made me think of old tapes, like the reruns of comedy programmes we listened to on the radio when I was young. My father used to do *The Goon Show* voices for me, creating a bizarre world in which tragedy lurked around every corner. *You have deaded me. He's fallen in the water.* In later years, he remarked: "Spike Milligan's genius was in the way he used sound to create impossible images. He simply doesn't work on TV."

They're all gone now, of course: Milligan, Sellers, Secombe. They've fallen in the water. My father's generation saw the sixties as a new start, a chance to say goodbye to everything that was sour and twisted about being English. By the end of the seventies, it had all come back. The drunken colonels and sadistic headmasters were back in charge, running the economy, running down the National Health Service. There were no more surrealists, only goons.

When the government changed in 1997, my father said it was too late for any real change to happen. "We've missed our chance." By then he'd taken early retirement from his engineering job, worn out by the battle to defend the union against the company's relentless greed. It was a battle you could never win. But that didn't mean you gave up. I remember him once telling me the story of the old gambler who was going into the faro house when a friend saw him and said "Don't go in there. The house game's crooked." The old man smiled and said: "I know. But it's the only game in town."

The next Friday night, I was sitting in the living room when I felt the air turn cold. I'd been drinking vodka and listening to Miles Davis to try and calm myself down. Jean was in the bedroom, deading. The muted horn seemed to fill with dust; the air became grainy. I could see my own breath in front of my face. All the colour had drained out of the room. I finished the glass, but couldn't taste it. Jean had told me she wasn't pregnant. The doctor didn't know what was wrong with her; he'd referred her to a specialist at the hospital for a biopsy.

As I climbed the stairs to the bedroom, I briefly imagined my parents would be waiting to say goodnight. The dusty green carpet on the stairs became the pale grey of the house where I was born. But there was no one there. Jean was slumped at the foot of the bed, her long hair falling down around her face. I lifted her and eased her back onto the duvet. A trumpet wailed from the staircase. Jean's body trembled, and I thought she was waking up.

But it wasn't her. It was something inside her, or behind her and moving through her. I watched its brittle limbs and dark, swollen body take shape in the air as it struggled and lashed out. One of its legs whipped her cheek, and her neck twisted away from the blow. Its eyes were black, but I knew they could see me. Its frantic gestures softened, became sly and caressing. I could hear its voice in my head, like fire in dry twigs. *I am more than your tears. I am not something your friends or a helpline or a cup of tea can help with. I am more real than you are.*

I stepped back and stood in the doorway, my hands twisting and clawing at myself. My vision blurred and I dropped to my knees. I was crying the way you cry in the playground when you've been beaten to shit, and your tears are thick with disgust and shame and fear. At the time, you think the crying will never stop. But it did stop, and *Kind of Blue* was a mournful pulse in the air, and Jean was lying still on the duvet. I got up and stood beside the bed, where I could see her face. See her lips stir with breath. She was asleep.

Some time after midnight, she came down and asked me if I wanted some cocoa. "I must have dropped off," she said. "Why didn't you wake me?"

"You were really tired. You needed a rest." The colours had come back to the house, but they were subdued, as if seen through a filter lens. I could hear the wind scouring the road outside, breaking twigs. Jean made some cocoa and we settled on the sofa, in front of the fire.

Eventually Jean decided it was time for bed. I would rather have stayed where we were, but I didn't tell her that. She got up and stretched, throwing her hair back from her pale face. I looked up at her and said, "Would you like to move in with me?"

She looked startled. "You do pick your moments." The wind made some ash fall inside the chimney, behind the gas fire. "I think so. Yes, Neil." Her neck and left cheek twitched, as though she were trying to shake off an intrusive hand. I didn't feel confident about touching her until she reached out and gripped my arm.

CONTRACT BRIDGE

It had been a few months since the four of them had last got together. Gerry, who'd been volunteered as chauffeur for the evening, was driving his familiar black Metro with the death-rattle gears. Steve was in the passenger seat; Carl and Louise were together in the back. The plan was to drive out to Ravenshaw, have a drink or two in the pub this side of the lake, cross the bridge on foot, visit the pub in the next village, then stagger back across the lake to the car. None of them were sensibly dressed for this. It was a clear, frosty night in early March. Black trees hung at the edges of the road like witnesses, unable to look away.

Somewhere between Olton and Solihull, a white clock stood at a fork in the road. Beyond that, traffic poured in from both sides and then, just as suddenly, flowed away again. The bridge loomed overhead before Steve was ready for it; the car's headlights glinted off its metal ceiling. He bit his tongue and tried not to feel its walls around him. A cat's cradle of stone, filled with light. Before it had gripped his mind, the car broke free and was back on the open road. Stars trembled like cracks in the windscreen. "Are you ok?" Gerry said. "You've gone pale."

"Yeah, I'm fine." Steve realised he was soaked with sweat. It would probably freeze and crack off him once they got out. The stone arch printed itself again and again behind his eyelids. There was a taste of blood in his mouth, like tinfoil. *Jesus. Less than a second.* "Touch of flu, maybe." Gerry slowed the car. "Don't worry. Keep going."

"Long as you don't give it to me," Gerry said.

"Well, maybe I won't stick my tongue down your throat this evening." Steve felt the trembling recede within him, shells within shells like a Chinese puzzle, until it was too small to see or feel. But still there.

Gerry snapped his fingers in annoyance. "Damn. And I'd even cleaned my teeth." A giggle came from the back seat: Carl or Louise, or both. They drove on, away from the built-up areas, down silent roads that were lined with naked trees. A bat swooped in front of the windscreen. Conifers shivered behind a

135

moonlit field where ridges of soil stood out like ripples in a frozen black sea. Out here, there was nothing overhead but the sky. Steve began to feel safe. The village was asleep: cars parked in driveways, TV sets flickering behind curtains. They passed a Gothic church built from huge stones, its windows cobwebbed with iron. Steve blinked, trying to see the figures in the stained glass. But there was only darkness.

The car park outside the Broken Arms was nearly empty. A few motorcycles were chained to metal stands by the wall. The tarmac was speckled with quartz; it glittered faintly, like the night sky. To the right, Steve could see the murky outline of the lake shore: an earthenware mug full of black coffee. To cross it, they'd have to follow the narrow road that went round the pub. He looked ahead and saw an arched stone bridge, there at the start of the road. A Gothic arch: Victorian railway architecture, like the bridge near the station in Leamington where Steve travelled to work. Once he'd stood there, sheltering from the rain, when a train had passed overhead. The vibration had entered deep into his bones, like the music in the groove of a record. Steve blinked. The others had disappeared. He followed them into the pub.

Maybe they'd come here before, but it didn't seem familiar. The rooms were huge, and most of the partitions had been removed. The pattern on the carpet was one of exploded roses, the colour of drying blood. Carl went to the bar and the other three sat at one of the varnished oak tables, close to the open fire. The smell of burning wood, faintly acrid and threatening, masked the usual pub smells of stale cigarette smoke and beer. Gerry was subdued, gazing into the fire as if trying to read it. Perhaps the prospect of drinking mineral water while his friends got pissed didn't really appeal to him. When the latest Bon Jovi single faded on the jukebox to be replaced by the same song, he exclaimed "Fucking hell," and went to find the machine.

Steve had a momentary sense of time standing still. He glanced at Carl and Louise, who were already snuggled together drowsily on the bench, whispering and giggling like teenagers on their first date. In reality, they were in their mid-twenties and had been married a couple of years. The firelight reduced them to a snapshot, pale and red-eyed. They both affected a postmodern take on the familiar Kevin and Tracy look. Carl Lamb was wearing a mock-velvet waistcoat with crimson and mauve chevrons. Louise was wearing a black PVC skirt that crackled when she moved. When they'd started going out together, Louise had been nicknamed Bama after the girl in *True Romance*. But once they were married, the nickname had faded away. Possibly because she wasn't keen on being called Bama Lamb. Steve closed his eyes and listened to the fire. As if tuning into an old radio station, he heard someone at the next table discussing a local news story. *They think it was an old man... Half inside the stone, he was. Like it had hardened around him. But it wasn't concrete... How did his fucking bones get into it?*

Steve turned round and looked at the man who was talking. But there were three kids at that table, and he couldn't focus on their voices. When the record faded to silence, he could hear them talking about the respective merits of Pizza Hut, Pizza Express and Bella Pasta. Gerry returned, looking happier, as the opening chords of Nirvana's "Scentless Apprentice" tore through the calm of the evening. As usual, he was wearing a black denim shirt and a silver bracelet. With his long, dark hair, sad eyes and pasty skin, he could have been an opium-haunted poet or the bass player in a Goth band. In fact he was both, but he worked in a factory that made plastic flowers. Carl and Louise were inclined to tease him about this in restaurants.

After a second round of drinks, it was time to move on. The warm haze of alcohol evaporated in the chilly brightness of the moonlight; but a kind of driven feeling remained inside the skull. They walked along in silence. Under the railway bridge, Steve paused for a moment. He could smell the faint odour of rot and mould, like unwashed skin. The bridge in Leamington was different: it stank of pigeon shit, loose feathers and bile. He closed his eyes and summoned up the memory of a train. The cables overhead began to sing. He touched the brick surface, felt it vibrate. Then, suddenly, the train came past. Its wheels pounded him through the stone. The rhythm grew louder and louder until he knew the bridge was going to explode.

It echoed in his head as he walked away. There was no train. His shirt was dark with sweat. He wiped his face with his sleeve, and saw a reddish dust smeared across the cotton. He could taste it in the back of his throat. The others were some distance ahead, close to the edge of the lake. They paused to wait for him. He tried to speed up, but felt too dizzy to run. "Are you all right?" Louise said when he reached them. "You don't look well."

Steve just shrugged. "Don't worry." The road shrank to a footpath going across the lake. It was a low, flat bridge, built up like an embankment from the ground. They crossed in single file. The wind across the lake was freezing and ragged; it flapped around them, smelling faintly of pond-weed. "It's good here," Louise said. "Where I used to live in Kidderminster, there's a pond that used to have ducks and stuff. Now it's full of blue-green algae. Looks like a huge bruise. Nothing can live in it. Signs all round saying not to touch the water. I don't know how…" Carl turned and squeezed her arm, gently. The surface of the lake was matt black, a layer of felt creased with ripples. Steve could see the bare outlines of trees in the moonlight, and stars jittering overhead; but there was no reflection in the water. We all need something to build on, he thought. Like Carl and Louise. We all need stability. To stop us coming apart.

The other village beyond the lake was more lively than Ravenshaw had been. It was still only ten o'clock. The narrow roads echoed with the roar of speeding cars and motorcycles. Outside a pub called the First Stone, a boy with a fresh cut across one cheek and a rosette of blood on his white shirt was being questioned by two policemen. Behind him, a girl with spiked hair and black eyeliner stood and waited, her loyalty reduced to patience. An extremely young couple crouched together by the wall behind a parked car, waiting for the police to leave.

Inside, the pub was crowded; but the people were too varied to be threatening. Probably a lot of them had escaped from the city. As he stood at the bar, Steve noticed someone watching him from a table close by. A man in a black leather jacket, slightly older than Steve. He glanced back, meeting the other's eyes, before realising that to do so was to invite a signet ring across the mouth. Strange, the way "You looking at me?" was the natural prelude to a fight. As if hatred were as spontaneous as courtship. There was nothing friendly in the stranger's face.

When Steve rejoined the others, Meat Loaf's "Read 'Em and Weep" was playing on the jukebox; Carl and Gerry were competing for Louise's sympathy by singing along to the final chorus, with suitable dramatic gestures. Carl's voice was an octave deeper than Gerry's. It worked well, because the final chorus went round again and again, with subtle modulations and a drop in tempo. The three were giggling helplessly by the end, and Steve had some trouble holding onto the drinks. "Tell me something," Louise said when she could speak. "Why do you love Meat Loaf when you despise Bon Jovi?"

"It's quite simple," Gerry explained seriously. "Meat Loaf *tries* to make great records, and there's something noble about the effort. It's like a kind of failed grandeur. Bon Jovi is like, *this'll do.* It's all slick and calculated, there's no passion in it. Like a Yuppie boyfriend who gives you a digital watch for a present. It's expensive, but you know he can afford it—in fact, he's probably found a way to count it off against tax. Meat Loaf is like a boyfriend who gives you a really dire present, say a crystal dragon—but you appreciate it, because you know he's been working late all week at the market stall to pay for it." He lowered his eyes before Louise's expression made him crack up.

"You know," Carl said, "that's something I admire about you, Gerry. You give good bullshit." Steve's mind was still crossing the lake. He poured a bottle of Diamond White into a thin glass and looked at the bubbles in the colourless liquid. Like flaws in a sheet of ice. Its taste was acid and pure, filling him with light. A hand touched his shoulder.

"Scuse me." The group fell silent. As Steve turned round, the pub seemed to expand to the size of a cathedral. "Sorry, mate, I thought…" It was the man in the leather jacket. He frowned as if trying to look through a misted-up window. "It *is* you. Mike's brother." Louise breathed in sharply. Steve began to shake his head, then stopped. He reached for his glass, fumbled it to his mouth and drank. Now he remembered the face. One of Mike's friends from school, looking pale and confused at the funeral. The face had changed, grown up, hardened with stubble and experience. But the eyes were the same.

"Yes, it's me." I'm still here, he thought. And Mike still isn't. What do you want with me? There was a pause. "I'm ok. Are you?"

The stranger nodded. "Stephen. I remember you. It was such an awful time. Look… I'm sorry. I've no business to remind you. But I'm glad you're all right." The question in his eyes was sharper than ever. Steve drained the last mouthful of Diamond White, felt its bubbles sting his throat. "You know, we all thought… like the *Express and Star* said, you were saved by a miracle." He'd been drinking whisky; Steve could smell it on his breath. "I lost three friends, you know? That's why seeing you means so much. I'm sorry." He stood up, looking embarrassed. Steve wanted to embrace him, tell him it was ok to talk about Mike and the others, it was good to remember them. But the unspoken question clung to him like a mask. *How the fuck did you survive?* He'd been trying to heal over that question for fourteen years, hiding it under layers of skin. Now this drunk had cut him open to expose it. He sat unmoving, all the life drained from his face. The man backed off slowly, avoiding Steve's eyes.

Cold as stone. That was what Joanne had said to him. The girl he'd dated for a few weeks after he'd left school, before he'd got used to living alone. He'd fucked her in the park by starlight, lying on the fluffy side of a Woolworths parka that had always been too big for him. They'd split up at work the next Monday, by reason of mutual dislike. She'd told him his eyes were as cold as stone.

"Steve." Louise touched his hand. "You're shivering. What's the matter?" He smiled at her. The Diamond White churned in his guts. "You looked like you were going to pass out."

"Have you eaten?" Carl said. "Drinking on an empty stomach can really fuck you up." All three of his friends were looking at him now. The palms of his hands felt gritty; sweat clung to his forehead like dew.

"Yes, I ate earlier. In Leamington. It's not that…" He tried to retreat into himself, become as young as he felt. "That guy. He was a friend of Mike's. My brother." His lips were dry now. The words came out like pieces of glass, bright and painful. "He died when I was ten. You know that." The others nodded. He could feel their eyes on him, their silence making him go on. "I was with him and two of his friends, out walking. A derelict railway near where we lived." He could remember the tall, purple fireweed, the white seed fibres that clung to his jacket. "The four of us were standing under this old bridge. Shouting to hear the echoes. Then it was like a train went past. But it couldn't have. The line was dead. That's all I remember."

He paused. "You don't have to go on," Carl said. Carl was always trying to be helpful at the wrong time. Louise squeezed Steve's hand and waited. He felt as though he were struggling for breath. First the words, then whatever else came up.

"I have to," he said. "Or you won't understand... I woke up in hospital. They told me the bridge had collapsed. Nobody knew why. I was bruised, but not really hurt. Just in shock. Some tramp had seen it fall with us underneath. They dug me out. And Mike and his two friends. They were dead. I didn't have a broken bone, and they were all dead." Steve felt tears running down the sides of his face. "The local paper said that bridge was so old, the bricks crumbled when they fell. Must have been as dry as dust. They said the bodies... Mike and the others, they'd lost so much blood. It was like they'd been dead for ages. Dried out and coated with brick dust." Steve put his face between his hands and sobbed. "Why?"

Silently, Louise put her arms around him. He felt other hands touch his shoulders, then drop away. "It's all right," she said. "It's not your fault. You're still here. And we'll look after you." He couldn't speak. The roaring in his skull gave way to the tinny chorus of the jukebox. Feeling a tightness in his throat, he stood up and made his way to the Gents'. His shirt was drenched with sweat, but his skin felt dry. The song on the jukebox was unfamiliar. He made it to a cubicle just in time, dropping to his knees on the cement floor.

A few minutes later, he wiped his mouth on a handful of toilet paper and rubbed his eyes with a sleeve. He couldn't remember when he'd last felt this tired. The smell in the cubicle was acrid and metallic, like a car battery. He glanced at the toilet bowl before pulling the flush with some violence. There were still traces of blood left around the seat, and a few half-digested shreds of meat floating in the water. The blood wasn't fresh, but who'd know the difference? Unable to face cleaning up any more, Steve backed out of the cubicle and staggered towards the nearest washbasin. The cold water on his face and neck helped to restore him to some kind of reality. As he was drying his hands, Gerry appeared in the doorway. "Steve? You ok?"

Steve nodded and smiled. "I'm fine." He felt as though he'd voided himself of the past. The emptiness inside him was familiar and safe. "We'd better be going now. It's late." He followed Gerry back to their table. The pub seemed brighter and smaller than before. The man who'd been at school with Mike was still sitting near the bar, but didn't look up as Steve and the others passed. I should have asked him his name, Steve thought. Too late now.

Outside, it was darker than before. The moon lit up a patch of cloud, like a face in a window. At the bus shelter, a lad was throwing up into a litter-bin while his girlfriend pretended not to see. Pigeons moaned from back gardens. Louise and Carl held each other up, walking unsteadily along the narrow pavements. Gerry, though sober, had absorbed some of their euphoric state. He was swaying from side to side, the village framed between his hands: a timbered house, a graveyard, a willow tree. Being drunk was only an amplification of what you were like anyway. Bigger speakers, but the same music playing through them.

A cold wind scratched waves at the lake's edge. Steve felt exhaustion shadowing him. Not far to walk now. Something rose to the dark surface and splashed twice. The moon reappeared; but the water still didn't reflect. The outlines of trees on the shore were like cutouts from black paper. Halfway across the bridge, Carl and Louise paused to admire the view. Their hands joined, and they pressed their faces together as if for warmth. Gerry stared at the trees, the ripples on the still water. Tiny ridges of frost glittered on the footpath. Steve muttered something about going for a piss. He needed to be alone.

In between the roadside lamps, there were long stretches of darkness. Steve walked as fast as he could. They'd catch up soon enough. Like they always did. His own breath seemed about to freeze in his mouth. He clasped his hands together and blew on them, feeling next to nothing. The village lights were a bright cluster above the road ahead. Near the railway bridge a dog barked at him, the sound echoing in a built-up darkness.

"Steve?" Then another voice: "Where are you?" The sound of approaching footsteps. Steve waited under the bridge, feeling the tight kiss of stone against his hands. The frost on the wall was like a galaxy of faint stars. There were spikes of lime under the brick ceiling. Not birdshit but real lime, the mortar of Victorian brickwork slowly dissolving in the rain. *You can't get away from us, you little cunt. This time we'll kill you.* He wondered who'd be found alive this time. It would be better with no survivors. No one to take up the contract, to live the way he'd lived the past fourteen years. Maybe the love and friendship some people had needed this coldness as its foundation. Like the family. Whatever, it didn't matter now.

"Steve! What are you doing there?" But he couldn't speak. He pressed his hands to the wall, feeling himself let go, his body drawn into the brickwork like a stain. Just as he felt the strength of the bridge gripping him, his own weakness made the bricks lose their hold. As Carl reached for his hand and tried to separate it from the wall, a deep mechanical shudder passed through them both. The whole structure was about to come down.

BEYOND THE RIVER

It's a surprisingly long way from London to Devon: a tilted line across the map of England, from the wealthy South East to the poorer South West. The landscape becomes more stark and elemental the further you go. It took me three hours to drive to Exeter on a warm September afternoon, the setting sun ahead of me painting the edges of rock that showed through the hillsides. The fires of late summer had left blackened patches on the rusting wheatfields. I drove through run-down little towns too far from the coast to benefit from tourism. At last, the silver gleam of the Dart estuary was in sight. I could smell the rich odours of marine salt and river mud, faintly tinged with the chemical traces of industry.

Beside my road atlas on the passenger seat was a page from an A–Z map, with the road I was looking for circled in red. Underneath both was a hardback copy of a children's book: *The Secret Dance* by Susanne Perry. The front cover was a colour version of one of the interior illustrations, showing a forest in twilight. The trees were ancient, their branches twisted into bizarre shapes. Living things were just visible among the trees and in the tangled undergrowth: a few squirrels, two owls, a fox—and many cats, whose eyes glowed a deep undersea green. The copy was a first edition. I'd had it for thirty years; it had been a present from my parents on my fifth birthday.

The Perry house was set back from the road, behind a tall privet hedge. The front garden was full of roses: tangled, overgrown bushes with heavy, blood-red flowers. The appearance of neglect surprised me; Susanne had sounded calm and relaxed on the phone, but perhaps the stress of the last year had got to her. I was here to interview her for the *Observer*, and expected she'd have things to say about her former publisher. But I wanted to tell the readers that she'd risen above the corporate nightmare: the world of her imagination couldn't be touched by business. That was what I wanted to see.

Wind chimes rang behind the panelled door. Susanne opened it. She was taller than I'd expected, and was wearing a blue-black dress that made her appear willowy rather than skinny. Her loose, dark hair was flecked with grey, rather like Patti Smith's on a recent *Later With Jools Holland*. She looked no more than fifty, but her eyes were older. She grasped my hand with her long, narrow fingers. "Hello there. Julie, isn't it? Do come in."

The house was decorated in tasteful shades of dark green and auburn, with abstract pictures and carvings that might have come from Italy or Spain. Susanne led me through into the living room, whose window overlooked the river. You couldn't hear the boats go by, but you could see them. The back garden was mostly long grass and weeds. Susanne made coffee, and we sat on her green couch at the end of the room. Her writing-desk faced the window; there was a small electronic typewriter on it, but no sign of a computer.

"Beautiful house," I said. "How long have you lived here?" As far as I knew, she lived alone. There'd been a marriage in the past, but no children.

"I was born here. It was my parents' house. I inherited it when my mother died, and moved back in. I used to travel quite a lot, but lately this is all I need. I like living close to an estuary. Where the river becomes something else, the movement flowing into what doesn't change." She said this as casually as if she were talking about the availability of parking spaces at the local supermarket.

"Are there any forests nearby?" I asked. "I didn't see one when I was driving here."

She laughed. "You have to know where to look."

I wondered about asking her to sign my battered copy of *The Secret Dance*. Maybe later, at the end. She was probably sick of maudlin fans trying to relive their childhood. I wanted to appreciate the person she was now.

"How do you want to do the interview?" I said. "I can show you the questions and let you think about them before we talk, or we can just start chatting and see how that goes. I'd like to get a photograph as well, if you're happy with that."

"Fine. Let's start there. Maybe by the window?" I fished my Nikon digital camera from my bag, then stood back so I could photograph Susanne with the river-boats as background rather than the forsaken garden. She ran her delicate fingers through her hair. Her face took on a lost, haunted expression, as if she were dreaming with her eyes open. I took three shots.

Afterwards, it took her a few minutes to come back from whatever thoughts she'd given herself up to. She sipped her coffee quietly, her eyes closed. Then she smiled at me. "Would you like something to eat? I can have some dinner ready in half an hour. Be easier to talk over a glass of wine."

"That'd be lovely," I said. "If you're sure."

"It's nice to have someone here. I haven't felt like company in a while." She led me into the kitchen and prepared a light, elegant meal of grilled salmon with fennel and toasted ciabatta bread. I admired the tapestry that hung on the wall opposite the stove: an undersea scene of fish swimming through tangled weeds, coral and the drifting hair of mermaids. It reminded me of Susanne's illustrations, though she always drew forest scenes since her books were set in a forest world.

We ate at a small table in the living room, and shared a bottle of Chablis. I reckoned I could get away with two glasses if I wasn't driving for a couple of hours. And to be honest, I hadn't felt like company in a while either. It was nice, I thought, to share a drink with someone who didn't have an agenda, whether business or personal. The light dimmed in the bay window, and the small oil-lamps on the fireplace filled the room with trembling strands of light.

And she told me about the Forest of Scriffle. The imaginary twilight realm Susanne had developed as a background for the dreams, mysteries and visions that she had wanted to explore as a young writer. The forest tales began as picture books with text and illustrations on alternate pages, and ended as short novels with a few pages of artwork. Like Tove Jansson, she had always drawn her own illustrations. The forest had grown over time, becoming more complex and more strangely populated.

"Did you read that interview with Simon Maxwell-Hoare in the *Sunday Times*?" she asked. I nodded. Maxwell-Hoare was the Managing Director of Neotechnic, the edutainment and educommerce publishing company that was trying to sue Susanne for breach of contract. He had asserted that "Susanne Perry is incapable of understanding the needs of her readership." The interviewer might have pointed out that, as the executive publisher of the magazine *Children As a Market*, Maxwell-Hoare viewed the cultural needs of children primarily in terms of their need for Neotechnic's products. But he hadn't.

Susanne drained her glass and refilled it. "The thing that infuriates me most about what he said is that the whole idea of the Forest of Scriffle was always quite commercial. But it gave me a peg on which I could hang my ideas about faith and imagination. Behind the dancing cats and the nervous squirrels and the world-weary owls were themes drawn from Wicca and nature worship. But I expect you know that."

"I think I did even as a child," I said. "The pictures suggested something more than just a bunch of cute little animals. The patterns, the swirling effects. Things going on in the background that you couldn't quite make out."

"In the seventies, some teachers said my books were a bad influence. They'd lead people to take drugs." Her eyes widened. "Which I never did, of course." I suspected she was being ironic, but wasn't sure. "But whatever I was putting into the books, Neotechnic didn't want any of it. They wanted the new books to be like papier-mâché: the surface repeated all the way through. I was supposed to let Marketing decide on the content. My job was simply to write and draw what they told me."

The grilled fish was rich and crisp, served with a sharp mustard sauce and a variety of boiled vegetables. I relaxed, drank some wine and kept the dictaphone supplied with miniature tapes as Susanne told me her story. Part of me was still five years old, dreaming with my eyes open, running with the little lost creatures through the ancient shadows of the Forest of Scriffle.

"I started writing those stories when I was a student at Bristol University. My lecture notes were annotated with little silhouettes of cats and distorted trees. I searched the university library for books of folk tales, and wrote a dissertation on archetypal themes in the tales of Hans Christian Andersen. By the end of my final year, I'd written an early draft of *The Secret Dance*. And drawn most of the pictures.

"Then I got a job in a Bristol museum. I kept putting the book away, then taking it out and doing more work on it. Eventually I had a typed draft with a set of pen-and-ink illustrations. I sent it to Dunwich Books because they were my favourite children's publisher. Once I'd sent the book off, I decided to put my youth behind me and never write or draw again. Then I got a letter from their editor, Judith Williams, saying they wanted to publish the book.

"They had a wonderful office building near Scarborough, full of pictures and book covers. Judith and I became good friends. She encouraged me to write more complex stories, aimed at slightly older children, so that my readership could grow into the series. *The Sleepless Forest* took me three years to write and illustrate, while I drifted from one museum or art gallery job to another. Then I met a teacher called Steven who was taking a group of kids round a dinosaur exhibition. We got a flat together, and got married a year later.

"When the third book, *Shadows That Dream*, won a literary award and became a best-seller, I was able to give up my job. By now I had an agent, Roanne Smith, who kept me busy with school visits and readings. Felicity Kendal read *Shadows That Dream* on the BBC's *Jackanory* programme. I had an offer from Puffin Books, but I wanted to stay with Dunwich—or at least with Judith. She was the only person who really understood the Forest of Scriffle. I did a painting of her in the forest, surrounded by cats. It stayed on the wall of her office until... the end.

"Steven was never comfortable with my success. He didn't mind me writing my little books and doing my little sketches, but the fact that I was earning more than him made him angry. Things were different then. He wrote a novel for teenagers but couldn't sell it, and things began to sour between us. Maybe if we'd had children it would have been different. Anyway, he met someone else.

"Then my father became ill and died. I was spending a lot of time here, which meant I was reliving things just as they began to slip beyond my reach. Do you know what I mean? The Forest of Scriffle became an escape for me, but also a place where I could try and make sense of things. That's why *The Moon Cats* was a darker book. I was trying to help children see that life can't always be a happy thing. It didn't do as well as the third book, but I was proud of it.

"I wrote three more books in ten years, then decided that was enough. Dunwich Books kept them in print, and I was making enough money to live on. When Roanne retired, I didn't look for another agent. I suppose I didn't feel confident about writing another Forest of Scriffle book. I started working on an adult novel, a historical novel set in this region, but I still haven't finished it. People are harder to understand than cats. I drew some cards for Dunwich to print as merchandise, but that was all. Until the year before last."

By now, we had finished the meal and drained the bottle of Chablis. I thanked Susanne for her hospitality, and changed the tape in the dictaphone. She disappeared into the kitchen, then returned with blueberries, ice cream and coffee. The daylight was fading in the window, and I could see the lights on the riverboats floating beyond the tangled shadows of the garden. The coffee was strong; its bitterness filtered through me as Susanne resumed her story.

"I'm sure you know most of it. Dunwich Books was bought out by Neotechnic, an American publishing corporation. Dunwich had to close their offices and move to the Neotechnic building in Telford. Have you been to Telford?" I shook my head. "It's a new town, all shopping malls and identical streets, nothing built before 1980. Judith hated it. Then after six months, they announced a 'restructure'. Dunwich Books would cease to exist as an imprint, and its line would be absorbed into the Neotechnic list of children's fiction.

"Judith was called into a meeting to discuss her future. She told me about it a few days later. At that time, Simon Maxwell-Hoare was the Marketing Director, not the Managing Director. But he completely controlled the meeting. It all revolved around him. Judith was asked to explain her publishing programme. She got out about three sentences before he said: 'There's no market for fancy books.' Judith tried to talk about the reputation of the Dunwich Books list, its status in the field, and he cut her off again, 'I call a spade a shovel, dear. I don't give a shit about literary awards. This meeting has five objectives: increase profit, increase our market share, increase the visibility of the Neotechnic brand, reduce overheads, and increase profit again. I don't see that you have much to contribute.' The MD sat there like Buddha and said nothing.

"A month later, Judith and two other Dunwich editors were made redundant. Neotechnic put out a press release expressing regret that the extremely tough market had made this measure necessary. If Judith had stayed in children's publishing I would have tried to move with her, but she decided to take early retirement. She and her husband moved to France. Meanwhile, Neotechnic sent me nothing except a royalty statement and a subscription form for their magazine *Children As a Market*.

"Then I got a personal letter from Maxwell-Hoare, introducing himself as the new Managing Director and claiming to be a lifelong fan of children's fiction.

He wanted me to come in and discuss the relaunching of the seven Forest of Scriffle novels in a new edition. As I recall, he said, 'The Scriffle series is a key product within the Neotechnic brand, and we look forward to increasing its market share.' He wanted me to write a new book in the series.

"I wrote back asking them to release me from my contract. That provoked a much less friendly letter informing me that Neotechnic would block any attempt by other publishers to reissue my work. It was their way or nothing. Of course, I should have got an agent. Or at least a solicitor. But I lost my nerve. This was just after my mother's death, and I was moving back here. I was very low, and short of money. Somehow I convinced myself that writing a new book would be good for me.

"So we had a lunch meeting at the only restaurant in Telford. There was Maxwell-Hoare, and the new Marketing Director, and the head of the design department. And Sally Black, my new editor, the only woman in the executive management team. Her contribution to the meeting was to smile and agree with everything that Maxwell-Hoare said. I recalled that Judith had mentioned Sally Black, but I can't quote her comments for legal reasons.

"It wasn't a very memorable meeting. Maxwell-Hoare informed me that he called a spade a shovel. Then he spouted some incomprehensible crap about market penetration and brand visibility. One of the phrases he used was 'old wine in new bottles." I wish I'd paid closer attention, but I'd had a couple of glasses of red wine and wasn't at my sharpest. So when he said that I'd be working with Sally and the design team to make sure the new book did well for Neotechnic, I didn't ask what changes they had in mind.

"The next day, the contract arrived. It looked normal enough. There was a mention of touching up some of the old covers to give them more impact, and I thought that sounded quite reasonable. To be honest, I just wanted to get back into the Forest of Scriffle. I realised that ideas for an eighth book had been creeping around my head for years, waiting for me to notice them. I wrote the first draft of *Trees Never Forget* in about three months, and sent it to Sally Black.

"Then I was sent proofs of the new edition of *The Secret Dance*. That was a shock. They'd broken up paragraphs, replaced longer or less modern words with simpler ones, and introduced a hundred or so typing errors. Every illustration now had a small version of the Neotechnic logo in one corner. You know, that distorted N in a circle. The one on the cover was red on black; the others were grey on black.

"I sent the proofs back to Sally covered with corrections, and said I wasn't happy about the logos. When the new edition came out, hardly any of my corrections had been done and the logos were still there. I phoned Sally, and she said it wasn't cost-effective to make so many changes. 'It won't affect sales.' I said I had never agreed for the earlier books to be re-edited. She said, 'You can't expect us to publish them unless they're appropriate for today's market.' I hung up the phone.

"A week later, my manuscript came back with Sally's comments. She started by saying that the language was too difficult for today's young readers. She wanted it 'rationalised' in line with the changes she was already making to my other books. And she insisted that I use American spellings, in line with Neotechnic's house style. Then she started on the story itself. She felt the hints of nature mysticism and Celtic magic were inappropriate for a mostly Christian reader-ship. She wanted the cats to be friendlier and less mysterious, so that children could 'identify' with them. She didn't like the territorial hedgehogs or the sinister grass snakes. And she wanted me to mention a little blue dog, in order to tie into another Neotechnic product.

"A letter from the Marketing Director was attached. He wanted the illustra-tions simplified, made more 'accessible,' with more cats and fewer animals that the readers might not recognise. He wanted the little tie-in dog added at least three times, and shown in blue on the cover. A scanned image of said pooch was enclosed. Finally, he wanted the Neotechnic logo drawn into the forest background in every illustration.

"What could I do? I wrote to Maxwell-Hoare, saying that these demands were a violation of my rights as an author and a corruption of the relationship I had built up with my readers. I got a letter from the Neotechnic company lawyer, telling me that I had to comply with their demands; otherwise, my contract would be null and void. So I tore up the contract and sent them the pieces. I got another letter from the company lawyer, serving notice of legal action for breach of contract. The story got out, and here we are."

It was dark outside by now. Susanne looked at me as if I had come with the bailiffs. I wanted to hug her, but didn't know whether that was appropriate. I rubbed my forehead nervously. "I'm really sorry," I said. "It sounds like you've been fucked upon. But that's corporate publishing for you."

Susanne raised her eyebrows in mock surprise, then smiled. Her eyes looked terribly weary. "Julie, would you like some more wine? Or a drop of brandy? It's getting late, and you're welcome to crash out in my spare room. It's a long drive in the middle of the night."

Ordinarily, I would have suspected an attempt at seduction. Especially as I'd put on a nice outfit for the interview. But my spider-senses weren't picking up any such vibes from Susanne. At the same time, her tone was too level for this to be simple helpfulness. She had an agenda, but I didn't think it was sexual.

So I accepted the offer of more wine. Susanne found a bottle of Chianti, and put on a Dr John CD to murmur darkly in the background. She drew the curtains, but left a window open. We sat and chatted for a while about subjects of mutual interest: modern art, blues, cats, Paris. I complained about the sexism of male journalists. Then she asked me: "Would you like to visit the Forest of Scriffle?"

"Er… pardon?" What metaphor was this? Was she offering me a joint, or a folder of her illustrations?

"I mean it literally." She wasn't smiling now. "It's not far away. Like I said, you have to know where to look."

"Where is it?" I asked, still mystified.

"Beyond the river. We can walk there."

The full moon cast delicate shadows from the trees outside Susanne's house. At the end of the road, a footpath led between two tall hedges. She led me through a gap in a steel fence, and down a precarious slope to the river bank. It was the kind of route I imagined a cat might follow.

"I found the way when I was seven," she said. "I've been coming here ever since. But I think it might not be here much longer. I want to share it with someone while I still can." The bank was overgrown, and I could see a factory wall on the other side. Susanne paused. "Look."

She was pointing down to the water's edge. The river was a dark skinless muscle with threads of moonlight. Just where the grass ended and the river-mud began, I could see two stone steps. The water smelt brackish. Susanne gripped my hand and pulled me forward. I felt a sudden, overwhelming sense of strangeness, as when you develop a fever or get caught between sleep and waking. I didn't think about my clothes, or my inability to swim. I just followed.

The steps led down under the water. It didn't feel cold, just a little more dense than the night air. Even breathing wasn't difficult: my chest just seemed to fill with air, and exhale thin white plumes through the dark water. Fish or eels slid around my ankles. I walked for some time, holding Susanne's thin hand. It was much darker down here. Then she paused, reaching forward. Her drifting hair touched my face. She moved on, and we began to climb another flight of stone steps.

The moon's reflection shimmered on the water surface just above our heads. My foot slipped on river-weed, but Susanne drew me on. The surface broke, then healed below us. We stood dripping on the mossy bank. And there, just a few yards in front of us, was the Forest of Scriffle. The trees were silhouetted in the moonlight, their twigs as intricately patterned as medieval carvings. Drifts of dead leaves rustled in the night breeze.

I stepped forward, open-mouthed with wonder. My nostrils filled with the scents of wood and leaf-mould, ferns and decay. But Susanne didn't move. I glanced at her and saw the growing terror in her face. "What's wrong?"

"I don't know. It's not the same. This time of year, the leaves should all be on the trees." She walked slowly forward. I followed her. Close up, I could see that the trunks were streaked with decay. The branches looked grey and brittle. "What's happened to it?" Susanne said. "The trees are all dead. And I can't hear the birds.

At night there should be owls hooting, doves calling. It's silent."

Then something came towards us out of the dark undergrowth. It reached a clearing and stood in the moonlight, uncertain. A black cat. It was sniffing the air, but didn't seem to see us. Susanne walked slowly towards it, reaching out a hand. "Hello, little one. How are you? Where are your friends?" Then she stopped. "Oh, no."

The cat was blind. Its eyes were blank sockets. Its fur was patchy, and its ribs were visible through the taut skin. Susanne dropped to her knees and stroked the cat's neck. "My God, what's wrong with you? What's happened here—" Then she screamed. I saw her rise to her feet and beat her hand violently against the trunk of the nearest tree. Some of the dead bark flaked away at her touch.

I went to comfort Susanne, but she backed away from me. The cat was lying on its side, no longer moving. I knelt to examine it. In the moonlight, I could see things moving through its fur. Crawling rounded shapes, like bugs or lice. Each one had a raised marking that glowed faintly with a terrible light of its own. A shape like a twisted letter N, red on black.

Now that I had seen them, I became aware that they were on the trees also. And on the dead leaves beneath my feet. And on a dead owl that was lying within my reach, its beak stretched open to receive the night. They were everywhere in the forest, infesting every living thing, leaving nothing but grey, brittle remains and silence. The rustling I could hear was the lice, hunting restlessly through the dead vegetation in search of something further to eat.

Then another sound reached me. A living sound. It was Susanne, weeping. I couldn't see her at first, wondered if the forest had claimed her for its own. Then I found her crouched behind the dead hair of a willow tree. In one hand, she was holding the clean-picked skeleton of a leaf. I pulled her to her feet, held her until she stopped shaking. Her tears were cold against my cheek.

"We have to get out of here," I said. She didn't respond. "Come on. There's nothing to stay for."

"There's nothing to go back to either."

"You know that's not true." I gripped her hand and led her back towards the river. Behind us, I could hear the sound of dead trees creaking, breaking and falling into the mounds of dead leaves. But something was calling to us through the night, from beyond the river. A heron.

Somehow we made it back the way we had come. The moon was lower in the sky, and it was colder than before. As we reached the house, Susanne began to shiver violently. She was pulling at her sleeves, checking them for signs of infection. I held both her hands, made her look at my face. "Come on. Let's go inside."

As I'd expected, Susanne seemed calmer indoors. She poured us both a large brandy, drank hers in a slow painful gulp. Then she walked up to the bathroom and closed the door behind her. I sat on the couch, drank my brandy and reflected that I hadn't asked Susanne to sign my copy of *The Secret Dance*. It didn't seem appropriate just now.

To my relief, Susanne emerged after a while. She was wearing a dark green dressing-gown, and her hair was wet. I poured her another brandy. She sat on the couch for a while, lost in thought. Then she said, "I have to go back there."

"What for? You can't save the cats."

"No, but I can burn them. Like a cremation. The wind will scatter the ashes in the river."

I shook my head. "There's no point, Susanne. If you go back, the forest will trap you. You'll die there. Your life is here."

She looked at me then, and her eyes were full of ashes. "What makes you so sure?"

"Because when things die, they don't stay the same. They rot. They become less than they were." I could feel a bitterness in my throat like nausea as I spoke. "You can't go back like that. No one can."

Susanne didn't say anything more. She finished her glass, then pointed to mine. I shook my head. She spread a thin duvet and a few cushions over the couch, then went upstairs. I turned off the light and spent a sleepless night on the couch, imagining that I could feel dead leaves dropping onto my face.

In the morning Susanne was brisk and efficient, making breakfast and filling a flask with coffee to help me get through the long drive home. We didn't talk about the midnight trip. I never did get that book signed.

The feature article came out a week later. I glossed over most of the Neotechnic business, focusing on Susanne's earlier career and the enduring magic of the Forest of Scriffle. She sent me a card at my work address. On the front was an original sketch, showing two cats walking along a river bank by the light of a full moon. Inside was the message: *To Julie, a moon cat who keeps her feet on the ground. With love from Susanne.* Soon after that, Neotechnic dropped the lawsuit and stopped reprinting her books.

We've been in touch occasionally since then—phone calls, an exchange of Christmas cards—but she hasn't invited me to go back. I like to think that she's able to keep the river between herself and the ruin of her dreams. Sometimes I remember her smile, and it warms me. But sometimes I wake up shaking in the night, clawing at my skin, and nothing can take away the image in my head: an army of sleek black and red lice, working efficiently to pick the bones of a cat.

THE PLANS THEY MADE

These days when I think about Kieran, it's like he's always been dead. He'd have liked that. I knew him for nearly eight years. The first job I had after leaving school was in a video shop. He and I were assistants, and mostly our shifts didn't overlap; but sometimes I'd be unwrapping and cataloguing stuff while he was checking it for defects, or vice versa. We'd chat about new films or the shit everyone was renting. Sometimes, we'd compare muttered notes on what a patronising cunt the manager was. Same as any job. You never think about where the people you work with might end up. From working in a video store, Tarantino went on to become a famous director. Kieran went on to become a statistic.

We stayed in touch after I went to college. A few years later, I got a job that required me to be near the South Birmingham train line. So I moved to Olton, the district where Kieran had always lived. He was still in the same rented flat as before, though he was working as a garage technician now. It was piecework, so his income was sort of uneven. He made up the deficit by copying and selling pirate videos. Mostly bootleg copies of films not yet available, plus some Dutch porn that seemed pretty mild to me. It's sad when minor copyright infringements are legislated into some kind of moral abomination. Kieran loved films. I tended to go for particular kinds of film—horror, crime, brooding European stuff—but Kieran would look directly into particular characters and scenarios that meant something to him, wherever they came from.

Back in the video shop days, he got me to watch *Running on Empty*. If you don't know, it's a film about a family on the run from the FBI for a crime the parents committed in protest against the Vietnam War. The children inherit everything: the guilt, the anger, the loss of freedom. The eldest son, played by River Phoenix, has to decide between his parents and his own needs. It was that conflict of loyalties that really moved Kieran, I think. His parents were divorced, and he'd never been able to distance himself from the feud between them. Later, we both saw *My Own Private Idaho* in a bootleg copy of the cinema print. River Phoenix

153

stood out in that film, because he was the only good thing in it. A similar role, in some ways. Not rebellious youth, but youth in pain—unable to reconcile his origins with his life, trying desperately to make sense of a damaged world.

I think Kieran was envious of that intensity. He might have felt it inside, but he didn't live it. He bought an electric guitar, but could only play strictly R&B stuff: pub music. He lacked the confidence to travel. Alcohol and films loaned him the gift of freedom; he didn't possess it. Mind you, he wasn't bad-looking in a solid, Brummie kind of way. Women either mothered him or played games with him, depending on their own past history. He'd been going steady with some girl for a while, I knew; but by the time I moved to Olton, he was alone.

One of the things that damaged Kieran—that stopped him moving on from a rather destructive background—was his involvement in fandom. There's like a hardcore of *Dr Who* and *Star Trek* fandom in the West Midlands. I'm not sure why. Kieran used to say it was like the Bible Belt in America. The fan belt, sort of thing. He was capable of getting very wrapped up in TV series like *Twin Peaks*; but it was the idea of an alternative worldview that appealed to him. The fandom thing of taking something intrinsically trivial and using it to replace the world wasn't really what Kieran was after. But he found the people in the fan subculture attractive. What he didn't realise, at first, was that they applied the same fucked-up rules to their own lives as to their viewing habits.

"They're just like children," he said to me. "You're either their best friend or their worst enemy. They'll fall madly in love with someone and then forget them a week later. All they can see is some image of themselves. Fucking roles."

One particular episode, when Kieran was about twenty, had left a mark on him. A young woman known for her imperial manner (her background was middle-class, but devoutly Catholic) had started going out with him. After a couple of months, she'd invited him to stay at her parents' house in Leeds for the weekend. When they got there, with no warning or apparent reason, she ditched him. He spent two days in a state of shock, feeling unable to leave. No one spoke to him. On Sunday, he went home alone on the train. She phoned all of their mutual friends and told vicious lies about him—Kieran never told me what exactly. The entire group froze him out. According to Kieran, "they needed someone to reject." One of them told me Kieran was immature. I thought he was naïve, but not frozen into childhood like they were.

That wasn't his longest or deepest relationship, of course. But it damaged the more important ones that followed. His series of bad jobs hurt him just as deeply. But then, the nineties are the first postwar decade in which working hard doesn't mean making a living. Changes in the employment laws mean that unless you've got the right background, the right voice, the right friends, then poverty is just a fact of life. Class has come back with a vengeance. The people hit by that generally blame themselves, of course. But round Olton everyone was blaming

Europe, or blaming immigrants. Poor fucking Brummies—the poverty of the North combined with the prejudices of the South. It's not all like that; but there are some districts—Acocks Green, Olton, Northfield—where the hatred of life is branded into the air like a skid mark on a pale sheet of tissue paper. At least there's a kind of truth about inner-city violence. Suburban misery is something else again. It's unreal. The smallness of it.

We used to meet up on Friday nights, go to the Westley Arms or the cinema in town. Sometimes Kieran's friend Steve, who played bass guitar on the pub circuit, would drive us out to one of the little villages strung on the main road to Warwick. There were usually a few of us, crammed into the car and singing along to one of Steve's compilation tapes. Too often, there was some bad news—a friend losing his job or getting robbed, a couple breaking up, a death—to be talked over and dissolved in alcohol. I used to feel it would be unlucky to miss one of these sessions, as if being there guaranteed the continuity of other things. It was a ritual, obviously. A communion of pints and talking and late-night balti and music and more talk. But if I had to say what it was about, I wouldn't say it was male bonding or machismo or any of that stuff. I'd say it was a fear of dying. Or of never having been alive.

Sometimes in midweek, Kieran would phone me up to say he had a new video. We'd drop into the off-licence and then go back to his flat to watch it. I'll always remember him in that room, lit only by the flickering screen. His intent, stubbled face, the slanted fringe of black hair. The posters on his walls, constantly working free of the Blu-tack. The little statues: aliens and religious icons. The dark crucifix. The battered electric guitar, rarely plugged in those days. But the video recorder was the chief occupant of the flat. Brand new films in blurred, pirated copies. Crackly old prints of *film noir* or German Expressionist classics. Inexplicable one-offs like *Eraserhead* or *The Tenant* or *Kanal*. Nothing was too disturbing for Kieran's taste. But increasingly, his real passion was for American road movies. *Easy Rider, Badlands, Thelma & Louise, Wild at Heart*. It was odd. For someone who didn't like travelling. He used to say everywhere was the same. But he adored those films. It made sense in a way.

Money was always the great worry for him. As a tenant, he'd never paid rates; so the poll tax and council tax fell dead on top of the rent. He kept hoping that sooner or later, the pieces of his income would all fit into place and he'd be out of debt. When the National Lottery started, he tried to conjure up winning lines out of serial numbers or ISBN codes on videos. By then, the repair work was drying up. Whenever he had any spare cash, it went on films or music or cheap brandy. He ate next to nothing and always wore the same few clothes: black sweaters or T-shirts, black jeans. When he started going out with a local girl called Theresa, in the spring of 1995, I used that as an excuse to see less of him. He was bringing me down. It sounds bad in retrospect, but you try being there.

I assumed he'd get his act together with Theresa's help. Whatever.

A typical incident from that phase of Kieran's life was the evening I went round to give back a Nirvana bootleg tape he'd lent me. Nobody answered the bell, though I could see the light was on. I rang three times. Then Kieran opened the door. He was a bit shaky and very pale. The flat smelt of alcohol.

"Sorry Dave," he said. "Been up late."

His voice was slow, childlike. His glasses were missing; I assumed he'd been asleep. Then I saw the empty frames on the table, and the pieces of shattered glass. "What happened? Are you ok?"

He nodded, looking confused. "It's all right," he said. "I don't want better eyesight, Dave. I want vision." Then he sat down on the couch and gazed at the TV, which was off. Something on the floor caught my eye: a glint of metal. I stepped towards it. Kieran didn't react. By the wall, in shadow, a few coiled lengths of steel wire. They seemed to flicker, like embers in burnt coal. I looked beyond them to where Kieran's guitar hung on the wall. Its neck was twisted, the face smashed open. "Did someone break in?" I asked. Stupidly.

Another time, Theresa phoned me to ask if I knew where Kieran was. He wasn't at home or at the garage. She was worried. "He's been really strange lately. Like he's seen a ghost. Or *not* seen a ghost when he was expecting one." He came back late the same night. Later, I found out where he'd been. He took me there.

From Olton to Acocks Green is a very brief train journey; but there aren't many trains these days. The Acocks Green station is on a long road lined with old trees. It was November. Rain had printed the outlines of leaves on the pavement. Branches waved their tatters of skin in the fragile light. Torn pages from a girlie magazine were scattered outside the wire fence of a primary school. A stray dog, or possibly a fox, emerged from behind a railway bridge and ran down a side road. Kieran walked in silence, glancing around as if trying to photograph the view in his head. I'd seen him like this before. In a group, it didn't stand out so much. Suddenly he turned and said to me, "You're the only person who could understand what I'm about to show you."

On the edge of Yardley, we came to a bridge over a canal. Kieran stopped and looked down through the trees to the black water. Dead leaves, bottles and cans floated on the surface. There was a steep slope down to the canal towpath on either side. From the trees lining the roadway to the cutting was not so much a steep slope as a drop. Just beyond the cutting, a derelict house stood in a narrow strip of wasteland. Years of exposure had stripped all the paint from the woodwork. The windows were boarded over. The door was open on a nest of darkness. There was no roof, only a few rotting beams framing the skyline. Kieran walked on. The next building was the local Baptist church, where a footpath led through to the cemetery. We stopped there, in a roughly circular clearing marked by several fir trees, with headstones and monuments all around. I noticed inscriptions dated as far back as the 1890s, and some stones that might have been older but were eroded to blankness.

Kieran wrapped his arms over his chest and stared at a white angel on a marble block. Its wings were beginning to flake way. He glanced suddenly through the forest of headstones, as if looking for someone who wasn't there. Then he turned to me. "I've been coming here since I was a kid," he said. "Ten, fifteen years. Nothing's changed. That house has been empty, just the same. The canal, the derelict house, the graveyard. Don't you get it? First you're born…" His eyes glinted. I touched his arm. He smiled emptily at me. "Do you know what it's like being in a house with two people who don't talk to each other? Who use you as an emissary, so they can go on moving apart? Until you're stretched between them, like a road that goes on forever? Why doesn't that fucking house fall down? Nothing ever changes." He walked away, rubbing his eyes viciously with the sleeve of his coat. I followed him. I couldn't think of anything to say. We passed the empty house to the line of bare trees above the cutting. Kieran stopped. Then, without looking back, he pushed his way through the trees and kept going.

He didn't reach the water. Part way down, he bounced off a hidden bit of rock and flew sideways into a tree stump. He lay still, curled on his side like a baby. From the road he seemed impossibly small. His mouth darkened with blood. I screamed helplessly. There didn't seem to be any safe way down. The road was empty. I ran to the nearest house that had a light on, knocked and asked to use their phone. Within a few minutes three paramedics had got him down onto the towpath. It took much longer to get him back to the street. Night fell as we drove to the hospital. It was very quiet in the small ambulance. Kieran was unconscious. I went to phone Steve, asked him to contact Kieran's parents or Theresa. When I came back, he was dead.

The next few days were a confused blur. I felt hopelessly tired and slow-witted. Quite a few of Kieran's friends were at the funeral. Nobody felt like organising a wake. There's something wrong about funerals. Watching a coffin go into a hole in the ground, like a dentist filling a cavity. And Kieran's parents trying to be polite to each other. That was the worst aspect of the whole business. I kept imagining some noisy, drunken funeral going on just out of earshot. Kieran's real friends welcoming him into their underworld. A few days later, the images started.

Always in poor light, like silhouettes folded into depth. And only when I was on my own. On street corners, in alleys, coming down staircases. A boy smashing a train window with his head, leaning out and laughing. Two silent women in a car, going over the edge of a ravine. A man with a flute, walking blindly around the same narrow tunnels. What I *actually* saw with my eyes, I couldn't tell you. They were only outlines, twisted like scraps of burnt celluloid. Black tinged with red. Cheekbones but no eyes. Gone before I could focus or reach out.

There were others that seemed more real. One night, I was passing by a city centre nightclub on my way to the bus. The street was empty. I saw a boy stagger through the doorway, take a few steps and collapse onto the pavement in a pool of light. His pale hands twitched violently. His mouth opened. The darkness of it spread across his face until there was nothing there. A few days later, I went back to the Acocks Green cemetery. The derelict house was unchanged, its door still half-open. I pushed the rain-soaked wood, felt it shift. Inside, a man was crouched on the floor, pushing a shotgun into his own mouth. A broken syringe lay by his feet. The room had been in darkness before I opened the door.

There was more. A lot more. But I tried not to remember. It would have been easy for me to cross-reference these ghosts. At Theresa's suggestion, most of Kieran's videos and tapes had been passed on to me. I'd hidden them away in the attic of the house where I was lodging. The one time I'd gone up there, I'd seen a young man with staring eyes slowly tying a rope to the top of a clothes rack. There was no one I could talk to. When the grief subsided, the images would surely go away. But it wasn't so easy. I began to lose my nerve: hiding in the flat on weekends, panicking whenever a car approached me in the street or a train went past.

Early in the New Year, I decided it had to end. The attic was unoccupied when I took down all of Kieran's stuff. Not strictly all—his family had kept the TV series and some of the commercial films—but I had the stuff that mattered. The offbeat stuff, the bootlegs. I packed it all into suitcases, and borrowed my dad's car to take them across town to the Sandwell Valley. I drove carefully, hoping the police wouldn't stop me for any reason. Kieran's collection was enough to get me jailed for possession alone.

It was getting dark as I stopped the car on the gravel track, just before the ground became too uneven for driving. Behind me was something that looked like a wartime shelter. In front, the trees thickened into a forest. Youngsters came here to fuck or take drugs. There was nobody in sight, though I could hear a dog barking some distance away. I decided to go into the trees, for cover. The ground was damp; the smell of decaying leaves was like unwashed human flesh. I dropped two suitcases in a small clearing, emptied them and went back for the rest.

When I returned to the clearing, he was there. Crouching by the pile of videos, hands outstretched. Blue denim jeans, short hair just a shade darker than blond. Intense eyes that fixed me through the still air. *I love you, and you don't pay me.* I spilt the remaining boxes onto the pile. He didn't move; he just flickered like a trapped frame on a screen. "Fuck off," I said. "Where were you when he needed you? It's too late." Now it was over, these fragments of myth still hung around, like stale food at the back of the fridge. I poured a can of lighter fluid over the boxes and lit a match. His face dissolved into the column of smoke.

This wasn't an act of censorship, I told myself. It wasn't the films themselves I was destroying, only Kieran's copies of them. Bootleg tapes. And bootleg ghosts. The heat exploded the plastic boxes, spreading ribbons of film like dried blood. Huge, complex ashes drifted in the heat, breaking where they touched the branches of trees. The smell of burning plastic made me feel giddy. I thought my mind was about to dry out and tear in half. Soon, there was only a black crust welded to the scorched ground. The leaf-mould was too damp to catch fire. I wiped my hands on a tree trunk and walked back to the car. I must have inhaled some fumes, because the chill took hours to leave me.

Kieran's not a legend. He doesn't live on in my dreams. But I miss him. Sometimes, these days, I see him in silhouette, staring at the TV screen from somewhere behind the wall. And it seems like the dead and the living are on opposite sides of a great pane of glass, trying to look through but only able to see their own reflections. Early this year, the house by the Baptist graveyard was demolished. The space had been boarded over. But anyone who wanted to could still jump through the trees into the cutting, into the cut.

For Chris and Linda Monk

THE DROWNED

To fall in love in a town like Worcester, you have to be on your way somewhere else. Preferably on motorbikes. There has to be a road in clear view, and a horizon that's either more rugged or more built-up. You have to be waiting to move on, see the unrest in each other's eyes, clasp in a fierce embrace, then share a narrow bed and leave together before sunrise.

But we didn't, of course. We tried to settle down and blend into the decaying woodwork. It was guaranteed to fail. The only time we went away together was pretty much a disaster. It taught us something about ourselves, but it wasn't knowledge we could use. That tends to be how it works most of the time. If you ever start to imagine that travel will drop existential truths into your lap, just remember that Jack Kerouac ended up an Oedipal wreck drinking himself to death in his mother's house. Which reminds me of one of Kevin's jokes: *My mother auditioned for a part in* Oedipus Rex.—*Jocasta?*—*No, she was crap.*

Worcester is a town surrounded by farms, which produces a certain insular mentality and a fear of city life. Kevin and I shared that, even though we consciously rejected it. It was always too much trouble to get out to Birmingham or Coventry. Instead, we both spent our teenage years sitting in pubs and putting the world to rights. I'd seen him a few times around the shopping malls and the library before we met in Worcester's only gay pub, one cold evening in January.

By then I'd left my parents' house and was living in a tiny flat near the Infirmary, where I was working as a hospital porter. I'd been through a few affairs, none of them as important as they'd seemed at the time. Kevin was different from the other men I'd met there. He was someone I could talk to about films and stuff—and though he was good-looking, he didn't need to be admired all the time. Also, he didn't want to sleep with me the first time we met. Which made me want to see him again.

We'd been going out together for a fortnight before he came back to my flat. It was a Friday night. We'd got caught in the rain leaving the pub, and our best weekend clothes were soaked. Kevin was shivering. I lit the gas fire and sat him in front of it, then dried his hair with a bath towel. Kevin's hair was deeply ambivalent: neither blond nor brown, neither straight nor curly. His eyes were blue in good light and grey in poor light, such as the light of a gas fire. I started to undress him, but he stopped me. That was when he told me he was HIV positive.

I was secretly impressed that his bloodstream carried an imprint of city life, the mark of someone not from around here. We talked for a long time. I didn't stop holding him, and eventually he began to relax in my arms. He told me he'd been infected a couple of years before, and was now on a course of prescribed vitamin and mineral supplements. They were training him for real drugs, he said. These days, AIDS was a serious chronic condition rather than a short cut to the crematorium.

When I started to undress him again, he didn't stop me. His body was pale and almost hairless. I wondered if he'd always been as thin as this. We were both a little uncertain about what was safe. Was it ok to kiss his cock, but not to suck it? Was it ok to rub together, but maybe not to let our cockheads touch? In a strange way, the restrictions made it more like how I'd imagined sex to be when I was going through puberty. And it was good—for both of us, I think.

He didn't tell me, and I never asked, how he'd contracted the virus. Over a period of time, I put the picture together from a number of things he said. A past relationship: a serious boyfriend who'd played the field. Maybe that explained the quiet rage I could sometimes feel burning through his touch. And the sensation I always had that he was looking through me at someone else.

I stayed at his flat a few times before he moved in with me. It was part of a converted house behind the racetrack. There were piles of books and magazines in every room, mostly Green and socialist stuff. He was never comfortable with fiction. His record collection was mostly vinyl, picked up from various second-hand shops around the town. His favourite singer was Richard Thompson, especially "Love in a Faithless Country." I was more of a Hüsker Dü and Nirvana kid, but I could appreciate the bitter lyrics.

There was always more going on with Kevin than was visible on the surface. I think he thought I was superficial because I tried to be direct about things. Not in public, of course: this was Worcester, after all, and telling our workmates or parents about us was out of the question. I got the impression that Kevin's parents were hard work at the best of times. A father who drank too much, a mother who prayed too much. Occasionally he'd drop hints about how painful his childhood had been. But when I told him he needed to rise above the way his parents had treated him, he became defensive: "You've got no right to criticise them. They were doing what they believed was right."

It wasn't in Kevin's nature to take a strong line on anything. Which was why he liked to mix with people whose opinions were direct and uncompromising, if not always well-informed. He took me along to SWP meetings on subjects like "Privatisation" and "Imperialism". I always felt vaguely patronised by his activist friends. And I could never get used to the way they used everyday conversation to reaffirm their convictions, as if they were in danger of forgetting what they believed. Also, I suspected that some of them disapproved of Kevin's sexuality but were trying to accept it as a matter of political principle. No doubt they'd had a meeting about it—*Queers: what we think.*

Underneath Kevin's idealistic statements about how "mankind" needed to wake up to the evils of capitalism and pollution, I always sensed a struggle against a very deep sense of futility. I could never have given him faith at that level, and I think he knew that. I tried to compensate by encouraging him to enjoy what was in front of him: films, music, nature, food, sex. I was very into him in a sensual kind of way. If I didn't really love him, it wasn't because I had someone else in mind.

One slightly strange thing that developed between us was that Kevin liked watching me swim and dive. He had a fear of water—not showers, but any body of water deep enough to drown in. As a result, he'd never learnt to swim. But he used to sit by the side of the swimming pools while I climbed onto the diving-board, flung myself into the water and got through most of a length without coming up for air. I liked swimming underwater: it made me less aware of where I was, the yelling kids in the shallow end and the tainted reek of chlorine. Afterwards, we'd rush home to make love.

In the summer of the year we were together, Kevin decided he was going to learn to swim. He had to start by persuading himself to get into water. I watched him sit at the shallow end of the pool for twenty minutes, shivering, before finally walking down the metal steps and across the hard floor. He looked as though he was trying to walk through fire. I showed him the movements for breast-stroke, but he wouldn't let his feet off the ground.

After half a dozen sessions, he was treading water uneasily and starting to move himself forward while floating. "Trust the water," I kept telling him. "Your body is lighter than water. Let yourself relax. You won't go under. It's instinct, like breathing." The smell of chlorine nauseated him; he couldn't eat for hours after visiting the pools. I didn't have the heart to tell him that the smell came from the reaction of chlorine with human piss.

By the end of July, Kevin could swim a width in the deep end. He still couldn't dive or jump in, and he refused to allow his head underwater. "If you think I'm getting this crap in my hair, you can think again." But after seeing the way he panicked when someone knocked into him and his face dipped below the surface, I knew there was more to it than vanity. He didn't want to see the world from within water. I liked that blurred, shimmering view: it made me feel at once free and contained. I wanted to make love to Kevin in a glowing Mediterranean bay.

But we couldn't afford to travel that far.

We got as far as Fleetwood, however, at the tail-end of that summer. I'd bought a second-hand car, and we booked a twin room in a cheap hotel overlooking the beach. Driving up from Worcester on a hot afternoon, the Charlatans' *Tellin' Stories* loud on the car stereo, I felt as though we were moving through a slow river of light and some inconceivable vision was just around the next bend.

That evening, we walked together along the coastline and listened to the gulls. Night fell quickly without streetlights to disguise it, and the unfinished moon was tinged with red. Kevin had said he wanted to swim in the sea; but when I suggested a moonlight dip without any clothes, he shook his head. "Too risky." I wasn't sure if he meant the undertow or the danger of being seen. A sudden wind brought cold air from the sea, and with it an odd, chemical smell. Kevin turned up the collar of his jacket and shivered. It was time to go back.

It felt odd to be sleeping in separate beds, even though we were side by side and our bodies were marked with each other's semen. I woke up before dawn and knew that Kevin was awake, but neither of us could speak. The steady rustling of the sea, like the crackle of static on an old radio, infiltrated the room. I felt as though we were being watched.

After breakfast, I stood on the hotel balcony and watched some kids heading out towards the beach. The sun was a flicker of white gold; the teenagers, boys and girls, were tanned and glowing with oil. Then I heard Kevin's voice at my shoulder. "John, do you know the difference between a visionary and a voyeur?"

I shrugged. "What is it?"

He pointed down at the cluster of youthful bodies. "Look. Sunflowers!"

That morning, we drove to Blackpool. We used the "driving south" part of my road atlas, a New Labour map in which everything was upside-down and left was right. The beach was too crowded, so we decided to investigate the Pleasure Beach fair. After winning a stuffed penguin in a shooting gallery, I watched Kevin obliterate a heart shape in a sheet of cardstock with a machine gun's pellets. He traced the outline with furious precision. "Where did you learn to shoot?" I asked him. He looked blank.

Then we tried the Revolution, a kind of panicky roller-coaster. You went up in a steep vertical curve, plunged back down to where you had started, then did the whole thing in reverse. "Evidently based on the Soviet model," Kevin remarked.

It was still bright and warm after lunch, when we took our towels and swimming suits down from the hotel to the beach at Fleetwood. It was an uneven shore of rocks and pebbles; the incoming tide had already covered the pale sand. A few couples were sunbathing on giant beach towels, and some children were paddling in the rock pools. We changed and walked down to the water's edge.

Kevin was silent. I could feel his tension from a distance.

Waves broke against my thighs, then against my belly and chest. I could feel the restless push of the incoming tide, the insistent drag of the undertow. The water was slightly murky. I could still make out that slight chemical odour from the night before. But I let the skinless muscles of the sea lift me and kiss my mouth with salt. I ducked below the surface and swam deeper, watching green trails of seaweed shift forward and back over the sand.

When I stood up again, barely in my depth, Kevin was beside me. I hadn't known he could swim so well. We groped each other under the water. "Take care," I said. "Don't go any further out."

"Just a little way," he said. "To that rock." He pointed to a small grey outcropping, only a dozen yards further out. We swam together. His arm movements were still a little wooden, but he had no trouble staying afloat. As we neared the rock, I slowed down to keep out of his way. Then something firm hit me in the face.

For a moment, I thought the water had turned into some kind of rubbery flesh. Then I realised I'd struck a floating object. Several more were bobbing on the surface around me. They looked pale. The chemical smell was much stronger now: ammonia, mixed with the sweetish odour of decay. They were fish. Dead fish, floating.

I reached down with my feet and couldn't touch the ground. A current had taken me past the rock, where Kevin was holding on and staring around him. In all directions, the water was swollen with the pale bodies of fish. As I trod water, hopelessly trying to avoid the creatures, Kevin closed his eyes and began to shake. Lifeless bodies drifted against my arms. They seemed warm, almost as if cooked. Their skin was pure white.

It took me a few minutes to reach Kevin. When I did, he'd withdrawn into himself. I couldn't make him respond or open his eyes. Instead, I held him until his arms dropped from his chest and his breathing slowed. The sun had clouded over, and the air was cooler. The rock we were clinging to was almost covered with water. "We've got to get back to shore," I said.

"They won't let us." His face was blank, as if he was sleeping. "They'll pull us under. Make us join them."

His fear affected me worse than anything else. But when the rock was completely covered by the incoming tide, I grabbed his hand and pulled him into the water. Half leading, half coaxing, I got him to swim through the bleached shoal of dead things until we stumbled on a bed of loose pebbles. As we emerged from the water, I saw that Kevin's lips were blue. I grabbed a towel and rubbed his shoulders with it, desperate to claim him for the land on which we knelt.

Two days later, we were back in our cramped flat. Kevin had some kind of breathing problem, and his hands were too shaky to hold a book. I wanted to take him to hospital, but he insisted on waiting until he could see his consultant. I lay awake listening to his ragged breathing, unwilling to touch him in case he was asleep. Within a fortnight he was in hospital anyway. I tried to prepare myself for the wasting away I'd seen in other people. But the drugs seemed to restore at least the appearance of health. A week later, he was home again.

Over the autumn, he stabilised on a combination of four or five different pills. The swimming was forgotten. He was back at work, but I could tell his confidence was shot. We were still making love almost every night—but I sensed he only valued the peace afterwards, the drowsy cuddle and the narcotised post-coital sleep. Our conversations became brittle and light, almost whimsical: the fear of depth had taken us both over. Kevin took up yoga, read children's books, became his own dreaming ghost.

I had searched through Lancashire and national newspapers for some mention of the shoal of dead fish that had trapped us. Nothing. Even Greenpeace had no record of it, and the woman at the end of the line I rang had no explanation to offer. I was left struggling with the absurd feeling that it had been a message of some kind. But weren't visions meant to inspire, not nullify?

When Kevin moved to Bromsgrove to become the manager of a health food shop, we agreed that we'd stay a couple. But within three months, it had all turned to dust. He told me he needed to get better at looking after himself. I met someone else and put him off until Kevin and I had discussed the future. As soon as it needed discussing, there was nothing to say. But we kept in touch.

I've not seen him in a year now. He knows I'd be there at once if he needed my help. For what it's worth. I don't think people can ever really save each other, but they can help each other to keep above the surface. This Christmas, Kevin sent me a card and a packet of sunflower seeds. I should have planted them, but I don't even have a window box, let alone a garden. So I baked them in a cake.

RESERVOIR

Men in prison come out with strange things sometimes. You can get to know your cellmate better than you know anyone on the outside. And in the long, hot nights, when you need something to distract you from the sound of desperate men screwing in the next cell and the weird, echoing song of your own loneliness, there's nothing to do except talk, and nothing to talk about except women.

When I was at Winson Green, for a few months I shared a cell with a guy named Fallon. Like me, he was a local boy. He'd lived in the district where I went to school, not far from the prison. I'd gone on school cross-country runs around Edgbaston Reservoir; he'd dropped an informer off the bridge there. That was the only red light district left in Birmingham, and he and I swapped a few stories of girls we'd had in those crumbling tenement houses. One night, when we'd both necked a few pills and couldn't sleep, he told me about the one he'd killed.

"It was in Gillott Road," he said quietly, "about three years ago. I was with the Forbes gang and we'd just done a warehouse in the jewellery quarter. So there I was, coked up and looking for something only money could buy. A mate had tipped me off about this place, said it was a pretty relaxed establishment. It was run by some posh woman who'd fallen on hard times, had an accent like broken china. I told her I was looking for a girl who didn't mind if I played rough.

"She sent me up to the top floor, no carpet on the stairs. No sound from the other rooms. For all I knew I was the only guy there. I'd been told to find room 14 and wait for Lena, so I walked through the door and waited. Usual shitty furniture, could have been a student's room. Then this thin, red-haired woman came in. Greek, Turkish, something like that. She didn't look like much until she smiled, and I could see she was pretty under all the make-up. No older than thirty. I said I wanted it all. She looked hard at me, then nodded.

"I wasn't trying to do real damage, just a few bruises. Money I paid her would have got me a night with any escort in Birmingham. Then I was getting near the end, and I put my hands round her throat. She went quiet and just looked at me. I couldn't help myself, I choked her pretty hard. She was getting off on it too. But then I heard her neck break." Fallon paused. His breath was loud in the cell. "Just a thing, a thing that had never been alive. I've killed before, but not like that. It did something to me. I got the fuck out of there as fast as I could. Forensic on the bed, I left traces, didn't care.

"The next few days, I was certain the police were going to come for me. Didn't even bother trying to get away. Fingerprints, DNA, they'd have me. But they never came. I thought the madam had covered it up to keep herself out of trouble. I never went with a hooker again after that.

"A few months later, I heard this story. It was going round the local pubs that there was a tart on Gillott Road who'd let you kill her. I mean almost. She had some weird thing with her neck, her breathing, she could fake death. And nobody ever came back to check. Nice little earner. Everyone was saying they knew someone who'd been with her. I kept my mouth shut. She was turning cold. Her lips were blue. I know death when I cause it."

I'd been out of prison a month when I started going to Edgbaston. It was hard sitting in pubs, having people behind you when you couldn't see them properly. The level of noise made me panic. And I was never much good at chatting up women. So it had to be the street girls. But I didn't have much ready money, as I was trying to stay out of trouble for the time being. When I could afford it I looked for the girls waiting at bus stops or outside pubs. They were the cheapest ones.

Sometimes I just walked around there, remembering my time at the old school in City Road. How much simpler life had been in those days, when a stolen packet of fags, a hasty French kiss or a porn magazine was enough to keep you going through the week. We'd talked about getting rich, getting famous, cracking the system open like a safe. Where were they all now? I lingered outside the school gates, remembering, hoping no one took me for a dirty old man. Virgins had never been my thing anyway. Not that there were many in the school, judging by the graffiti on the walls. U SAY U WAS RAPED COS U CANT GET THE MANZ. I had those words in my head for weeks.

One morning I walked around the reservoir, smoking filthy roll-ups and thinking about the school cross-country runs. Our football boots clattering on the gravel path. Willow trees stained grey by factory smoke, weeping their leaves into the black water. Dragonflies jittering above the long grass. I did well on those runs, because my slight build gave me an advantage over the muscle-bound thugs who could write me off on the pitch. I was always one for the distance.

On the far side, the place where the heavy mob slowed down to a breathless stroll, a long bridge crossed the water just inside the dam. You could see over the wall to the factories and rubbish tips of Smethwick. Out here, the water was deep; it glinted blue and silver, the reflections of tower blocks corroding faster than the buildings themselves. I thought of Fallon and his victim, which made me think of the mysterious redhead.

About a year later, I got lucky. Helped a friend to break into a student house in Balsall Heath, found ten grand's worth of Leb. Felt a bit sad to see a promising small business go up in smoke. I decided to try and find her. There was no word of any Lena in Gillott Road, but nobody stayed there for long anyway. That was why it was a red light district: there weren't enough permanent residents to make trouble. Most of the area was old family houses, converted into tenements. The only new housing was an estate of red-brick prefabs that looked like cockroach traps.

Three months and I'd got nowhere. The money was running out. Then I met a girl in a Bearwood sauna who said there was a skinny redhead, about thirty, living out on Reservoir Road. She shared a house with two other working girls. "Sort of foreign type, Albanian or something. Calls herself Magda. Go along there at night, you'll find it. You want to watch yourself though, some pretty dodgy blokes go there." I said I'd happily watch myself if they had a camera. "You're mad," she said in a tone of no special concern.

Some prostitutes work the days, others the nights. I had a feeling Magda would be the latter kind. I caught the last bus out along the Hagley Road and walked past the reservoir, avoiding the girls who were shivering in doorways. A police car drove past and I kept walking steadily, as if I had a legitimate reason to be there. At the top of Reservoir Road, I lit a cigarette and glanced at both sides. Terraced houses, shops, no lights on. I walked down the left-hand side, enjoying the sense of being alone. Then I saw a house across the road with its upper window lit. A pale face was watching me from the window. I finished my cigarette, then crossed the road.

The woman who opened the door was conventionally dressed in a blouse and long skirt. Her hair was dyed an autumnal shade of red. Her Mediterranean background showed more in her bone structure than in her skin, which was quite pale. "Come in," she said. The hallway was poorly lit, and smelt of damp. "I'm on my own here tonight. The other two girls are on holiday, together." She led me up the creaking stairs to her room.

The single bed was freshly made up. Perhaps I was the first client she'd had that night. She drew the curtains, switched on a red bedside lamp and turned out the main light. "So," she said. "What do you want?" I couldn't place her accent, except to say that it was foreign.

"I want it all," I said.

She looked into my eyes for a few seconds, then smiled. "So does everyone. But they can never get it. Perhaps you will."

I reached into my left sock for the money I didn't dare keep in my wallet. She asked me for five hundred; I paid it. Then she undressed. I could see faded bruises on her thin arms and over her ribs. I didn't want to hurt her, only to take her life.

We made love twice. The first time I just wanted to hold her, to savour her, as if we were lovers. I had never felt such tenderness towards anyone. Her eyes were sad, but her face was calm, and there was a playful smile on her mouth as I kissed her. The second time, I put my hands around her throat. When she didn't try to stop me, I gripped tighter. It felt as though there had never been anything but the two of us, naked on the cheap cotton sheets, as close as life is to death. I pressed my thumbs into her throat until I felt the tension leave her body. The room was very quiet. I could see a white trace in the air between us: her last breath.

I held her as our sweat dried and her warmth escaped into the cold room. A car went past outside, the changing pitch of its engine marking seconds that were no longer part of time. I felt destroyed and redeemed at once. Magda's eyes were open, reflecting the red lamplight; I closed them with a fingertip. Then I pulled away and cleaned myself up. I went to the washbasin, soaked a flannel in cold water and washed her still body. Then I sat on the edge of the bed and waited.

An hour went past. Then another. Her lips and fingers were turning blue. I could see the muscles beginning to stiffen, the skin losing its resilience. If she didn't come back, I would sit with her until I was found. I felt physically tired, more tired than I had ever been, but I didn't want to sleep. After a while I went to her dressing-table, found a brush and, very carefully, brushed her long auburn hair.

The darkness behind the curtains began to melt into a grey dawn. I could hear birds singing from the reservoir, and the sounds of traffic going past. I stirred, and cramp gripped my left leg. I struggled to stand up, then leant on the bed to get my balance. Magda's eyes opened, and she turned her head towards me. "Why are you still here?" she said.

That was it. I hadn't been afraid up till then. But her voice opened something that screamed inside me, and I put my hands over my eyes. Stumbling like a drunk woken up by angry bar staff, I threw myself through the doorway and down the narrow staircase. The front door wouldn't open; I fumbled with the bolt, terrified that she would follow me down the stairs. The thought of her hands on me almost made me lose control. Then the door was open, and I was out on the street.

Nothing much has changed. I'm still a villain, though if they catch me again I may try to give it up. I'm getting too old for prison. And I don't go with prostitutes anymore, because I don't like what they make me feel about myself. I go to pubs, drink myself empty, then walk home gazing at the stars. The stars never change. Once in a blue moon I meet a woman who'll share my bed for the night. It doesn't set my world alight, but it helps.

Every night, I think about her. Where she's living now, what might be happening to her. Nearly all of the time I think of her as a kind of freak: a mutant, perhaps even an alien creature, trying to fit in as best she could. Using her different nature to make her way in the world. Trying to belong.

It's easier to believe that than to think that she might have lived in this world before, and come back to redeem herself. And it was fucked up, she got it wrong again. She used her power of resurrection in a way that didn't help anything.

She wouldn't be the first.

AN UNKNOWN PAST

People occasionally still ask me why I gave up singing. I just say I lost my voice. If I know them well enough, I say it was the drugs. The drugs were part of it, but the true reason is something I've never wanted to explain. I'm not even sure that I can. But I'll give it a try.

It was back in 1990, when The Chosen Few were just starting to take off. That first album hadn't sold particularly well, but it had a kind of cult following in the fanzines and the more indie corners of the music press. The *NME* said we were the new Cure, but we felt more like the new disease. We were broke, living in bedsits, piecing together new tracks on cheap equipment. Of course, we were in the wrong place. Birmingham's a heavy metal city; it's not kind to Goths. We should have moved to Leeds.

But when we got the advance on the second album, we all got a bit greedy for a while. Delayed capitalism. Peter bought a red Jaguar, Mike bought three new guitars, Dave went to Amsterdam for a fortnight. And I bought a flat in the south part of Moseley. Got all my records and books out on shelves, new posters on the walls, new stereo with a speaker in every room. I started calling myself a musician.

At the back of my mind, there was always a kind of doubt. Stuff we'd come up with on lonely nights, keeping warm over a shared joint, was being talked about as "work." I didn't know where the music came from, but I knew we couldn't sit in an office and plan it to meet a production target. I was afraid of losing the voice, or the meaning. That fear probably had a lot to do with the way things started to change.

It was early November. The first tissue-thin coatings of frost appeared on the roads. I'd just split up with my girlfriend and was staying home a lot, drinking and listening to morbid records. My flat was lit with floor lamps, so I always had darkness overhead. I tried to drown Sakina's image in the voices of women like Nico and Patti Smith: singers who were intimately present in their songs, yet somehow mysterious and remote.

Not long after I moved in, I woke up in the middle of the night to find myself crouching by the window, naked, shivering violently. For a few minutes I couldn't seem to move. Then I felt my way back to bed and lay there unsleeping until dawn. It happened a few more times: I'd wake up away from my bed, or even in the bathroom, and become kind of trapped. The worst thing was a feeling that if anyone had been there, I couldn't have called for help.

I invited Sakina round for lunch, in the hope of getting her back. But the flat put her on edge: she said it was gloomy and smelt of damp. "Did you get it cleaned properly before you moved in?" She relaxed after a couple of glasses of wine, and I played her a couple of the band's recent demo tapes. But when I tried to kiss her, she backed off: "Don't, I'm coming down with something. My throat feels raw."

That weekend, I met a girl at the Moseley Arms and brought her back. We sat up all night, smoking heroin. She showed me how to melt the powder on tinfoil over a lighter, then suck up the pale wisps of smoke through a rolled-up tenner. We had sex in a kind of blurred, stumbling dream. Time seemed to flake apart, so that every moment hung in the air and could be seen, heard, felt over again a few minutes later.

I woke up in the afternoon to find that she'd gone and I'd thrown up over the bed. The smell of vomit hung around for weeks. But having finally tried the drug helped me to appreciate the sombre dream-world of Nico's songs. I'd seen her on stage in 1984, playing with a bunch of inept chancers who fucked up half the songs. Apparently her drug habits were so bad she couldn't get real musicians to tour with her. She seemed lost, terrified, yet still majestic in her ability to create a different world with her voice. I went home drunk and scribbled an adolescent poem about her that ended with the lines:

we are frightened to find you alive
with this voice that blows out our torches
these hands that break the moon's neck

After her death, the keyboard player of that hapless backing group wrote a snide, mocking book about her last years. He didn't give a fuck about her songs, her music or the complex tragedy of her life: he just thought it was funny that he'd seen her concealing smack inside herself before going through a border checkpoint. I wanted to find him and work on his face with a hammer for a couple of hours.

Listening to *The Marble Index* with every speaker in the flat connected, so that the music became the building, I wondered where lost voices went to. Did the sound fall away into nothing? Or did it echo permanently in space, waiting for the correct recording device to bring it back? I thought of Nico's death, the fall that broke her skull. And the oddly similar death of Sandy Denny, a mysterious voice at the sacred heart of folk music. And how Linda Thompson was still alive, but her voice had withered and died while Richard's had grown stronger. Perhaps they'd only ever had one voice between them.

I told the guys in The Chosen Few that I was working on new material. In reality, all I was doing was playing Nico's songs and trying to find a way into her world. I saw glimpses of European decay and American glamour: ruined buildings, armed police guards, trains in the night, silver aeroplanes, the Hudson Bridge, the ghostly face of Andy Warhol.

But it was my knowledge, my imagination supplying these images. What I saw in my dreams was much closer to home. A thin girl, her dark eyes trapped in the mirror, tying a scarf around her upper arm to make the veins stand out. The same girl trapped in the flat like a moth in a lampshade, beating helplessly against the walls. The crash of breaking glass; a rain of pale, gleaming fragments. White powder dissolving in a trickle of blood. I couldn't make sense of it.

A strange girl's face and body. A dead singer's voice. Crumbs of frost on the window. Grains of salt on the kitchen table. Which shoulder were you supposed to throw them over? Peter and Dave came to see me one evening and were shocked at the state of the flat. I said I'd been ill and hadn't felt like tidying up. Dave said, "Are you the only one living here?" In that moment, I began to understand.

One evening, the flat's pull on me became so overwhelming I just had to get out. I felt like a prisoner in a cell. Someone was trying to reach me, but it might take her forever to get through. I had to pretend I was taking out the rubbish just to get through the door. It was snowing: hard flakes like tiny razor blades swirled out of the darkness overhead and melted in the streetlight. I wished I'd thought to put on a jacket. After a few minutes, I began to shake. My breath felt liquid. Probably the onset of flu, I thought as I took refuge in the nearest pub.

At once, the sound of a teenage male voice stumbling through "Two Out of Three Ain't Bad" almost made me turn around and head back. I hate karaoke with a passion. But I was so shaky by then that I bought a double Scotch and slumped against the wall, struggling not to pass out. When my head began to clear, the cheap sentiment of the music was vaguely reassuring. Maybe all karaoke fans are ill in some part of themselves, and need comfort.

Then a tall, dark-haired woman stepped up to the microphone. As she waited to sing, the opening chords chimed and vibrated fiercely: John Cale's electric viola. The screen was blank, but I knew the song at once. "All Tomorrow's Parties." One of the songs her backing group had ruined. But this was the Velvet Underground version, heavily rhythmic and nervously atonal at once. I felt the darkness at the core of the song shudder through me, and pressed the cold glass against my cheek. Then the rhythm softened, the light grew stronger, and the dark-haired woman was singing an Abba song. "Fernando," if memory serves me.

In mid-December, we played a gig at the Foundry. The audience reacted well to the songs from our album, but the new material we were planning to record left them cold. It was my first taste of the innate conservatism of audiences. Peter and I decided to change the set list, dropping two new songs and playing an adolescent love song that local followers of the band would remember from our earliest gigs. It got more applause than anything else that night.

Then, with no other material to hand, we tried out a cover version we'd just started rehearsing: Nico's "One More Chance." It was the song that had worked best when I'd seen her, and it offered plenty of dynamics for the band to get their teeth into. But something went wrong. At the start of the last verse, the microphone went dead and the vocal disappeared. I'm sure the rest of the band thought I'd forgotten the words.

Afterwards, we got drunk on cheap vodka and started chatting up a bunch of Goth babes who'd come from Redditch to see us. We finished the rider together and had a long, serious talk about the respective merits of the Sisters of Mercy and Fields of the Nephilim. After a while, it became clear that they didn't want to go home. I left the rest of the band, who all had girlfriends, to make their own decisions and took one of them back with me in a black cab. Her name was Karen.

In a ritual that I was getting used to by now, we chased the dragon together. Then we went to bed, but were too stoned to fuck. Karen passed out in my arms. I put her down on her side, so she wouldn't choke if she threw up. Then I lay back and stared into the shadows of the high ceiling. An impulse gradually took shape in my numbed mind. I wrapped a glass in a handkerchief and smashed it against the wall. Then I picked up a handful of glass shards and pressed them into the hollow of my throat. Blood trickled between my fingers, warm and sticky.

At last, she had reached me. I understood her message now. There were no words in it. Its meaning was need. Slowly, I reached down to the foil packet of heroin. We'd only used half of it. I licked my finger and put a few grains on my tongue. Then, using a lighter and a rolled-up banknote, I smoked the rest. But I didn't get any higher. Indeed, I hardly felt the effect of what I'd already taken. The need wasn't mine.

I had to go all the way to Glasgow to find him. Several hours on a train plagued by electrical problems, feeling worse with every mile of distance from the flat. My hands were shaking too badly to drink coffee. It was early January; grey handfuls of sleet were rattling the windows, a jittery Cale percussion to which my empty head supplied the vocal.

Patrick lived in one of the "schemes" or estates on the edge of the city. A loose collection of tower blocks on a floor of concrete, with nothing visible between them except the pale sky. I felt terrified by the lack of shelter. Not the people, who couldn't be any more desperate than me, but the limitless hunger of space.

After several map-reading errors, I found the block where he lived. I'd already phoned him from Glasgow Central Station. We'd been no more than acquaintances in the Moseley pub-rock scene, but he'd not seemed very surprised to hear from me. Maybe he'd been waiting for an opportunity to talk.

His new flat looked rather like the Moseley flat when I'd first seen it. That wasn't surprising: it had had all his stuff in it then. He shook my hand. "It's good to see you. Coffee? Whisky? I've nothin stronger."

"No thanks." I sat down on his black leather sofa and looked at him. He'd put on some weight since moving back to Glasgow, trimmed his beard. He still looked rough, but in a hard way rather than a manic way. He looked like he was at home. "She's still there," I said.

He rubbed his face, then leant back. "I'm sorry. I really thought it was just me. My guilt."

"What was her name?"

"She went back to Germany. Still alive, for all I know. Christa. Like that Velvet Underground singer, you know, the one who went mad. Nico, that's it. Her real name was Christa. I think my Christa wanted to become her. Used to drive me mad, playin her records."

"Nico? Wasn't she in *La Dolce Vita*? Didn't know she was a singer as well." Patrick looked at me, trying to establish whether I was taking the piss. "So what happened to her?"

"She fell off a bicycle in Ibiza and died of a fractured skull." He caught the look in my eye and raised his hands. "Hey, you started it. Just relax and I'll tell you."

He lit a cigarette, offered me the packet. I shook my head. "We met in Birmingham," he said. "She was nineteen, workin behind the bar at Edwards No. 8. Wanted to be a singer. She liked The Chosen Few, saw you a few times. I think she fancied you. But I'm kind of a jealous guy, so she never talked to you. She might have got somewhere as a singer, if she'd found a good band. Her lyrics were really... I don't know, just weird. All about the afterworld, spirits livin underground, the darkness eatin people's souls. Didn't reckon much to it myself. But she was too fucked up on drugs to get a career together.

"She was into smack long before I met her. It went with the Nico thing, the whole child of despair business. I've tried it, done a wee bit of everything, but it's not for me. I've seen it destroy too many people. Strong people, it rotted them from the inside. Christa wasnae strong. Heroin ate her for breakfast." He paused, blowing pale smoke. A coil of it hung around his face.

"It took over everything. She didnae want to go out anymore, not even to gigs.

Just sat in the bedroom listenin to fuckin Nico. Went from smokin to injectin an all. Soon I wasnae just feedin both of us, I was feedin her fuckin habit as well. Then she decided to deal the stuff. I could see the police tearin the flat apart. Told her I'd cut her hands off if she started. But she was desperate. I didnae know what she was goin to do next. Neither did she.

"So I came up with a plan. You might think it was a terrible thing to do. You weren't there. I tied her to the radiator, like Terry Waite. Gagged her so she couldnae scream for help. For nine days I fed her, washed her, made sure she was ok. Every day I untied her so she could walk around while I stood with my back to the bedroom door. We didnae have sex. I slept on the couch in the livin room. Told her she could have me and her freedom back when she was straight. I wasnae even sure what that meant.

"The first few days, she was a mess. The hatred in her eyes made me want to kill myself. Or kill her, so she wouldnae feel that way anymore. Then her body started to settle down, the withdrawal started to wear off. I wasnae sure when to let her go. I had this kind of romantic plan of cookin her a meal, takin her to bed, showin her the life she'd be missin if she went back on junk.

"So I took off the gag, and we talked. She wasnae tryin to plead and bargain anymore. She said she wanted to be with me. A week earlier she'd been callin me a maggot-ridden, crawlin piece of shit. But now she said I'd been right. We were goin to live again. I cooked a really nice meal for us both, brought her a glass of wine in the bedroom. In front of my eyes, she smashed it against the wall and rammed the broken glass into her throat."

He touched the soft spot just above the collarbone. "I used to kiss her there. The glass went through into her voice-box. She never spoke again. I phoned an ambulance. They saved her life, but they couldnae save her voice. All she had left was a kind of mewin sound, like she was bein fucked. I told her I'd look after her, but she didnae want to know me. Her mother came over from Germany and took her back there.

"After she'd gone I had nightmares about her. The needles, the broken glass, the blood. And the hunger for smack. I knew if I didnae get out, I'd become an addict too. There was no other way to make her stop. Because she didnae have a voice, the only way she could talk to me was through the drug. And the pictures in my mind. And Nico's songs. Which I'd always fuckin hated anyway."

He stubbed out the cigarette. We sat in silence for a few minutes. Then I stood up. "Cheers," I said. "I don't know whether to shake your hand or smash your face in."

He smiled. "Do you want to get out of here alive?"

Maybe I should have gone to Germany and tried to find her. The mute, bitter remnant of a teenage Goth. I tried to recall her face from the band's early gigs, but wasn't sure. She was probably dead in any case. Maybe I should have given up drugs and put all my energy into making The Chosen Few something like their name. What I should not have done was, inevitably, what I did. Stay in the flat.

It wasn't because of Christa. At least, not the Christa who'd stabbed herself in the throat in the flat I'd bought a few months later. I stayed for the other Christa. For Nico. For the three women I'd loved since I was a shy, obsessed teenager. The thin, blonde woman who'd emerged like a sardonic angel from the ruins of Germany. The melancholic, dark-haired singer who'd created a mysterious other Europe with her voice. And the bitter, exhausted woman who'd summoned up precious fragments of grace on a stage that reeked of beer and defeat.

I fixed myself up with a few good, dependable suppliers. Got a friend to show me how to inject, what precautions to take. And I tracked down virtually every Nico recording in existence: bootlegs, studio out-takes, live albums made for release in Japan and Russia. I filled the dusty, mouldering flat with the stink of heroin and the cries of a dead addict.

The Chosen Few had to fulfill their contract, so I sleepwalked through a month of recording sessions at Moseley Shoals. The second album sank without a trace. Critics said it was just a pale imitation of the Velvet Underground. A few no-mark Goths loved it like nothing else. I didn't care anymore. We stopped playing live, then drifted apart.

I spent nearly ten years playing host to Nico. I cooked for her, poured wine for her, played her records until they wore out and I had to replace them. Night after night, I walked down into the underground cavern where the lost voices dwelt. But I couldn't find her. Nico was a fiction, the dream of a traumatised and brilliant woman named Christa Paffgen. She was pure spirit. And I failed to reach her, just as the girl who'd been kept a prisoner in this flat had failed to reach her.

That's why I didn't go back to singing. When I quit the drugs, got my voice and my guitar-playing ability back, I still knew that I had failed. Deep down, I didn't have what it took to make the dead live again. When Orpheus came back from the underworld, he made the comeback album to end them all. Then he turned gay. I didn't do either of those things. I just wanted to leave it all behind.

YOU COULD HAVE IT ALL

The last time I saw Paul Wyken, he was neither alive nor dead. They'd dressed him and put him in a wheelchair to receive visitors, but it was a pointless exercise, like trying to light candles underwater. His only movement was a slight trembling in his hands, which were lifted just above the arms of the chair. His face was a mask that had been left in a garage and warped by the damp. My first, idiotic thought on seeing him was *You don't look well.*

I talked to Paul for a few minutes. He didn't seem to respond. There was no message in his eyes. His lips trembled faintly with breath. I told him about friends who'd asked after him, might be coming to see him. Then I began to wonder if reminding him of life was hurtful. Perhaps he needed to accept this stillness, not try to think beyond it. I didn't know. I'd seen him asleep and I'd seen him comatose from drink; he'd never looked like this. It was like watching him turn to stone.

We sat for a while, but my silence was only an imitation of his. Eventually I stood up and grasped his hand. It felt cold, despite the warmth of the hospital. "Take care," I said. "I'll come and see you tomorrow. You'll feel better soon." We always say things like that to people who are dying. It's not really a lie: it's an act of faith. But maybe faith is a lie. Paul would have said it was.

I spent the evening on my own, drinking and trying to remember the only night I'd spent with Paul. It was early in our friendship, and luckily neither of us expected anything to come of it. We'd both gone to a party at some time in the mid-eighties. The house was full of young executives head-banging to Iron Maiden. We'd escaped to the garden and ended up kissing in the winter moonlight, dazed by cheap wine and the need to belong to something. Around midnight we'd caught a taxi back to my rented flat. Paul had been chasing a girl at the party, but then he was notoriously fickle. And booze makes people gravitate to their own sex.

I remember how pale his skin was, the hairs on his chest a light corona of red. He seemed to want something he couldn't express. As we kissed, he stroked

181

my hair and throat. He was embarrassed when I noticed the scars on his arms. During the night, I woke up and saw him watching me; I'd forgotten to draw the curtain, and the yellow streetlight turned the bedroom into an alley.

I went back to the hospital the next day. The staff nurse told me Paul had died around seven o'clock that morning. Another stroke. "He was never a morning person," I said. She nodded, unsure whether I was joking. I glanced at the empty bed and felt a guilty stab of relief. This kind of death was easier to accept.

Paul Wyken's death was hardly a shock to anyone who'd known him in recent years. But many of his readers saw him only as the passionate, tender young man who'd written *City of Ghosts* and *Like Drowning*. Or when they thought about his books, they remembered themselves at that time. Whatever the reason, his death infected the literary world with a brief Wyken fever. Features on his work appeared in all the serious newspapers. The BBC commissioned a three-part adaptation of his last novel, *Beneath the Ice*. His shadow became a celebrity.

But all of that happened weeks, months after Paul's death. His funeral was a muted, conventional affair that he'd clearly had no hand in planning. There were a couple of dozen people there: his half-sister, his niece, his agent, a number of local writers and editors, a few of his drinking buddies and a vaguely familiar man who might have been his drug dealer. The music at the committal was something from Enya's *Call Centre Classics* that his half-sister probably chose because she knew Paul liked folk music.

Within a few days of the funeral, I had a call from Paul's agent. It was a strange, dislocated conversation. Did I know that Paul had named me as his literary executor? No. Was I willing to take on that responsibility? Yes, ok. Had Paul finished *The Wasted Streets*, the novel he'd been writing for the last six years? Not to my knowledge. Would I be willing to edit and, if necessary, complete the manuscript? I wasn't sure.

Paul's death made me feel less human than I had been. The way he'd been slowly taking himself apart had gnawed at me for years. And now this loser of an agent, whom Paul had badmouthed to me any number of times, wanted the absence of me to collaborate with the absence of him. It made no sense. But I agreed to look at the unfinished novel and see what could be done. Paul's solicitor would lend me the keys to his house. I could take away whatever books or papers I needed.

Of course, you already know that it didn't happen. Some people have blamed me for that. If you're one of them, please try and understand that I went into the project not only with positive hopes, but with good intentions. Paul had mentioned the book to me several times, but never described it clearly. He'd always intended to finish it. I saw *The Wasted Streets* as his final message, the words his stroke had silenced. Even if no one read them, it was still necessary to put them out there. It was like scattering his ashes. Or like the task I'd performed for him that night in my rented room, his cries merging with the rhythm of traffic in the narrow street.

Paul and I were friends for almost twenty years. When we met, he was already well known as the author of *City of Ghosts*. I expected a quiet, dreamy, almost spectral young man. In reality he was a fierce little bastard, at war with every norm and convention the Thatcher years had to offer. His inner self was protected by walls of sarcasm and defiance, ringed by a moat of alcohol that grew wider as the years passed.

He always lived alone. I was initially surprised at the roughness of his private life: sudden pickups and ill-judged liaisons, a chain of women and men who never seemed to ease the hunger inside him. He used to mock my dreams of settling down with some nice Celtic boyfriend. "The family is an ideological state apparatus," he said. "It's a prison we carry in our heads."

We used to get drunk together, go and see late-night films at the Triangle or local bands in the city centre pubs. While he was hard to impress—very little struck him as either original or authentic—he was always able to lose himself in the moment, swaying open-mouthed as the music played or staring like a child at the screen. Like sex, it was something he could escape into. And Heaven help anyone within several yards of him who started talking during a film or a band's performance. He was small, but you wouldn't take him on.

Paul's literary reputation declined in the nineties. He was writing less, and his work was considered weaker. The politics had become more overt, the vision less generous. *Beneath the Ice* was largely ignored by the reviewers. Its closing image—the skating couple on the reservoir completing their dance and falling through the ice together—was an apt summary of the book's commercial performance.

It didn't help that by then, Paul had become a liability as far as public readings and interviews went. Scruffy and pissed, he seemed to concentrate his mental energy on projecting bad vibes. For the detached observer, the results could be hilarious. I remember the last time he appeared at a literary festival, on a panel of Midlands authors chaired by a West Midland Arts director. Invited to comment on the changes in regional writing over the last two decades, he declared: "The Midlands literary community is quite incestuous."

"In what sense?" the chairman asked, intrigued.

"In the sense that that they have sexual intercourse with their parents."

One of his trademark gestures at public readings was to conclude by throwing the book to the ground and leaving it there. In the early years, his fans would pounce on the discarded copies. Later on, no one bothered.

Much of his published writing in the last five years of his life was political journalism. He wrote a regular opinion column for the *Morning Star*, though he'd left the Communist Party in the mid-eighties. I still have his article "The Liberal Faith," pinned to my wall. I'd heard many earlier versions of it over a pub or balti house table, whenever Paul got onto the subject of "the Radio 4 mentality." I can still hear his slightly nasal Birmingham accent as I read the words: *The trouble with the reformist, gradualist model of social evolution is that it sounds wonderful in theory, but always fails in practice. Liberals go through life bent double with woe, wringing their hands, intoning "When will we learn?" They are unable to face the truth that there is no "we," no "mankind" at the controls. The ruling class acts only in its own interests. It chooses war, racism and inequality, not because "mankind" is incapable of learning, but because war, racism and inequality are good for business.*

As the nineties limped to a close under a Labour government more right-wing than the Tory government it had displaced, Paul seemed to give up. The drinking had become relentless, and other drugs were joining it at the table. Most of them were prescribed: sedatives, antidepressants, tranks. By the time he realised the medication was itself a problem, there was no way out. Life had become a chemical imbalance. "You're better off with whatever you can buy in a Moseley pub toilet at closing time," he remarked to me after hunting through his backpack for six different pill bottles.

I once saw a Michael Leunig cartoon of a man walking along with an umbrella on a sunny day. Rain was falling on him from the inside of the umbrella. It's funny how, when Paul would never let anyone abuse him or control him, he let alcohol do both. He said it helped him cope. But with what? With the consequences of his drinking. I got fed up with it, to be honest. I was tired of being the only one who understood. Why couldn't I not understand for a change?

My anger cracked open on a rainy Wednesday evening in 2002, when Paul phoned me to ask if I wanted to join him for a "session." My head was full of the kind of optimistic, creative thoughts I could have shared with him in happier days. "Not tonight," I said. "If we arrange to meet in the pub, I'll arrive to find that you've already been there for hours. I'll spend the evening trying to keep you out of trouble, while you get more and more fucked. I'll end up trying to decipher your incoherent expression of some personal secret you've forgotten the words for, which is just as well since I don't want to hear it. I'll guide you to the bus and try to pretend that your kissing me goodbye isn't putting us both in danger.

"Then I'll go home and wait a couple of hours for you to call from some bus station in the middle of nowhere. To say that you've just woken up in someone else's vomit after being thrown off the bus miles beyond your stop, and you need me to check my A–Z and tell you where the fuck you are. If that's the plan as usual, can't we have a night off instead?"

Paul chuckled. "That's good. You should write it up, put it in a comedy sketch. After you've FUCKED OFF AND DIED, that is."

But it was Paul who fucked off and died. Not at once, but within a year. The last time we talked was on the phone, early in 2003. We'd bought coach tickets for an antiwar demo in London, but he cried off due to a chest infection. Too much smoking—tobacco and other stuff. I'd have gone to see him, but I knew he didn't like to be visited at home. He said he was planning to do some work. "I need to get the voices back," he said. "I've lost them. The voices in my head. My mum and dad, my brother. Friends who died years ago. I can't hear them any more."

One of Paul's drinking buddies told me he'd collapsed in the Prince of Wales at the end of the night. "The stress of last orders," I said bitterly. They'd had to clear the place while the paramedics worked on him. He was forty-six.

The house would have to be sold. It was a thin terrace in Balsall Heath, bought cheaply before the property boom of the nineties. There were debts to pay. But that wasn't my concern. My job was simply to find and collate the manuscript of *The Wasted Streets*, and any other manuscripts or notes that Paul had left behind. Once I had the book, I could work on it at home.

At first I thought I had the wrong key. The lock was rusty, and the door stuck in the frame. Eventually it jerked open, scattering junk mail across the pale carpet. The walls of the front room were lined with bookcases, their contents grey with dust. The gas fire had been ripped out, leaving a gaping hole under the mantelpiece. A few woodlice stirred as I switched on the light, then crept back to the cover of the rotten skirting-board.

In the living room, the floor was barely visible. Heaps of books, newspapers and magazines were scattered everywhere. Mugs and glasses were balanced on every flat surface. There was a smell of damp and decay. Along one wall, CDs and cassettes were heaped at random around the bulk of Paul's ancient stereo. His LPs were mostly in a cheap wooden cabinet under the window; what I initially took for a net curtain was in fact a tissue of cobwebs obscuring the glass. The massive TV set in one corner was blind with dust. How had Paul managed to live like this?

More rubbish was heaped in the kitchen. When I opened a cabinet to find a clean glass, a pile of letters fell into my hands. I began to realise that Paul's inability to shake off the past had a direct physical aspect. The sink was half-full of plates, bowls and broken glass. Rusty pans were heaped on the gas stove; from the atmosphere, I suspected that not all of them were empty. The doorway to the bathroom was smeared with pale cobwebs. I decided not to look further.

Upstairs, I found the study that must have been Paul's comfort zone—the one room he'd felt at home in. Though dusty, it was free of cobwebs. A small computer perched in the middle of the desk, surrounded by notebooks and stacks of paper. The walls were covered with pictures: Picasso, Rodin and Schiele; photographs of urban decay; jackets from Paul's books; some framed erotic sketches that looked decades old. The walls were lined with bookcases, but there was a small portable CD player on one shelf, and a stack of CDs beside it. The topmost one was a recent Johnny Cash album. His face on the cover was a pale death-mask, the eyes shut behind glasses.

Some preliminary investigation revealed that Paul's literary papers were divided between three rooms: this one, the living room and the hall, where more notebooks were piled up by the phone. Most of his actual manuscripts were in unmarked folders, wedged in amongst the heaps of newspapers and bills and political pamphlets. It was a task that S. T. Joshi might have flinched at. And I couldn't face going back into the kitchen to make some coffee. I took a deep breath and sat down at Paul's desk.

Several hours later, the desk was covered in folders and notebooks that contained as much of *The Wasted Streets* as seemed to exist. I still felt sure there must be a master document somewhere that could guide me through all these fragments. It's a common archivist fantasy. Paul seemed to have started the novel five or six times under various titles, including *Ruined in a Day*, *Sing This Corrosion*, *Permanent Bruise* and *Views of a Black Earth*.

One draft was an unbroken stream of consciousness, handwritten on sixty sheets of paper, with the biro pressing through whenever Paul became drunk. It ended with the words: *The only real life is decay.* Another draft, printed on the computer, got as far as page 97 before giving way to a repeated error message that went on for three pages: *The file is corrupted.*

What I'd found of the novel didn't make much sense. It was a kind of love story, like *City of Ghosts*, but had none of the idealism of his early work. Nor did it have much of the sarcastic energy and venom he'd become famous for. It described Birmingham seized by a kind of rapid decay—of life and the non-living alike—that reduced it to almost nothing within a year. Newspapers rotted before they could be read. Mounds of dead pigeons choked the city streets. Thousands of dying people were crammed into hospitals that were crumbling by the day. New cars became rusty deathtraps over a weekend.

Through this ruined landscape, a teenage lad and a teenage girl carried out a desperate romance. They fled from one blighted district to another, searching for food and shelter. The passion between them seemed to keep them free of corrosion, while their world literally fell apart. Paul repeatedly compared them to Hansel and Gretel, the hungry children finding a gingerbread house in the depths of the forest. He devoted many pages to achingly detailed portraits of their lovemaking.

The last part of the book was the hardest to follow, and I wasn't sure that Paul had ever really finished it. With only the lovers remaining alive, the stark ruins of the city became populated by ghosts. For a while, the streets echoed with the voices of children. And then the memories began to decay and the ghosts became sick, fell apart, rotted. Paul seemed to be saying that the past was not immortal. I could agree with that.

It was impossible to decide which draft, if any, represented the most recent version. Perhaps the computer files would help, but I didn't know his password. For now, I gathered all the papers that seemed relevant to *The Wasted Streets* into a box file. I also took a box of unmarked discs to try at home. Outside, it was getting dark. Rain spat at the window, leaving it stained with flecks of yellow light.

Walking to the bus stop, I was more aware than before of how the streets had deteriorated in recent years. Houses had become tenements, shops were boarded or whitewashed over, doorways were filled with rubbish. This had been a red light district a decade earlier, and the poverty had lingered. I imagined Paul walking home through an avenue of tall, skinny whores. Had he ever tried them? I doubted it. When sober, he knew how to get laid. When drunk, he didn't bother.

A bus approached but didn't stop. It had no lights on inside. The driver was a thin silhouette behind a grimy windscreen. One of the rear windows had been smashed; I felt spied on by the darkness. The rain became heavier, and I was afraid it might get into the box file I was clutching. At the top of the road was a pub, The Earth Shovel. Paul and I had gone there for a drink once. It was open, so I decided to catch the bus later.

The lighting inside the pub was so poor that I wondered if it had closed early. But there was a man behind the bar, and a few people sitting at the low tables. The carpet's pattern had faded to the point of invisibility. As I reached the bar, I saw that most of the optics were either broken or empty. The barman looked over my left shoulder, as if someone had come in with me. I asked him for a double Scotch. He found a bottle somewhere among the empty glasses and poured from it. There didn't seem to be any ice. The glass looked murky, but I didn't say anything.

Surely it hadn't been like this when Paul and I had come here. Avoiding the misshapen sofas, I perched on a wooden stool. An ageing drunk at the next table leant over and started mouthing some kind of nonsense at me. I couldn't make out any of the words. Maybe Paul had done the best thing, dying before he became like that. Would I be able to say the same? Would I be able to say anything at all? The whisky had a sour aftertaste, like milk on the turn.

The drunk gave up and returned to his past. I gazed at the long framed photographs on the walls: forests, ruined abbeys, bombed-out cities. Weird choice of décor. No doubt chosen in a hurry to help cover the blotches on the walls. A few grey legs twitched from the bottom of a frame. I jerked upright and felt one leg of my stool come loose from its socket. *Even the stools are falling apart.*

My body made the pun faster than my mind. I walked quickly to the back of the room, through an empty second bar to the Gents' toilet. There was only one cubicle, with a broken seat and a cold smell of ammonia. The dark inner surface of the door was covered with graffiti. Obscene anecdotes, offers of money for sex, urgent pleas for a hard cock and a mouthful of sperm. All written in black felt pen, all in Paul's neat handwriting. I'd always thought he preferred women. Was he mocking me?

I bought a double gin to steady my nerves. It didn't look clear, but I was past caring. The first gulp spread inside my stomach like a pale, cold hand. I closed my eyes and saw Paul drinking up. Had he really got pissed in here? Had he spent long minutes of drinking time writing those desperate messages? Looking around me at the decaying old men and tired, expressionless women, I saw the bitterness of the joke. It wasn't me he'd been mocking.

The rain had thinned out, and I could see a reddish moon above the black rooftops. Within a few minutes the bus came. Some drunken teenagers were arguing at the back, so I went upstairs. The box file was damp; I checked the papers and notebooks inside, but nothing seemed to have been damaged. The image of Paul's ashes came back to me, and I wondered what his family had done with them. There wasn't really any place he'd felt at home, except the bottom of an empty bottle. They should have dissolved his ashes in whisky and poured them into the gutter.

The window was misted over. I cleared a porthole with my sleeve and tried to see where the bus had got to. It was nowhere I recognised. Rain darkened the bricks of thin terraced houses, glittered from coils of razor wire on factory walls. A road sign said "Weoley Castle." Had there been a diversion? I realised I should ask the driver whether we were still heading for Cotteridge.

Then we passed through an area that was still under construction. I could see fragments of walls, heaps of loose bricks, braziers smoking in the night. The streetlamps were less frequent, and there were no street signs. The bus lurched as one wheel caught in a pothole. It righted itself, lurched again and stopped. I could smell fire. Suddenly afraid that the bus might not be a safe place to stay, I rushed down the stairs and through the open door.

As the bus drove away, I saw the slow flame of rust warp its chassis and flake away its paint. The road ahead of me was pitted and scarred as if by mechanical diggers. On either side, the buildings were little more than half-formed sketches of brick. What was ahead of me had less form than that. It was a slowly expanding vortex of rain and fire and shattered glass.

As I watched the ruin take hold around me, a lean shape ran from a side alley into the chaos: a cat or a small dog. I saw its bones drop to the pavement, still driven by muscles that had been eaten away in seconds. Vague forms stirred in the dimness ahead, and I wondered if the cells of my retinas were decaying. I couldn't breathe properly. The rain tasted of rancid milk. I walked on into a crater that sucked in everything real and turned it to nothing. An abscess of infected brick and concrete. A pit where every kind of loss found its true meaning. Pale streaks moved at the edge of my vision, like silverfish. I thought I could see through the ground to some kind of dark shower of burned-out debris moving randomly through space. I was no longer walking, but being held and drawn in.

I came to in the dark, on the floor. The smell of dust in my nostrils. Torn paper and hard plastic cases under me. My limbs felt clumsy, numb. My back hurt. I could hear myself crying. It was a seizure, a fit, a what? A what? I curled up tight and waited for the dark to go away. It didn't. Eventually I stood up and reached around me. I knew I was in Paul's house. This must be the study upstairs. I could feel the desk, the chair, the wall behind me. The light switch. It didn't work. The electricity must have been disconnected.

I waited until my hands had stopped shaking, then felt my way down the stairs. Convinced at every moment that I was about to touch a cobweb or something worse, I managed to stumble over the heaps of rubbish to the kitchen and find a box of matches on the sideboard. The box was damp, and the match took three strikes to light up. I held it until my fingertips began to hurt, then lit another. With the fifth or sixth match I found some candles in a drawer and lit one.

Leaving a trail of wax behind me, I went back up to Paul's study and tried to collect his papers together. The first file I opened on the desk seemed to contain only notes for a political pamphlet. The next was filled with e-mail printouts regarding some dispute between himself and West Midland Arts, in the course of which he accused them of political conspiracy and monogamous sexual relations with domestic animals. One of the notebooks I'd knocked onto the floor contained some barely coherent poems in praise of various brands of hash. Another appeared to be some kind of pornographic journal. A third contained the outline of a screenplay based on *City of Ghosts*.

There was no sign, anywhere, of his novel *The Wasted Streets*. No synopsis, no scribbled notes, no abortive drafts. I looked through everything on the desk and the floor, and even some boxes in the hallway I hadn't opened before. It was nearly three A.M. when I gave up. The rain had stopped, and the streets were unexpectedly quiet. I walked to the centre of Moseley to find a black cab. In a pub doorway, an old man was coughing his lungs out. I offered him a handful of change. He wheezed: "Fuck off. I'm not a beggar. I'm just a dying man." I offered to phone for an ambulance and he laughed. "No fucking point."

I left him there. Just as I'd left Paul to choke on his own stored-up rage. There's no point in trying to exorcise what's part of you. Whatever ending I tried to think up, for Paul's story or my own, the truth was already there. I didn't know who to trust, what to do or how to live, and I realised I'd always felt that way and been unable to admit it.